KICKING
OVER
THE
Traces

ELIZABETH JACKSON

ROBERT HALE · LONDON

ISBN 978-0-7198-1758-8

Robert Hale Limited
Clerkenwell House
Clerkenwell Green
London EC1R 0HT

www.halebooks.com

2 4 6 8 10 9 7 5 3 1

Typeset in Palatino
Printed in Great Britain by Berforts Information Press Ltd

Your daily life is your temple and your religion.
Whenever you enter into it take with you your all.
Take the plough and the forge and the mallet and the lute,
The things you have fashioned in necessity or for delight.
For in reverie you cannot rise above your achievements
   nor fall lower than your failures.
And take with you all men:
For in adoration you cannot fly higher than their hopes
   nor humble yourself lower than their despair.

Kahlil Gibran – *The Prophet*

Acknowledgements

First of all I would like to thank my good friend, Barbara Bos. Without her endless support and encouragement while writing this book it would not have made it beyond the first three chapters.

I would also like to thank Gill Jackson, Nick Chaytor, and the rest of the team at Robert Hale Publishers for their diligence.

Last, but not least, a huge thank you to my readers who have waited patiently for the completion of *Kicking Over the Traces*. I hope you enjoy it.

A sequel is underway …

Chapter One

THE WINTRY SUNSET cast an eerie light over the little Norman church and the handful of mourners standing on the bleak hillside by the open grave.

'We therefore commit her body to the ground ... earth to earth ... ashes to ashes ... dust to dust...' the priest droned. He glanced across at the girl and was instantly touched by the rawness and beauty of her grief-stricken face. Her hair was as black as a raven's wing, caught loosely in a ribbon of black lace at the nape of her neck, and her sapphire–blue eyes brimmed with unshed tears as they followed the coffin.

Florence Grainger shuddered as her mother's coffin was lowered into the dark earth. Her father roughly yanked her hand and deposited a cold clod of wet soil into it. She looked into his face for a trace of comfort; it afforded none. She crushed the cold sticky earth between her fingers before throwing it into the gaping hole. It landed with a heavy thud on the coffin lid concealing the brass lettering: *Esme Grainger 1884-1922*.

Florence's mother, Esme Grainger, had celebrated her thirty-eighth birthday barely a month ago whilst attending Yarm Gypsy Fair. They had been travelling north intending to camp within striking distance of Appleby in Westmorland for the ensuing winter months. And it was then that Esme fell dreadfully ill. She died quite unexpectedly in the rear of the bow-top wagon just prior to reaching the nearby village of Stoneygill in whose graveyard she now lay buried.

Blood poisoning, the doctor said: septicaemia, due to a small cut on her hand that had somehow become infected. Esme had developed a temperature and a high fever. Her daughter and husband suggested she rest in the back of the wagon for a few hours. But when they halted their journey to rest and water the horses, Florence looked in the back of the wagon to check on her mother to discover she had died.

I'm so sorry, Mother, Florence mouthed silently, to leave you here ... in this strange and lonely place. But I'll come back ... and visit you ... I promise, she vowed, gazing up to the heavens.

She felt the touch of a hand on her shoulder and turned to find the priest was standing close behind her.

'What will you do now, my dear?' he enquired. His voice was soft and full of concern; the warmth in his eyes gave her a measure of welcome comfort.

'I ... I'm not sure what I'll do,' Florence replied hesitantly.

'Will you come back to the parsonage and have a bite to eat, please? My wife will be glad to—'

'Thank yer kindly for givin' my missus a decent burial – and for your invitation,' Benny Grainger interrupted. He then handed a thin roll of notes to the priest. 'Me and my daughter have a fair way to go and it'll be dark soon. C'mon, let's away, Florence,' he said sharply.

The priest stood watching until the bow-top wagon disappeared down the road and out of view. There was something about the girl that he couldn't quite put his finger on; something that had stirred an exaggerated concern in him. But it was too late now – they'd left. And there was no way her father was going to hang around. The priest tried to shake off the uncomfortable feeling the man had imposed on him; and shivering, he headed back to the warm cosiness of the parsonage as the first snow of winter settled on the footpath.

And, unbeknownst to Florence, she would be included in his prayers that night.

'Look sharp an' take them over to t'barn!' Benny Grainger growled impatiently. 'I'll go and see if it's all right for us to stay here the night.'

Florence jumped down from the wagon and led the horse into the barn and waited for her father's return. They had arrived only just in time for the snow was coming down thick and fast and blowing across the moor, causing deep drifts; the road they'd driven along was no longer visible.

Florence placed her hands on the warm chest of the horse and buried her head in his neck. 'It's all right, Ginger Dick, I'll soon have you fed and watered, lad,' she said, hugging him.

'What d'yer think you're doing!' her father bawled. 'I thought I told you to get that bloody horse seen to! Are you bloody deaf?'

She hadn't heard his approach and the flat of his hand struck her sharply across the back of her head, causing her to stumble. The pain was blinding, but she swiftly regained her balance and spun round to face him.

'Your mother's not around now to protect you. Yer an idle git an' you'll do as yer told from now on; an' I don't give me orders twice! Understand?'

His cold eyes blazed down into hers, and Florence, too stunned to reply, started work on Ginger Dick immediately. She relieved him of the heavy wet harness and quickly making a straw wisp she proceeded to rub him down briskly. Father's never liked me, she thought, tears flooding her eyes. What on earth will I do without Mother here? He'll be hell to live with. Well, he's not going to beat me, she resolved in that moment. I'll leave first. I'm a good worker, 'specially with the horses. And since the war things have changed … maybe not so much in the travelling community … but women are doing men's work on farms and suchlike.

After Florence finished grooming Ginger Dick, she took the empty water-jack to fill at the pump in the farmyard. It was five in the evening and it had stopped snowing and the sky had cleared, allowing a full moon to emerge which lit up a snow-covered landscape. She turned up the collar of her worn tweed coat and trudged through deep snow to where the pump was located. She looked up suddenly when the back door of the farmhouse was flung open and a woman scurried out carrying a pail and hurried over to the pump. Florence instantly relieved the woman of the empty pail and began to fill it for her.

'Thank yer kindly, girl,' the woman said, pulling a battered ex-army greatcoat tightly round her. 'Come on in and have a cuppa and get thissen warm, lass, I've got a grand fire goin' in the kitchen.'

Florence hesitated for a moment, but the thought of a warm fire and a cup of tea were too much to resist. 'Thanks, that'd be most welcome,' she said. Then setting down the water-jack, Florence picked up the other woman's pail of water and carried it back to the house.

A blazing fire crackled in the grate of a shiny black-leaded range. The woman gestured one of the spindle-back chairs at the fireside to Florence before disappearing into the scullery. The woman returned carrying a plate of buttered tea loaf. She then poured tea from a teapot resting on the range before sitting down opposite her.

A log shifted in the grate, producing a shower of sparks which lit up the room.

'Thank you, missus, it tastes lovely,' Florence said, biting into the moist, sweet loaf plastered with butter, 'and thank you for letting us shelter in your barn.'

'Oh, that's no bother to us. Now, tell me, lass, how on earth do you manage to get through these harsh winters?' she asked, frowning and shaking her head. 'It's hard enough here for me and my husband with a solid roof over our 'eads.'

'Aw, you get used it, missus,' Florence said, "specially when folks are kind – like yourselves.'

'And yer mother? I couldn't help notice there was only you … and er, yer dad is it?'

'My mother died the other day. We … we buried her … this morning, at … Stoneygill.' Florence's voice was thick with emotion and tears began to well in her eyes and clog in her throat.

Mary Dalby set her cup aside and reaching out took Florence's hand in her own. 'Ah, I'm sorry, lass, here.' She handed her a clean white handkerchief from her pinafore pocket. 'What's yer name? I can't keep calling you lass.'

'Florence Grainger,' Florence snuffled, wiping her eyes and

blowing her nose.

'And I'm Mary Dalby. So you can call me Mary, and me 'usband's name's Arthur. He's just feeding up and shouldn't be too long. Stay and have a bit o' tea with us, love, eh? You'd be more than welcome.'

'No, no I can't. My dad will be wondering where I've got to and er ... sometimes he can get a bit angry.'

Aye, I bet he can, thought Mary. On meeting him she'd concluded he was a mean-looking man; and had she not seen Florence at the side of him when they drove into the yard, looking pale and tired, she'd have told him to keep moving. She and Arthur hadn't any children, unfortunately, but they'd been happy through the last twenty years. Glancing across at Florence, Mary couldn't help but wonder how that man had managed to father such a pretty daughter and assumed the girl's mother must have been a very beautiful woman.

'Here, take the rest of this loaf with you. I've got more in the larder,' Mary said, wrapping the remainder of the tea loaf in greaseproof paper.

'You're very kind, missus, thank you again.'

'Think nowt of it, lass, I mean, Florence. My, but it's a pretty name, Florence, it suits you.' Mary smiled at her. 'Now there's no need to be rushing off in this bad weather, love. Tell yer dad, I said it'll be all right for you to stay on a while; if you want to, that is.'

'I'd like that very much, thank you,' Florence said, beaming with delight at the prospect of spending a few days here. 'And in return I can help you if you like. I can turn me hand to most things; cooking, cleaning, washing ...'

'You just come over in the morning,' Mary said, interrupting her and gently patting her arm, 'an' I'll find something for you to do. Be nice to have a bit of female company about the place; it can get lonely in these parts, particularly during the long hard winters we get up here.... Aye, I'll see you in the morning, Florence. Fetch that handkerchief back with you and I'll have a clean 'un for you.'

Florence's spirit soared with delight as she made her way back to the barn. She liked Mary Dalby and it would be nice to spend a few hours in that nice warm house every day, away from *him!*

Benny Grainger eyed Florence suspiciously as she entered the wagon.

'Took yer bloody long enough to get some water!' he snapped, 'an' what's that yer've got there?' he yelled, snatching the tea loaf out of her hands. 'Ah, good … so you've got friendly with the farmer's wife, eh? Now that could be useful. What's she say? Does she want us gone in the mornin'?'

'No, Dad. She said we could stay. And I can help her in the house in return for us stopping here.'

'Not gonna pay yer anything for working? Bah, bloody cheek of some folk – typical bloody gorgios taking advantage of us gypsies … thinking we 'ave to be grateful for any crumb they toss our way …'

'Well, at least we've got somewhere to stay through this bad weather and I don't mind helping her out in the house – honest I don't. Please, let's stay here. It'll be Christmas soon.'

'Get summat cooked for me tea! Never mind harpin' on about bloody Christmas!' he snarled. 'And I decide how long we're staying 'ere for.'

'What's the matter with you, Dad? What's wrong?' Florence pleaded. She was fed up with his shouting and bullying. He'd changed: the coolness he'd always displayed towards her in the past, had, these last few days, deteriorated into extreme, downright cruelty. 'You've been nasty to me ever since Mother passed away and it's not my fault she's dead!'

'Well, now she's gone I don't have to pretend to like yer any more, do I?' His voice was low and menacing. 'Cos I don't like you … and I never have – it's all been a bloody sham, and when the time comes to leave here – I'll be leaving on my own.'

Florence gasped aloud hardly able to believe her ears.

'Aye, that's shocked yer, hasn't it?' A grim smile creased the corners of his mouth.

'W-what about me … Dad, d … don't you care?' Her voice held a tremor and was a mere whisper as she struggled to take in what he was saying. He didn't want her with him … Her own father didn't want her!

'Dad? Hah! You can stop calling me Dad now your mother's dead. Cos I'm not yer father. Yer mother was carryin' you in her belly when I married her! That's why she married me; cos no bugger else would 'ave her. 'Ad a fling with some gorgio, she did, at Topcliffe Fair.'

Benny Grainger raised his head, his eyes examining her carefully; he was enjoying the pain which was evident in her face. 'Yer ill-gotten whatever yer breeding – an' it's no bloody concern of mine.'

'What?' Florence felt physically winded and her hand shot up to her mouth to stem the sharp pain shooting through her. Her eyes were wide with horror and as she stared in disbelief at this cruel man before her a chill began to steal over her. What an ugly nasty man he was, she thought; it was as though she was seeing him for the very first time. He had small pinched features, and his nose and cheeks were reddened by a network of fine broken veins. And then with a sudden realization of this truth, she thanked God it wasn't his blood coursing through *her* veins. Then lowering her hand from her mouth, Florence started to laugh; quietly at first, but it wasn't long before her whole body began to shake with laughter.

'You think it's funny, do yer, your mother being nowt but a whore?'

Florence's laughing ceased. She looked into the face of the vile being standing in front of her and saw a complete stranger; a callous man whom she detested and wanted no connection with ever again for as long as she breathed the breath of life.

He would be easy to forget. The sooner he was gone the better.

Garrett Ferrensby looked out from the drawing-room window across to the snow-whitened moorland, illuminated by a full moon in a darkening sky. A log shifted in the grate, disturbing the Great Dane which slept peacefully on the rug by the hearth. He jerked his head and looked from the fire to his master. Garrett picked up a long iron poker and leaning forwards pushed the log back into the flames.

There was a tap on the door and a young girl entered the room.

'Mrs Baxter says I've to see if yer want the fire buildin' up an' the lamp lighting, sir?' she said. The girl's thick Yorkshire accent belied her refined features; there was nothing delicate about the folk born and raised on Hamer Moor; they were as tough as the sheep that roamed the moor and could withstand whatever hardships life threw their way.

'No, I do not want the fire building up and I'm quite capable of lighting a lamp. Now you can go back and tell Mrs Baxter that I am not completely useless!'

The girl was no longer taken aback by her master's rudeness. She nodded, turned, and hurried from the room. The dog opened his eyes at the sound of his master's harsh tone and, seeing that this was not directed at him, he discharged a contented groan before slowly letting his eyelids fall closed again.

Garrett struggled to his feet with the aid of a walking stick and prodded the dog. 'Move, move Bruno!' he griped. Bruno clambered to his feet and stretched before retreating to a safer distance on the other side of the fireplace. Garrett hobbled across the room with difficulty and lit the oil lamp. Then, grimacing, he made his way back and crumpled wearily into the chair.

The door opened with a simultaneous knock. Ivy Baxter blustered into the room. She stood before him with her hands on her hips. Garrett stiffened and waited. His housekeeper was not only beginning to get on his nerves, but getting out of hand and forgetting her station since his return from the war.

'Are you wanting rid of *all* my staff?' she demanded, 'Because if you are you're going the right way about it!'

'Don't you talk to me in that manner! How dare you?'

Ivy Baxter ignored his counter-blast. 'I'll tell you how I dare, *sir*, cos no bugger's going to come and work up here in the middle of nowhere if you keep shouting at them and biting their heads off. Your dinner will be served in the dining room in fifteen minutes,' she concluded in a civil tone before marching from the room.

Garrett stared blankly at the closed door. I've taken my meals in this drawing room ... what? Ever since ... since I came home! What's got into that blasted woman? Damn her! Damn that woman!

Garrett unconsciously ran his hand down his thigh, allowing it to rest upon the damaged limb. If it hadn't been for that brilliant young surgeon I'd have lost it, he thought, gently massaging his leg. He recalled the Belgian doctor who, thankfully, had ignored his superior's advice to amputate the leg, thereby saving it. Most of Garrett's regiment had been killed. They'd been blown to smithereens that day at Passchendaele in October, 1917, five years ago. Still, the graphic nightmares continued, and he would wake up sweating and crying in the middle of the night. In the recurring nightmare Garrett would be fighting his way through the heavy, stinking sludge, where thirty days of heavy rain had converted soil to mud so deep that men and horses drowned in it; nothing less than a grinding swampy slaughter.

He looked at the clock on the mantelshelf, which said seven o'clock.

'It looks as if Mrs Baxter means what she says, Bruno.' The dog rose from the hearthrug at the mention of his name.

'There you go now, sir, I'll put your stick where you can reach it,' Ivy said. Her tone was gentle, like that of a mother to her child. She was smiling broadly at her employer as he made his way to the dining table.

'Grouse,' she said, 'shot on the moor last week, and poached pears for dessert. Enjoy yer meal, sir.' Ivy quickly examined the table, ensuring everything was within easy reach before leaving.

'Ahem!' Garrett coughed and Ivy stopped at the door. 'Just a moment, please, Ivy.'

'Yes, sir?'

'Thank you for … for all of this,' he said in a quiet voice, waving his hand over the table, 'and, err, the young girl … tell her from me, please … she's doing a grand job.'

'Aye, I'll tell her. It's good to have you back in the dining room, sir.'

Garrett looked around the huge room. He sat at the head of the table that seated twelve, twenty when the extra leaves were inserted. Two silver candelabras were positioned at each end separated by a large ornate silver fruit dish which stood in the centre. Dark, heavy Victorian furniture graced the sides of the room, and a strong smell of beeswax filled the air. For a moment he remembered the laughter that had rung in this room years ago, before his parents had died ... and before the God-awful war.... His older brother, Robin, was now married and living in London with his wife, Felicity. He rarely visited nowadays, but when he did, he would only came for a few days during the grouse season; often accompanied by two or three colleagues longing to get away from London and its frequent smog.

Robin, it appeared, had returned from the war physically and mentally unscathed by its horrors, unlike himself. And having taken up politics he was fast becoming a big noise at Westminster.

The next morning Garrett woke up feeling rested. It was the first night since arriving home from the war he'd managed to sleep through till morning undisturbed by his usual hideous nightmares. His leg felt stiff and sore as he hobbled without the aid of his stick to the bedroom window and drew back the heavy curtains.

Dawn was breaking.

The sun's weak ascent cast a watery glow across a landscape of vast barren moorland; a moorland formed thousands of years ago when the ice sheet melted, and which rambled all the way to the east coast, diminishing in height on its approach along the way.

High Agra had been in the Ferrensby family now for four generations. The estate was some twenty thousand acres in total and boasted one of the best grouse shoots in Yorkshire. The land was tenanted to sheep farmers who lived in the tiny cottages dotted about the moors. These farmers scraped a meagre living from the harsh moors as had their ancestors before them; many were old and since the war deprived of sons to carry on farming. Their bodies lay buried on French soil with the thousands of other young men who'd lost their lives; a loss which had echoed throughout Britain – nobody could avoid the impact of war.

All of a sudden his eyes hardened. They settled on a fold in the moor beyond the long drive and the main gates to where a tumbledown hovel, Hamer Bridge, crouched in the depression and interrupted his panoramic view.

Old Tom Pickles, who owned the property, died more than six

months ago; and as yet, there was no indication of a *For sale* sign. Only last week Garrett had paid a visit to his solicitor in Ryeburn instructing them to make enquiries regarding the property but so far had not heard back from them. He craved ownership of the property and who other but himself was the obvious buyer, he'd pointed out to his solicitor.

And after I've bought it I'll damn well demolish it! It's a bloody eyesore! What the hell was Father doing selling a piece of land and a cottage – ripping the very heart out of High Agra? And to bloody Old Man Pickles? I can only assume Father must have been a bit strapped for brass at the time …

Garrett straightened his back and brought his attention back to the present. Looks like a fine day, he thought, scanning the clear blue sky.

'Come on, Bruno!' The dog jumped to attention immediately, his tail beating madly against him. 'It's about time I was back in the saddle, my friend, and *you* can come with me. We'll ride into Ryeburn together – that should please Ivy Baxter, to get me out from under her feet.'

Friday in Ryeburn was busy and there was an air of activity. It was market day, and people from the neighbouring villages assembled in the open square to sell their wares. Their voices rang out from beneath canvas-covered stalls crammed with home-made chutneys, jams, cheeses, butter, rabbit skins; anything they could barter with – or exchange for a few pence.

Garrett made his way to the Three Feathers Hotel where he liveried his horse. He then weaved his way through the busy market square to his solicitor.

'Mister Ferrensby, what a pleasant surprise. I didn't know you had an appointment? Is Mr Hatch expecting you? I don't think— '

'No, Miss Brown, he is not. But, I happened to be in Ryeburn and hoped he would give me a few minutes of his valuable time. Ah, here's Hatch now,' Garrett said, glancing to where a tall, thin, cadaverous man emerged from the office.

Clive Hatch extended a bony white hand which Garrett shook. 'Have you got five minutes, Clive, please? As you've probably already guessed I haven't got an appointment.'

The solicitor took out his pocket watch and checked it.

'Ah, it's almost lunchtime, Miss Brown,' Clive said to the middle-aged spinster who'd been with the firm for as long as Garrett could remember. Her pursed lips softened a little when the solicitor leaned towards her and affectionately rested his hand on her elbow. 'I'll be back in an hour or so. Come, Garrett.'

Clive Hatch wiped his mouth and dropped the napkin on the table. 'I can't find out a damned thing about Hamer Bridge, Garrett, I'm afraid,' he said, with a puzzled expression. 'I've made enquiries for miles around: Thirsk, Northallerton, Malton, every town within thirty miles of here – and nothing! God only knows who's dealing with the man's estate. I take it that no sign has been put up at the property, then?'

'No,' replied Garrett, shaking his head, 'and nobody's been to view the place either since the old boy died. The workers keep their eyes open for me and promise to relay any comings or goings, but not a dickie bird. Well, thank you, Clive, I'd better be making my way back. No, no, my pleasure,' Garrett insisted, taking out his wallet.

He paid the bill and then pressed a shilling into the hand of the young waitress who attended their table. The waitress looked up and rewarded him with a wide smile when seeing the generous tip he'd given her.

Garrett smiled back and the noisy chatter of the other diners muted into the distance. All he was aware of was the smallness and softness of her hand, and how it impacted greatly on his senses and that he didn't want to release his hold; he didn't want to lose the warm glow which spread unwittingly throughout his entire body. Nor did he want to relinquish the stirring sensation in his loins, something he hadn't experienced in a very long while. The girl blushed as he continued to stare wordlessly at her, but Garrett didn't care.

Most of those taking lunch in the hotel were well aware of who Garrett was: his family was respected and well known for miles around; the Ferrensbys were the local gentry. The townsfolk were also aware that the squire had sustained injuries during the war and that he didn't venture far from High Agra, so today would set their tongues wagging, especially those observing him now smiling down at the pretty young waitress. The room had fallen silent as the diners stopped eating and chattering and turned to look at him.

The solicitor coughed loudly.

'I'd better be getting back to the office,' he said, hauling Garrett's attention away from the young waitress. 'I'll let you know if I hear anything.'

'Yes, do that, Clive,' Garrett said, watching the young waitress retreat to the safety of the kitchen – the glorious moment gone.

On leaving the hotel, Garrett was mindful of his faltering stride. His leg ached terribly because of the ride into town along with the effort of trying to hide his limp. But he didn't mind too much. What mattered most to him then was that he felt alive inside again. The desire to take that young waitress in his arms and crush her to him was proof enough for him.

There was a stiff breeze blowing across the moor as Garrett made his way home with Bruno running alongside his horse. A red-brown flash of a grouse rose from the snow-covered purple heather. It took flight with a deep whir from its strong wings, its plaintive call fading into the lonely distance. The cold wind whipped his face, but Garrett couldn't stop smiling to himself as he recalled the young waitress smiling her thanks at the tip he'd given her and he pondered her warm, soft young body. It had been a long time since he'd made love to woman – too long.

'Something I must rectify, Bruno,' he said to the loping dog. 'Come on, boy, we're almost home!'

Chapter Two

THE LONG HARD winter had released its hold in the lower reaches of Westmorland, but higher up, above Stoneygill, the talons of winter retained their icy grip until the bitter end. It was late March and the last pockets of snow that had lain deeply packed against the stone walls were finally surrendering to the warmth of spring.

Florence had been at Arthur and Mary Dalby's farm for almost six months.

Benny Grainger stayed true to his word and deserted her just as he said he would.

The Dalbys kindly took her in, providing her with a room and work. Although she was paid a mere pittance, Florence didn't mind; she would gladly have worked for them for nothing. She loved the stone-built farmhouse. It was the coldest yet most comfortable winter she'd ever experienced in her entire life. And much to her astonishment the very thought of returning to a life on the road filled her with a sense of sheer dread.

Florence milked the cow and saw to the hens before going in for breakfast. A wonderful aroma of bacon and eggs frying wafted through the back door. She removed her dirty boots and went into the kitchen.

'Morning, love,' Mary Dalby said, greeting her with a warm smile. She placed a huge plate of food in front of Florence and then one for herself. 'Last of the snow's gone I see. It must've warmed up through the night, not a bit of white to be seen anywhere, thank the Lord!'

Life up here was one of: waking, working, eating and sleeping. There was nothing besides the family Bible to read which Florence found a great pity; for she'd had the advantage of being taught to read and write at the numerous schools she'd attended at the insistence of her mother. Although her attendance had been intermittent, this was all that was required for Florence's quick brain to pick up her alphabet; she learned this twice as fast as the other pupils. Although she'd never owned any books herself she was surprised that anybody living in a house this size didn't possess any.

'That tweed coat will be too heavy for you now it's getting a bit warmer, Florence. I'll see if I can find you summat lighter and more suitable for you, eh? Put that one away till the autumn,' Mary said, smiling at the dark–haired young woman. 'Never had a kind winter up here yet, lass.'

Florence wanted to leap for joy. Mary was in fact telling Florence that she'd still be here next winter! Her heart soared at the prospect of not having to leave this place she considered home.

'Thank you, Mary, that's kind of you. I've still my mother's old red coat which isn't as heavy … and she'd be right glad to know I was wearing it and putting it to good use.' A lump rose in Florence's throat whenever she spoke of her mother.

After breakfast Florence cleared the breakfast table and washed up, then went to her room to change her coat.

Benny had taken what few possessions she owned and the red coat was the only thing he'd left behind; discarded like an old rag and tossed in the corner of the barn. He's probably already pawned mine and Mother's stuff by now, she thought bitterly. She opened the drawer and carefully lifted out the red coat, and burying her face in it tears pricked her eyes. 'Oh, Mam,' she cried, trying to breathe in any faint trace of her mother that might remain.

'Are yer ready, love?' Mary called upstairs.

Florence wiped her eyes and put on her coat, then went downstairs.

'Ooh, you look right grand in that, lass. The colour suits you,'

Mary said, tilting her head to a side and studying her. The girl's hair contrasted magnificently against the bright-red coat and fell about her shoulders like a black cape. What a beauty she is, Mary thought. Living here on the farm here these last few months has filled her out.

'We'll fetch the sheep down from t' top field first and then we'll get ready for market tomorrow. Thought it'd make a nice change for you. You've been stuck here all this time and not been anywhere. Mind you,' Mary continued, unaware of the beaming smile spreading across Florence's face, 't' weather's not been fit for man nor beast!'

'Oh, thank you! I'd love to go to market with you,' Florence said excitedly. 'I'll fetch the sheep down. Shep'll help me, won't you, boy?' The dog pricked his ears at the mention of his name. 'That'll leave you free to get things ready.' Florence and Shep were out of the door before Mary had chance to reply.

'Yes, all right,' Mary said as the door banged shut. Aye, that lass will turn a few 'eads in Kirkby Stephen tomorrow – I've no doubt.

Florence followed the steep well-trodden track to arrive at a summit in the undulating land where Shep gathered the sheep at her command. A sharp descent then brought them down to a stream and open fields beyond. It was a beautiful place: vast and silent and filled with peace. Florence stood breathing in the cool spring air – watching clouds racing on the wind and casting shadows on the barren landscape. I've been so happy here … she thought, but nothing's forever … 'Is it, Mam?' she said out loud, 'And by the way, Mam, I don't know how you carried this coat cos it weighs a bloody ton!' she laughed. Her shrill laughter rang through the sharp morning air, causing Shep and the sheep to turn suddenly and look at her.

She could barely contain her excitement for tomorrow. The opportunity to spend any of the money she'd earned hadn't arisen. Kirkby Stephen was the nearest town and, although Mary and Arthur had been a couple of times during the winter months when stock ran low, she'd remained on the farm. I might buy myself a summer coat tomorrow … or a length of material. Mary will help me make a coat, I'm sure – she's clever with a needle, I'll ask her tonight.

It was growing dark by the time Florence and the Dalbys settled down for the evening by the fire. Everything was ready for the market. All packed and stacked for an early start the next day.

'The weather's set fair,' Arthur said, walking across the room and tapping the barometer.

'I think I'll turn in now,' Florence said, rising from her chair. She usually went to bed early, believing it was only right Mary and Arthur have time together in the evenings without her.

'Aye, get thissen a good night's sleep, lass, cos you're in for a busy day tomorrow. It's a good market so you treat yourself to summat nice, Florence. Yer work 'ard and yer deserve it. By, it'll be grand to have such a bonny lass along aside of us, won't it, Mary? Err … Mary…?'

'It will. Now off you go, Florence, we'll see you in the morning.'

Florence left the room and was going up the stairs when she couldn't help but hear Mary say crossly, 'Now leave the lass alone, Arthur. D'you hear me?'

Florence went into her bedroom and sat down on the side of the bed feeling rather puzzled. I wonder why Mary was cross with Arthur? Poor old fella … he was only being kind … saying I was bonny.

The red coat she'd worn was still lying across a chair and she reached across and picked it up. She walked over to the wardrobe and was about to put it away when the hem of the coat caught on the lock of the door.

'Damn!' she swore, hearing the material rip. 'I need this for tomorrow.'

She sat down on the bed to examine the damage. The stitching had come away a couple of inches. But then on closer inspection she could feel something. There was something hard trapped inside the lining. Her fingers worked their way into the tear.

'What on earth is this I can feel? What the—' Florence gasped when a gold sovereign slid into her hand. She placed the sovereign on the bedside table and frantically began unpicking the rest of the hem. After unpicking the stitching, she placed the coat flat on the bed, then folded back the loose red lining. No wonder it was heavy, Florence thought. She stared in bewilderment at a felt padding which had been carefully sewn to the inside of the coat. As she ran her hands over it she felt the protruding bulges beneath her fingers. The dull grey wadding was not too difficult to tear, and using a hatpin, Florence prised out what she knew would be another gold sovereign. She glanced at the door at the sound of footsteps on the landing and quickly gathered up the coat and stuffed it into the wardrobe.

'You all right, Florence?' Mary said, stopping outside her door. 'Early start tomorrow, I'll knock you up at 4:30.'

'Yes, don't worry, I'll be up,' Florence replied, gaping at one of the sovereigns glinting in the candlelight on the bedside table. She hastily picked it up and popped it inside her boot. I'll take that sovereign with me tomorrow, she decided. There wouldn't be time to unpick the stitching to see how much money there was until she returned home from market tomorrow. She would have to exercise patience. Florence climbed into bed, but couldn't sleep and lay awake for hours. The sovereigns must be her mother's savings over all the years. She always did appear too grand for the likes of him, when she came to think of it. Her mother was a polite lady; and she had nice manners too ... Maybe this money was from her family; given her at the time she had to leave home and marry Benny. And who would blame her for not telling him about it? Yes, you've slipped up there good and proper, Benny Grainger, Florence sneered. That piece of rag you tossed aside was literally worth its weight in gold. And I'm not answerable to you – or anybody else.

And on that thought and a prayer of thanks on her lips for her mother, Florence closed her eyes and drifted off to sleep.

The small market town of Kirkby Stephen thronged with people. They poured in from the surrounding villages of Nateby, Raven-stonedale, and Mallerstang. The weather was fine with a cold northerly wind keeping the rain at bay.

The market square grew quieter by midday and Mary Dalby suggested Florence take time for herself to see if there was anything she wanted to buy.

Florence strode off and touched the pocket where the sovereign lay safely knotted in a corner of her handkerchief. Heads turned to watch her as she strolled along the street. Her jet-black hair swung about her shoulders and walking tall and straight-backed, Florence was oblivious to the attention she generated every time she stopped to gaze in a shop window.

'All right, are yer, lass?'

Florence spun round at the sound of her name. Arthur Dalby was standing very close behind her.

'Yes, thanks, Arthur. It's quietened off now and Mary said I could have a look round the shops.' There was something wrong with him, she thought. He had a strange look in his eyes. He leaned forward to speak and a strong smell of beer reached her nostrils and she recoiled.

'I'd better be getting back or Mary'll wonder where I am,' Florence said, stepping back from him.

'Yer all right, Florence, d'yer know that? Yer a right good lass … an' a bonny one,' he hiccupped. His body swayed and Florence raised her hands and placed them on his broad chest to steady him.

'Me friends are askin' who's the pretty lass we've got stayin' with us … hic … they're jealous cos I gets to rest me eyes on you … every day, hic …'

Arthur Dalby was a recognized figure in the town and a small group had gathered round them.

'I'll see you later, Mr Dalby,' Florence said, striding off quickly.

And what would Mary make of the drunken state her husband was in? Oh, Florence dreaded to think!

The journey home was a solemn affair. Florence drove the cart and Mary sat up beside her while Arthur lay in the back – unconscious and snoring loudly. Mary didn't utter a word all the way home. And when Florence dared to glance in her direction Mary's face was set in stone with her mouth clamped tight shut.

Arthur was still asleep in the back of the cart when Florence went upstairs to bed after a non-communicative supper with Mary. She slipped into her flannel nightdress before taking the red coat out of the wardrobe.

She'd borrowed a pair of small scissors from Mary's sewing box. Sitting comfortable on the bed knowing she'd not be disturbed, Florence carefully set about cutting away the felt wadding and released the gold sovereigns. Amongst the sovereigns she discovered tightly rolled-up pieces of paper tied with threads of cotton; which, when unfurled, turned out to be five-pound notes.

Florence looked at all the money strewn across her bed. She counted it. Two hundred and fifty pounds in total! Her eyes misted over as she thought about her mother going without any of the niceties in life; and again wondered how she'd acquired such a vast amount of money.

Sitting on the bed, Florence allowed herself to dream of a better future. I can afford to buy a little place; a horse and cart.... I could even sell my own goods at market. Do as I please. And after the atmosphere here today the prospect of moving grew more appealing by the minute.

She carefully collected up the money and stuffed it inside her boot. Tomorrow she would do some serious thinking about her future.

Florence woke with a start. The darkness was thick and black as pitch. She opened her eyes and stared into it knowing instinctively something was terribly wrong. She gasped and tried to scream when out of the darkness a hand clamped hard down over her mouth and pressed her head further into the pillow. Within seconds her wide eyes grew accustomed to the dark. Towering over her and standing by her bedside was Arthur Dalby. He was naked from the waist down. She couldn't move. He raised himself onto the bed and straddled her. He was twice her size with the strength of a bull and she was immediately rendered defenceless by his great weight. He leered down at her drunkenly through bleary eyes and tore open the front of her nightgown and groped her exposed breasts, squeezing them hard. She winced and tried to struggle free, but he was far too strong for her. Please God, no ... don't let this happen to me....

'Keep still, you bitch!' he said, his voice a harsh whisper. 'If Mary wakes up I'm gonna tell her you've been begging me to come to your bed ever since yer got 'ere, and she'll believe me, d'you hear? And you'll be out of 'ere an' walking that 'ard road quick sharp!'

Florence's eyes were wide with fright and filled with tears. He removed his hand from her breasts and planted his wet lips on her nipples and sucked on them hard. The feel of her body beneath him had him in full arousal. He placed his hand between her legs and prised them apart with his knee. A groan of horror escaped her clamped mouth. He tried to penetrate her and couldn't; and taking hold of his throbbing penis he pressed it against her until his juices exploded over her young naked belly and breasts.

He kept his hand firmly over her mouth and surveyed the beautiful young body in a long silence. 'Next time I come visiting yer – you're gonna enjoy it and let Arthur inside you,' he said. Then before clambering off the bed he added softly, as though he'd done nothing wrong, 'Don't make a noise, Florence, d'yer hear?' She moved her head slightly in acknowledgement. 'I'm goin' to take my hand away and if yer scream, you'll be for it! Right?' She closed her eyes and nodded again. He removed his hand – she gasped and grabbed the bedcovers, covering her nakedness.

She trembled with shock as she watched him leave her bedroom and close the door silently behind him. Florence couldn't cry. She laid there traumatized until the first sign of daylight pierced the thin curtains. When she heard the door bang shut and knew Arthur had left the house, she quickly gathered what few belongings she had and stuffed them into a cloth holdall.

Mary was in the kitchen preparing breakfast. Florence knew Arthur wouldn't be too far away and that Mary would shortly slip out into the yard and call him in for breakfast. Still brooding from her husband's drunkenness yesterday, Florence was no longer concerned for Mary's feelings. All she wanted to do was to get away as far as possible from the place; the place she'd considered a peaceful refuge until last night, but which was now untenable.

'Morning,' said Mary, not looking up at Florence. 'There yer are,' she said plonking a bowl of thick porridge on the table in front of her. She looked at it and a feeling of nausea swept over her.

'I'm leaving today, Mary,' she announced.

'What?' Mary stopped what she was doing and turned to look at Florence. 'Is it because of Arthur?' she asked. Florence stared back at her with a look of complete horror on her face. How on earth could she possibly know?

'He won't get drunk again,' Mary said. 'Anyway, it's not as if his drinking's bothered you; or caused you any 'arm, is it? It's me that has to put up with it – not you. You've seen men get drunk afore, haven't you? It's nowt fresh. Life can get rough up here … sometimes Arthur likes to unwind a bit, have a few pints …'

Florence gazed blankly at Mary. The woman's no idea what a monster she's married to, she thought. What would she do if I told her he's tried to rape me in the middle of the night, I wonder? She'd blame me, likely. Say I'd encouraged him.

Rough up here? Well, it's too rough for me!

'It's nothing to do with Arthur getting drunk,' Florence lied. 'I'm grateful to you for giving me shelter over the winter … it's time for me to move on, though.'

Mary eyed her cagily and Florence didn't know whether it was relief or anger she felt at Mary's lack of concern. A lump caught in her throat and her eyes stung with tears she'd no intention of shedding. There was a moment of awkward silence.

'Aye, well, it's in your blood, I suppose. When are you thinking of going?' she enquired brusquely.

'Now, straight away this morning … I've got my things gathered together.' Florence rose from her chair and left the room. Mary stood staring after her. She looked down at the bowl of cold porridge Florence hadn't touched, and picking it up emptied it into the dog's dish.

When Florence reappeared to say her farewell to Mary the house was empty.

She made her way across the backfields. It was a shorter distance and it was also less likely she'd run into Arthur Dalby. She paused on reaching the stone wall that ran parallel with the road and glanced back to make a last farewell to what had been a pleasant winter's stopover until last night's events. In the far distance she saw two figures that she made out to be those of Mary and Arthur Dalby. She could only guess at the conversation they'd be having and imagine Arthur's relief at Florence having left. A stab of pain shot through her as she recalled the horrific experience and she allowed the tears to fall. She wondered along the silent empty road; and by the time she'd reached Kirkby Stephen her tears were spent and her body exhausted.

It was midday and Florence was hungry. She hadn't eaten since the previous day and she found a small café serving lunches. It was whilst paying her bill that she asked a pleasant young waitress who'd waited her table if she could recommend a tidy, but inexpensive lodging house she might stay for a couple of days. The waitress suggested a boarding house not very far away and wrote the address on a slip of paper for her.

It was an hour later and Florence was settled into pleasant lodgings for two days. And it was from here she would make plans for her future.

Florence secured much comfort from the knowledge that her mother had known – somewhere in the back of her mind – Florence would be in need should anything happen to her. And in her wisdom, Esme knew the red coat would never be of use to her husband and that Florence would be its recipient.

The boarding house supplied breakfast and an evening meal and the next day Florence had lunch at the same café, and was delighted to discover the same friendly waitress was working again that day. Her name was Meg and when she served her she asked if she'd found the boarding house she'd suggested suitable. Florence said yes, and thanked her, then disclosed she was also on the lookout to buy a small property. She asked Meg whether being a local girl, she had any suggestions as to where she could begin her search? Meg said, although she was unable to help her she knew somebody who could. She proposed Florence meet her an hour later when she would be on her break.

Whilst waiting for Meg, Florence strolled into the square and chanced upon a ladies' dress shop with stock that was very reasonably priced. She kitted herself out, and bought two dark-coloured sensible skirts, a neat white blouse plus a pair of sturdy boots that would see her through the summer and the following winter.

Meg showed up as promised an hour later and she led Florence across the market square, then down a narrow side street.

'It's me uncle who has this place,' she said in a broad Cumbrian accent. 'He's an agent, a ... aw, now what's he call himself? Yes, that's it, he's a middleman. He finds what you're looking for and doesn't charge a lot. An' you don't 'ave to worry – cos he's as 'onest as the day is long,' Meg said, stressing her point with pride. 'D'yer want me to come in with you?'

'No, no thanks, it's all right, Meg. I'll make an appointment.' Then turning to her, she took the girl's hand in hers. 'I can't thank you enough. You've been so kind and helpful.'

'Aw, think nowt of it. I'm always glad to help where I can. Ta-ra then, and ... and good luck to you, Florence.'

The next morning Florence boarded a train in Kirkby Stephen.

The two days she'd spent in the town had been fruitful. Florence was now the proud owner of a cottage and two acres of land; and she carried the paperwork in a brown leather briefcase besides a solicitor's document to prove it.

There was also a small sum of money left to tide her over to live on for a few months if she was very careful. All that she required now was a decent horse and cart so she could earn a living; and Florence promised herself a visit to the next horse fair.

Chapter Three

THE GREY MARE walked slowly along the narrow well-worn path through the heather. Spring had arrived early on the moors. The red grouse that had paired off last autumn had finished laying their eggs and were now busy incubating them in well-concealed nests amid the thick heather.

Garrett Ferrensby climbed down from his horse and then removed his walking stick from a holster, specially adapted and attached to his saddle for when riding.

'Stay,' Garrett commanded the horse. He picked his way carefully through the heather until he came across what he was looking for; and a smile spread across his face. There were seven perfectly formed oval-shaped eggs that lay camouflaged in a nest lined with green vegetation. They were a glossy pale yellow covered in brown blotches. The female returned; she flew low above the ground and her wings made the familiar whirring sound when disturbed. She landed not very far away. The distinctive call of her mate in the distance challenged Garrett's intrusion: *Go-bak, go-bak – bak – bak!* the bird cried impatiently.

'All right … I'm going,' Garrett said, then paused a moment to watch the female scamper through the heather and disappear from sight.

A few months from now the moor would be flooded with strangers. The shooting parties would teem in from the towns and cities from miles away to shoot Agra grouse. And during this time much-needed money would pour into nearby Ryeburn; where gentry would take up residence at The Swan and the Three

Feathers hotels.

Garrett himself hadn't picked up his shotgun since his return from the war. He'd seen more than enough killing … and the sound of gunshot sent shivers through his body. He lit a cigarette and looked at his pocket watch. There was just enough time to get back and change before going to Ryeburn. And with a bit of luck … make contact with that attractive fair-haired receptionist at The Swan whom he'd encountered one evening when heavy snow prevented his return to High Agra. The hotel had been practically empty and he'd struck up a conversation with her. Then later that evening they'd taken supper together. Garrett discovered Daphne was a 26-year-old war widow – and a damned good looking one at that! She and her sweetheart had been married only a week before he'd been shipped across to France; from whence he never returned. From then on Daphne threw herself into her work; her life revolved around the welfare of the hotel where she devoted her attention to its patrons and the general running of the place.

He pulled up outside the The Swan Hotel in his yellow Austin Twenty and went inside.

Daphne glanced up suddenly from the paperwork she was attending to at the sharp ring of the handbell sitting on the reception desk.

Her eyes lit up and her heart skipped a beat when she saw it was Garrett Ferrensby standing there. She loved to hear his velvety well-spoken voice; and whenever he spoke to her she felt special – he treated her like a lady. Unlike the rest of the stuck-up toffs who frequented the hotel who looked down their noses at the staff.

'Are you working tonight?' he enquired.

'What? I mean, pardon? No, err, no, I'm not.'

'In that case, Daphne, allow me to take you out to dinner – I have the motor car,' he added. Then leaning over the reception desk he smiled – his face mere inches from hers. 'I know a superb little pub in Beadlam which does great food. What do you say?' he whispered.

Daphne inhaled the expensive cologne he wore. *If I turn my* head just a few degrees our lips would touch … hmm, I wonder … what would he make of that? The thought brought a smile to her face. 'Thank you,' she said. 'Just give me half an hour to change and wash my face, then I'll meet you in the bar.'

As soon as he left for the bar, Daphne bounded up the main stairs two at a time to quickly change.

A good fire burned in the grate in the bar making it cosy and welcoming. Garrett glanced round the half-empty bar and spotted Clive Hatch, his solicitor, sitting in the corner absorbed in a newspaper. He walked across to him.

'Hello, Clive. Can I buy you a drink?'

The solicitor's ferrety eyes peered over the top of the newspaper to see who had interrupted his relaxation. When he saw who had disturbed him he quickly folded the newspaper and, putting it aside, rose to greet Garrett.

'Garrett, what a pleasant surprise,' he said, shaking his hand. 'Thank you, yes, I'll have a whisky, please. I'm … I'm so pleased to have run into you,' Clive said awkwardly. 'It will save me sending you a … a … letter.'

Garrett frowned. He walked over to the bar and ordered two whiskies, then went back and sat down. They waited for their drinks to arrive and both men quaffed in silence for a few moments.

'Well?' Garrett asked.

'Hamer Bridge.' Clive said in a low voice.

'Hamer Bridge? What about it?' Garrett asked, irritated at Clive's reluctance to spit it out. He'd only walked around the property yesterday and peered through the windows. It was filthy! If something wasn't sorted soon it would be infested with rats– or God knows what!

'Have you found the agent who's dealing with the sale?'

'Nooo … I haven't, but, I've been told a land agent from London is dealing with it, and….'

'And what? Get it out, man, for Christ's sake!'

'I am afraid, Garrett, that Hamer Bridge has already been sold.'

'What! Sold to whom?'

'I'm afraid I don't know, Garrett. Someone from the South of

England, I suspect,' the solicitor said, shrugging his shoulders. 'I can't tell you anything else. That's all I could find out – and believe me the man who told me was taking a big risk divulging *that* information.'

Garrett didn't give a damn what risk the man was taking! He could hardly believe what Clive had said. Hamer Bridge, sold, and right from under his feet!

'Blast!' Garrett swigged back the remainder of his Scotch in one gulp and banged his glass down sharply on the table.

Beset with anger he hadn't noticed Daphne enter the bar. She was standing in front of them when Clive nudged him and Garrett rose to his feet with the aid of his walking cane.

'Oh, Daphne, sorry, I'm so sorry, I didn't see you there for a minute. Erm, do you know Mr Hatch? Clive, this is Daphne … err?' He'd forgotten her surname and looked at her apologetically.

'Bowman,' Daphne said.

Clive acknowledged the receptionist with a nod, but didn't bother to get to his feet.

Ignorant sod! she thought, nodding back politely. Daphne averted her eyes from the ferret-faced man, and smiling, she rested her eyes on Garrett. He stood six inches taller than her in her heels. His brown hair was neatly cut and swept back. He wasn't by any means what one would describe as handsome. Thick eyebrows overshadowed his soft grey eyes; eyes that told you very little and held you at a distance. She noticed the large Adam's apple sticking out above his collar and his face was pale from the long winter and too little time spent outdoors. He looked a little flushed now with the whisky he'd drunk and the anger he felt. His nose appeared overly large in his rather thin face; this was accentuated by the way it hooked slightly at the bottom – like a bird of prey's. But he had that distinctive lick of gentility and stamp of good breeding that negated any of his imperfections.

'You ready, Daphne? My, you do look lovely,' he added, appraising her. She'd exchanged the drab, dark-grey work dress for a pretty mauve two-piece suit.

'Bye, Clive. I'll drop by your office next week sometime. Hopefully you'll have more news for me.'

'Yes, of course,' Clive said.

The solicitor watched the couple leave together. He was filled with an urgent desire to follow the stupid woman and tell her to go home and find someone of her own class. Yet, Clive had to admit at the same time, it was good to see that Garrett was getting out and about again. The man had locked himself away at High Agra for almost two years until recently. He needs a woman to bed, the solicitor reckoned, but … don't we all. My own life would be a dreary existence had I only my wife for comfort.

'Thank you, Garrett, I've had such a lovely evening,' Daphne said.

Garrett had stopped the car and switched off the engine. He lit a cigarette and passed it to her before lighting one for himself. 'I enjoyed myself too.'

'Did you really?' she queried, and turned to look at him.

'Yes, of course I did. Have I done or said something wrong for you to think otherwise? Because I promise you …'

She didn't let him finish, but leant towards him … her face close to his. 'No, Garrett, I … I'm more than happy to be with you.' Daphne spoke in a soft whisper and saw a shadow of pain flit across his face and the soft caress of his gaze … then his mouth covered hers.

'Can I come up to your room, Daphne … please…?' Garrett said. 'I want you … and need you … so badly,' he whispered in her ear.

Daphne groaned with sheer longing. 'Oh, yes, Garrett …' she sighed deeply, 'yes … yes, please.'

They entered the hotel by the staff entrance and where a narrow flight of stairs led to Daphne's private quarters.

The fire in the grate was still glowing. Daphne deposited a few coals onto the embers and it burst into life, adding a soft warm glow to the room. She didn't turn on a light, but lit two candles on the mantelshelf. Then without asking she poured two glasses of Scotch and handed one to Garrett.

'Thanks.' His hand shook as he raised the glass to his lips and he hoped she hadn't noticed. They sat side by side on the sofa and Garrett rested his head against the high back. The whisky followed by the wine he'd consumed at dinner earlier was beginning to take effect and he felt his body relaxing. He reached across and took her hand in his. 'You all right, Daphne ... about this, I mean? I can leave ... if you really don't want this ... if you've changed your mind ... or feel uncomfortable...'

Daphne put her glass down on the table in front of her. 'Yes, I'm all right,' she said, meeting his eyes briefly before looking away. 'I'm nervous, that's all. There hasn't been anyone since ... since Bert.'

Garrett placed his arm about her and drew her close to him.

'I know, Daphne, I know ... we'll take it very slowly ... but together.'

There was a husky rasp to his voice ... and an edge of sadness.

Chapter Four

FLORENCE DREW THE cart to a halt on reaching the high point of the moor. She climbed down and stretched her arms high above her head. The sound of the wind howling across the moor was pleasing to her ears and she turned her face skyward, closing her eyes against the bright June sunshine.

The journey had taken much longer than expected. After learning of a reputable horse and cart dealer in Darlington she stayed in the town for a few days. Florence had purchased a strong young Welsh Cob and a useful cart from the man. Then after closing the deal he had asked her if she would also consider taking the dog that had come with the horse. Florence said she would if he was prepared to deduct some money off the price of the horse seeing as it was another mouth to feed. The dealer had demurred a while, but then realizing the lass was right, he'd agreed.

'What breed of dog is he?' Florence asked.

The dog was a strange-looking animal. One of which she'd not seen the likes of before. His coat hair was rough and brownish-grey colour. But what it was that won Florence over and decided her to take the dog was his eyes. They were kindly eyes; a dark soft brown topped with long sweeping lashes.

'Ah believe 'e's a cross between a lurcher and a wolfhound if I 'ad to tek a guess. But 'e's a nice-natured dog, and he'll look after thee an' not let thee come to any 'arm, lass,' the man told her.

That would account for his size, Florence thought – I only hope he's fully grown. 'What's his name?' she asked, stroking the dog's head. He'd sat obediently at her feet looking up into her face. She liked him.

"Aven't a clue. I call 'im Dog.'

Dog hadn't been with Florence for long before a name came to mind for him. It was Moth – which she believed suited him. For the large hound loafed about most of the day – not venturing far, but when nightfall descended, his energy increased considerably and he'd take off into the night and return with the welcome offering of rabbit or hare more often than not.

Yes, Moth was proving to be a good provider and a devoted companion.

Florence glanced at the pocket watch she carried. It was almost four o'clock and they had a few miles to go before reaching their destination. She filled a pail of water from the copper waterjack for the horse and then filled a bowl for Moth before taking a long drink from a flask of cold tea she'd prepared for herself that morning. We could be there before dark if we keep going, she thought, wiping her mouth with her sleeve.

'C'mon, my beauties, let's keep moving.' Florence tossed the empty pail into the back of the cart and clambered up. She flicked the reins and the cob broke into a trot and Moth leapt upon the cart beside her as it set off.

'Lazybones,' she said, and laughingly ruffled the dog's ears.

It was ten o'clock and dark when Florence eventually arrived at what could only be described as a tumbledown dwelling. A mist had crept in, shrouding the moorland and making it difficult for her to see. She jumped down and taking a small oil lamp from the cart lit it. She peered through the mist and saw there was a barn and stables behind the house. The horse was tired having covered a fair distance and Florence swiftly unharnessed and stabled the cob before giving him a bucket of bran-mash.

Moth patrolled the area with his ears pricked, but didn't wander far; it was as though he knew his close attendance was necessary.

'Here, Moth,' she called in a soft quiet voice, and Moth was at her side in an instant.

They walked round to the front of the cottage. Florence removed the large key from her skirt pocket and placed it in the door and turned it. The heavy door creaked loudly on its rusty old hinges as she pushed it wide open. It was too dark to see anything in detail and she raised the oil lamp in front of her for a closer look. 'Goodness me, it's a bloody hovel,' she exclaimed out loud. 'What on earth have I bought?'

As Florence's eyes slowly became accustomed to the semi-darkness her heart plummeted. But then the silence was broken by a sudden burst of flapping wings, causing her to jump. A cockerel leapt onto the hearth and its small eyes glittered in the light from the oil lamp. In its panic the bird had disturbed a deep pile of soot which now ensconced Florence and Moth in a dirty black film.

Moth barked loudly and the cock crowed!

Florence rushed to the doorway and shooed the bird out, which was closely followed by Moth. She sat down on a rickety chair by a table in the centre of the room and swept a hand across the table, removing a crust of dirt which beneath revealed an oak top. Surprised, Florence looked about, noting a number of pieces of furniture in the room. Feeling her spirits lift at her discovery she took the lamp and ventured into the bedroom. Although equally filthy, it held a bed, a wardrobe, and a dressing table. In the morning when it was light she would be able to assess the property, and establish what the probable cost would be to put it right out of her already dwindling savings, but then all Florence needed was to sleep; she was as tired as the cob that had carted them there. She'd take her bedroll and settle down under the cart for the night with Moth to keep her warm and safe.

Florence woke at first light. She'd slept in the same soot-coated clothes she'd gone to bed in and her first priority was to scrub herself clean at the water pump in the yard before changing into her working clothes.

She went back inside the cottage where the sunlight flooded the two small rooms through holes in the roof where the thatch was missing. I'll have that done straight away, Florence decided; already making a mental list of jobs she could not do herself.

Within a few hours Florence had the range cleaned and a good fire going in the grate. Whoever lived at the cottage before had been well prepared for winter, Florence thought, because there was sufficient peat stacked in the barn to last a long time. Another pleasing aspect on closer inspection was the furniture, which was of high quality. The scullery, pantry and cupboards were supplied with pans, crockery and cutlery; everything a person could possibly need to set up a home. She couldn't help but wonder why the family of whoever lived here hadn't cleared out its contents; or taken up residence themselves, for that matter. Florence was learning very quickly there was no accounting for some folk.

The pan of stew simmering on the range was almost ready. She set the table neatly for one; and whilst doing so she couldn't help smiling that this was *her* home. She owned it. Lock, stock and barrel. Nobody could turn her out or tell her to, move on, or, you're trespassing, as so often had been the case in the past.

And she had much to thank Mary Dalby for, who had played an essential part in Florence's life. Mary had taught Florence the significant requirements for running a house; one being how to lay a table properly, a detail people took for granted living in a house in the settled community and much overlooked by her own. Florence glanced at the frameless photograph of her mother smiling at her from the mantelpiece and a lump caught in her throat. Her mother's eyes seemed to be saying, Well done, Florence. I'm proud of you.

Garrett Ferrensby finished his lunch and requested that coffee be served in the drawing room. He was standing looking through the window when Ivy arrived with the coffee and he turned to face her.

'There's smoke coming out of the chimney at Hamer Bridge!' he blared. 'Get someone to go there immediately and find out what's happening!'

'Can't do that, sir, someone's living there.'

'Living there!' he yelled. 'When? When did this happen?'

Ivy shrugged her shoulders. She couldn't understand why he got himself all het up and bothered about Hamer Bridge. It was nowt but a hovel as far as she was concerned.

'Answer me, woman! Who–has–moved–into–Hamer–Bridge?'

'Yer'll 'ave to ask someone else, *sir*, cos *I–don't–know*,' she said. 'And what's more neither do I care!'

Garrett stared disbelievingly at the door as Ivy banged it shut behind her. That woman gets away with bloody blue murder in this house! Just because she's been here forty years doesn't give her the ... the bloody right to ... to take liberties!

I'll damn well go and find out for myself!

He continued gazing towards the fold in the moor where dark smoke rose, curling upwards into a clear blue sky. For a fleeting moment his eyes trailed the slow movement of the smoke ... as it drifted upwards, taking with it ... his anger and pain....

But not for long.

'Bruno!' he snapped. 'Come!' The dog hauled his huge frame from the rug where he lay and followed his master.

Florence had heaved the heavy Turkish rug she'd discovered rolled up under the bed outside and hung it over a cart shaft to clean it. Moth sat close by watching her as she thrashed it with a carpet-beater, mesmerized by the swirls of dust which rose into the air, covering them both.

Garrett drew his horse to a halt.

Florence and Moth had neither seen nor heard his approach.

'Stay,' Garrett commanded Bruno.

Garrett immediately detected a transformation about the place. The small windows sparkled in the sunlight and the peeling paintwork had been scrubbed clean. The clutter which had surrounded the cottage was now sorted into separate heaps.

Florence stopped thrashing the rug and taking a handkerchief from her pocket she wiped her brow; then she swept up her mane of thick black hair and dabbed the back of her neck. Garrett knew it was improper and ungentlemanly of him to stare, but he couldn't help himself. She was the most beautiful creature he'd ever laid eyes on ... dark, vivacious, and ... eternally female. He surveyed her as an artist would a sunset; his eyes following her every movement. She opened the top buttons of her blouse and ran the cloth over the top of her breasts before fastening it again. She leaned down and picked up the carpet-beater and the spell was broken the instant Moth glimpsed Garrett and began to bark loudly.

'Heel!' Florence shouted at Moth, who completely ignored her and bounded over to where Bruno stood madly wagging his tail. How she wished in that moment Moth wasn't such a placid animal, but one who would snarl and bare his teeth at strangers.

Garrett dismounted on his good leg, then removed the cane from its holster.

Blast! She's not going to walk over here. I'm going to have to damn well hobble to her!

Florence didn't move. She noted the thoroughbred horse and that the man was well dressed; everything about him signified wealth and position. He was attractive, but not handsome, she thought.

She grew uncomfortable and her heart beat rapidly when he withdrew a stick from the side of the saddle and panic began to build in her. The only thought racing through her head was he's going to attack me – tell me to pack up and move on ... Then something happened. Her mother's voice cut across the dark and terrifying thoughts; interrupting her fears. *Don't be afraid. Hamer Bridge is yours, Florence. Always remember that. It's bought and paid for. No one can take it from you ... this is your home. There's nothing to fear....*

'Moth, here boy!' she commanded, her confidence bolstered. The dog sensed the tone of authority in his mistress's voice and pricking his ears deserted his newfound companion and ran to her side.

'Yes, can I help you?' she asked, relieved to see he was using the cane because of some injury or other.

'Good afternoon. My apologies if I startled you. My name's Ferrensby, Garrett Ferrensby.'

She's almost as tall as me. And she didn't say, *sir!*

He looked into her eyes. They were a bright blue with clear flecks of green surrounding the black iris. As he scrutinized her, she held his gaze. But then he perceived a flicker of mistrust in them – and for a moment he was tempted to smile, but didn't. He held out his hand, 'And you are?'

'Florence Grainger,' she said abruptly, and briefly shook the proffered hand.

'How do you do, Mrs Grainger, is Mr Grainger around?' he enquired with a lift of his eyebrows. 'I … may have a proposition for him.'

'There *is* no Mr Grainger.'

For some reason she was unable to meet his steady gaze any longer and lowered her eyes, taking refuge in stroking the top of Moth's head. She didn't like the idea of a man knowing she lived alone – not even one who dressed fancy and spoke like a gentleman.

Garrett couldn't place her accent. It definitely isn't from these parts, hmm … so there's no Mr Grainger, eh? Well, hopefully that will make the task of removing her from the place a little easier.

'I live up at High Agra,' he said, pointing. 'You may have noticed it. It's the big house on the rise on your way here. This … erm, Hamer Bridge, was always part of the … estate in the past … and I am actually looking to buy it back. Whatever you paid for it,' he said, raising his hand, as if to assure her, 'I'll pay you double … treble. Now you won't get a better….' His words tapered off and he left the sentence unfinished. She was glaring at him. Her blue eyes had turned blue-black with rage. 'Are you listening to me?'

'Get off my land and property. Now! Right this minute! I moved in here two days ago and I intend to live here for a good many more – probably the rest of my life. Now leave, mister!'

Her directness took him by complete surprise. Garrett had never been spoken to like that before. He quickly regained his composure.

'It's hard up here in winter, Mrs … Miss Grainger. There are times when you can't get out for weeks … months sometimes. That road is blocked with snow so deep it can cover a man.'

'Is that so? Good job I'm tough, then, isn't it? I've wintered for years in a bow-top wagon! Do you honestly think I'd be suffering in a house? Pah!'

'A bow-top wagon? Goodness' sake – you mean to say you're a

… a damned gypsy?'

'Aye, that's right, I'm a gypsy, yes, but not a damned one, no, mister. It'll be you who'll be damned to hell before me!'

Moth moved to stand in front of Florence and started to growl.

Bruno backed a few paces, sheltering behind his master; and Florence couldn't help but smile.

Garrett mounted his horse, which shifted restlessly, ready to be on the move. 'You'll sell one day, Miss Grainger. People like you do – they can't settle.'

'Don't hold your breath, mister – or should I say, yes, *do* hold your breath!'

Florence waited until he'd disappeared from view before allowing her shoulders to slump and the inevitable tears to fall. Would it always be like this for her? she wondered. Fighting prejudice everywhere she went? Never permitted to acknowledge her roots proudly? And she *was* proud of them. But she had no family; how was it possible for her to travel the country lanes on her own? There were lots of unscrupulous people about ready to take advantage of a young woman – even amongst her own people.

Florence wandered back inside the house and set about curing a few rabbit skins. It was market day tomorrow in Ryeburn and she needed to stock up with a few provisions. She would take the cart and leave Moth behind to guard the place. She glanced down where the dog lay at her feet and smiled. He was her only friend. 'Good boy, Moth, you've turned out to be a grand dog.' She rose and disappeared into the larder and returned holding a pan of leftover rabbit stew and dropped a dollop into his bowl. 'That's for looking after me, you *kushti juckel*,' she said aloud in her Romany tongue.

The grandfather clock Florence had inherited with the house struck four, its resonant strike reminding her of the silence which surrounded her in her new home. She wasn't used to total silence. Living in a canvas-covered home, every single sound outside seeped in. She threw open the little windows and the front door and birdsong instantly filled her ears.

Next month it would be Topcliffe Fair. She would go and buy

herself a horse to ride and drive. Florence's spirits began to lift as she considered her future. Garrett Ferrensby was already proving not to be a friendly neighbour, that was obvious, but she'd withstood harsher conduct from worse people than him in the past... then instantly she thought of Arthur Dalby and his hands groping her, and shuddered.

A loud clattering of hoofs in the courtyard alerted the household. Ivy Baxter was in the drawing room putting a match to the fire and looked out to see Garrett striding with an ungainly lopsided gait with the aid of his cane to the front door.

Ah, I see it looks like he's met the new owner of Hamer Bridge, then, Ivy thought, grinning.

Ivy had met the young lass while taking a walk before bed last night. She'd been quite taken with her but had no intentions of telling *his nibs* that.

Florence had kindly invited her in for a cup of tea, which was more than Old Man Pickles had ever done. She'd cleaned the place up grand in the short time she'd been there and invited her to drop in any time she was passing. Not that she would. Cos if 'e found out there'd be all hell to pay!

'Bloody damned gypsy has bought the place!'

'Aye ... and good afternoon to you too, sir,' Ivy said, and brushing past him, left the room.

Garrett poured himself a large whisky from a decanter and dropping into an armchair flung his stick to the ground. Bruno lifted his paw and placed it on his lap. Garrett looked at the dog and managed to smile. 'Sorry, old boy. What a grumpy bugger I am. It seems every time I walk into a room somebody vacates it. Not surprising, eh?' He took another large swig from the glass and drained it.

The gypsy girl, now ... what was her name? Yes, Florence, that was it.

Garrett poured himself another drink and began to relax as the alcohol took effect. He could see the girl in his mind's eye. Jet-black hair tumbling about her broad straight shoulders; a narrow waist nipped with a man's crude leather belt. She wore a drab serviceable skirt ... and a cream-coloured blouse. He could visualize her breasts beneath when she wiped the perspiration from them....

Garrett closed his eyes, wanting to keep alive her image, but it wasn't long before the empty glass slipped silently from his hand onto the rug and he fell asleep.

Chapter Five

RYEBURN NESTLED ON the northern edge of the North York Moors. The gentle eminence of the twelfth-century medieval castle dominated the market town. Its ruins rose into the sky out of a dramatic landscape on a wave of ditches and banks where it had guarded the town for nine hundred years.

It was market day and the town was crammed with canvas-covered stalls where traders called out their wares for sale.

Florence's first call was at the blacksmith's. Her Welsh cob she'd named Barney had thrown a shoe. When she introduced herself and told the farrier where she lived the farrier took her by surprise.

'I know who you are, missus,' he said removing his grimy flat cap and running his hand through what few strands of hair remained. The blacksmith was broad and short; his head reaching no higher than Florence's shoulders. His brown arms appeared out of proportion to the rest of his body; they were strong and muscular from hard work and glistened with sweat from the heat of the furnace.

'I'll mek a good job for thee,' he said.

'How ... how do you know ... who I am?'

'Ah, nowt 'appens in Ryeburn without townsfolk gets wind of it!' he laughed, and slapped the greasy cap on the leather apron he wore. "Specially up at Agra – yer've bowt old Pickles's place, I hear. Well, tha's set a few tongues waggin', young woman, an' no doubt about it. Now, you git thissen to market and t'cob'll be ready for yer when you've done.'

Florence wound her way through the bustling market taking note of goods for sale while at the same time considering what she could sell here besides rabbit skins. She stocked up on provisions and sauntered away from the market square and crossed the bridge under which a narrow stream ran gently through the town. There was a little café which didn't appear too crowded and Florence was ready for a cup of tea. The bell jingled when she opened the door, and as she entered the room the voices ceased chattering. Florence made her way to a small table and flushed hotly, aware that all eyes turned to look at her. She was dressed decently enough; wearing the good navy skirt which almost reached her ankles. The long-sleeved white blouse she'd bought for best was cloaked in a dark shawl and tucked neatly into the belt at the front on her waist. A waitress poised with pencil and notepad walked over to where she was sitting.

'Tea and a buttered scone, please,' she said quietly. The silence was stifling, and the tension continued until she finished her tea and had eaten her scone. The waitress came and cleared away her things. Florence paid, then rose to make her departure; her chair leg scraped noisily across the polished wooden floor. It was as she grasped the door handle the chattering resumed. It was then that she heard the passing remark amid the babbling.

'She's that *gypsy lass from Hamer Bridge ...*' Florence shut the door with a firm hard bang behind her and caused the bell to jangle furiously. Hurriedly, she made her way back to the blacksmith's. And after paying the farrier Florence thanked him and left. The farrier stood watching her departure with a twinge of sadness in his heart. He'd seen the agony in her eyes when she'd glanced briefly into his. Aye, the womenfolk won't take kindly to a bonny young woman like you in the area, he thought, shaking his head. Mind you, it'll mek an enjoyable change for us old buggers tae 'ave summat decent to rest our eyes on, he mused. Then the farrier tossed his greasy cap into the air. It came back down and landed on his head before he disappeared into the forge.

The glorious sun-drenched moors blurred before her as tears pricked her eyes. There was nowhere Florence could run to: no refuge among her own people, no relatives to travel the roads with; her future loomed before her as lonely and empty as the moors she now drove over.

Absorbed in her despondency, time flew, and before she knew where she was Hamer Bridge came into view. In contrast, towering loftily on the moor above the tiny cottage loomed High Agra, standing impressively in all her splendour; looking down on the world below – and mocking it.

'Get on, Barney!' Florence said sharply, bringing to mind its occupant. She flicked the reins hard on the horse's rump. 'If they don't like us, Barney – they're gonna have to lump us – cos we're not going anywhere. C'mon, let's away home, lad!'

Topcliffe gypsy horse fair two months later

Ambrose Wilson stepped down from the brightly coloured bow-top wagon and strolled to the wagon pitched next to his own and rapped on the little door.

'Mam, Dad, cuppa tea's ready an' I've seen to the 'orses,' he called.

A few moments later, Bob and Mary Wilson joined their son beside the campfire and the family sat in companionable silence as they drank their tea.

The Wilsons came every year to the three-day gypsy fair supplying the local farmers with workhorses, and riding ponies for the children of the well-to-do. Sadly though, this time, there was only the one son accompanying them. The last time they'd visited the fair prior to the war they'd been a family of five, but two sons had died at the Somme. The bereaved couple thanked God every day Ambrose had not been accepted to go and fight for king and country alongside his brothers. His hand was disfigured. He had pleaded with the War Office to give him a position working with the horses. Eventually he'd been successful. And after receiving references he'd obtained from gentlemen of note, the ministry acknowledged Ambrose's expertise and exploited it in the training of horses to pull the cannons.

Ambrose glanced about the field remembering the time when

his heart had sung with joy; a time when he and his brothers had frolicked in the grass like young colts wrestling one another to the ground for hours in the warm sunshine. But it was a different scene today, he thought, looking around ... where old men out-numbered the young.

This was a journey he and his parents had had to make; not only for themselves; but in memory of their family members who had died. He glanced across at his parents immersed in their own memories and grief. Ambrose didn't possess the means to lessen their pain, but hopefully one day there would be grandchildren to fill the vacuum ... ease the pain of loss ... and bring them some joy before death.

The field where the gypsies gathered was overflowing with brightly painted wagons and fine-looking horses. At the bottom of the field flowed the river Swale where they watered and washed the horses prior to selling them on the village high street.

Ambrose tossed the dregs from his teacup onto the grass and set about the task of grooming the horses for sale. There were five in total; amongst which was a gelding he'd managed to pick up cheap a few months ago. But on closer scrutiny, the horse was much older than he'd been led to believe. He placed a bucket of bran mash down in front of the horse and patted his neck. 'All right, old boy, eh? You might be a bit long in the tooth, but you know how to pull a wagon.' The horse whinnied in response to his soft words and Ambrose smiled. There was a touch of Clydesdale in the animal, which Ambrose believed accounted for his size and remarkable strength; regrettably, though, he was wall-eyed. He had one blue eye and one brown. Not an attractive feature in any animal. But Ambrose had no intentions of selling him; he was the best horse he'd come across between the shafts in a long time. During the short time he'd owned the gelding he worked him to lead the younger ones he was breaking to drive. The big gelding's passive character and know-how quickly steered the inexperienced horse back in line when they objected to the restraints of the shafts and tried to kick over the traces.

Ambrose unfastened the buckle which held the leather glove in place on his left hand and removed it; it had become hot and itchy in the confines of the glove – felt sore and uncomfortable and he gently massaged the red lump of flesh. The fingers curled round almost to a fist where they had fused in the heat of a camp-fire one winter's day when he was only five years old. With the exception of being deemed unfit to fight alongside his brothers, the injury hadn't caused any further disruption to his life.

People poured into Topcliffe village from far and wide.

Florence stood among those lining the street. Four piebald were first down the street, moving at a fast trot. Bystanders gasped in admiration at the expertise of a young gypsy boy riding one bareback at high speed whilst leading three more.

However, Florence wasn't that concerned with the piebald horses – she had her eyes focused on the horse that followed. It was a young black colt, no more than three years old by her reckoning. At a guess he appeared to be about fifteen hands high and perfectly proportioned. Florence kept her eyes on him; not allowing the colt to disappear from sight. The crowds were now taken up with a collection of heavy workhorses being led into a maelstrom of bidders. Florence quickly made her way through the crowds to have a word with the colt's owner.

'Hello, mister. I'm interested in your horse. I take it he's for sale?'

Ambrose turned round to see who'd spoken. 'Aye, he's for sale,' he replied.

She looked vaguely familiar, he thought. She was the same height as him and he found himself gazing into the bluest eyes fringed in thick black lashes. Her jet-black hair was neatly drawn back in a chignon at the nape of her neck.

'I need a horse for riding. I've already got one for the shafts … and I like the looks of him,' she said, taking a step forward and running her hand along the colt's neck and along his back.

'Don't I know you from somewhere? You look kind of familiar.' Ambrose folded his arms and cocked his head to one side, study-ing her.

'Aye, mebbe,' she said, smiling. 'I'm one of you lot. Florence Grainger's my name. I – I've been to a few horse fairs in my time … before my mam died.'

'Grainger … Grainger … well, now, I'm sure I've heard that name somewhere recently.' He rubbed his chin thoughtfully with the leather-gloved hand, trying to recall where he'd heard the name … Grainger?

'Yes! That's it! I bought a horse from a Grainger a few months ago … but I don't think he'd be anythin' to do with you.…'

He saw the girl's expression change in an instant – and panic replaced the self-assurance he'd regarded in those blue eyes only a few moments ago.

'Oh, so you've another horse to sell? Have … you?' Florence asked, quickly regaining her self-control.

Surely not, she wondered … could it be Ginger Dick?

'Aye, I've a few to sell, but not the old gelding I've bought recently … he's too old, I—'

'Can I see him, please?' she asked excitedly.

Ambrose frowned and shrugged his shoulders. 'Yes, if you want to, I suppose. Come on down to t'field with me now if yer like. I'm on my way for the rest of the horses I've to flash,' he said using the local term for to show, 'there're lots of farmers 'ere looking for workhorses, but not for the likes of this young 'un, eh?' Ambrose said, roughing up the gelding's mane before gently slapping the side of his neck. 'C'mon, young 'un, let's get you back. Miss Florence Grainger here's taken a shine to yer, even if the others haven't, and,' Ambrose whispered loudly into the gelding's ear while winking at Florence, 'I'll cut her a good deal if she promises to spoil yer.'

Florence burst out laughing. The sound of her own laughter made her realize she hadn't laughed in a long time – it felt good.

She thought him a pleasant man and liked him.

And it was in this relaxed and easy manner that Florence fell into step beside him and the horse and they made their way back to the campsite.

Mena Hall was sitting by her campfire when she saw Florence walking over the field with Ambrose Wilson. She would have recognized that girl anywhere. Apart from her black hair – it could've been Esme herself. She had her mother's height and carriage; bearing no resemblance to that mean brute of a father. Mena's eyes followed them. And when they were in hearing shot she shouted, 'Hey, Florence! Come yourself on over here to see me when you've done, girl!'

Florence turned to see who had called her name.

Oh, how nice to see that dear woman's face. She hadn't seen Mena Hall for a very long time. The old fortune-teller was crouched on a stool by the fire outside her wagon. Yet even from this distance Florence could see the familiar clay pipe suspended from her smiling mouth, revealing her tobacco-stained teeth.

Mena had been a close friend of her mother. Florence recalled her mother saying that a lot of dukkerin' or fortune-telling wasn't to be believed, and more often than not it was nothing more than a load of old codswallop. There were exceptions, though, she'd said, and Mena Hall was one of them. She had the true gift of sight and that was why she was highly respected up and down the country. Mena had frequented the stately homes of the rich and noble – maintaining decade-long relationships with many of her distinguished clients.

'I'll be along for a cuppa, Mena, as soon as I've finished here, all right?' Florence called back and the old lady responded with a nod.

'Mam, this is Florence Grainger, she's interested in the young black colt.'

'Ah, I knows who it is. You're Esme's bairn, ain't yer?'

'Yes, I am … you knew my mam?' The sound of her mother's name on someone else's lips delighted Florence, causing her heart to flutter. It was little more than six months since she'd passed away and it was the first time she'd spoken to any of her own people or heard her mother's name mentioned.

'Aye, I did, lass. I'm right sorry to hear of 'er passing. God rest her soul,' the woman said, crossing herself. 'We were at Appleby Fair when we heard she'd passed on; someone must have spoken to yer dad.'

Out of the corner of his eye, Ambrose noticed Florence visibly flinch for the second time at the mention of her father.

'Right, let's put this colt through his paces, eh?' Ambrose said chirpily, and stuffed the halter lead into her hand. 'He's had a saddle on his back, but no one's sat him as yet. Now, you lead him on and I'll follow behind yer.'

Florence led the young horse away from the wagon and down the field.

He was a biddable animal, she thought, and quickening her pace allowed him to trot. She glanced back over her shoulder to where Ambrose loped at the rear in long easy strides. She glimpsed his leather-gloved hand and wondered why he wore it. Her concentration lapsed for an instant and her foot caught in a rabbit hole and she went flying head first. The young colt shied at the sudden movement and danced sideways seeking to escape her grasp, but Florence held on tightly to the lead.

'Damn and blast!' she cried, dragging herself up into a sitting position.

'You all right? You went a right old cropper there?'

'I'm fine, thanks … my pride's hurt more than anything.'

He held out his hand, Florence clasped it; the warmth of his touch spread through her fingers and up her arm and deep into her belly. Ambrose pulled her effortlessly to her feet. He was smiling with genuine amusement when he saw she was all right and had come to no harm. They were standing very close – their bodies touching – and for a brief moment their eyes locked; both acknowledging that silent sense of wonderment when lovers meet for the very first time. Ambrose's hand rested firmly in the small of her back to steady her, and the warm pressure of it caused her pulse to race with excitement. She didn't trust the sudden silence and quickly passed the rein to him. Then, averting her eyes she brushed the grass and dirt from her clothes.

'Come on, I'll get Mam to make you a cuppa tea, that'll put you right.'

'Thanks, but I'm all right. A-and I promised old Mena I'd have a cup of tea with her – can we settle up on a price for young Dancer here?'

'Dancer. Named him already, eh?' He chuckled. 'Hmm … yes, I like that; it suits him.'

'Couldn't really call him anything else after that performance

… an' I'm right glad you like it.'

'I can deliver him to you if you want me to. That's if you don't live a hundred miles away,' he added jokingly. 'It won't be till after the fair's finished.'

'That'd be a big help, thanks.'

'Now … come and see the old gelding I bought.'

Florence would recognize the horse anywhere.

'Ginger Dick!' she exclaimed, running to the dear old horse tethered behind the wagon. He threw his head up and whinnied loudly at the sound of her voice. She put her arms about him, burying her head in the horse's mane. The gentle creature turned his head and affectionately nuzzled her.

Ambrose watched in silence as a tear escaped and slid unchecked down her cheek before she could stop it. Something strange and unexpected was happening to him, and he wasn't sure whether he was enjoying it or was disturbed by the feelings he experienced. Here he was, a man of twenty-eight. He'd courted a fair few travelling lasses in his time and also one or two lasses from the settled community, but not one of them had ever had this effect on him before.

'Will you sell him to me?' Florence was asking. 'Please? I'll pay you a handsome price …'

Ambrose was shaking his head, not allowing her to finish. 'No. But if I ever do decide to sell him you'll get first refusal. That's a promise.'

Florence turned and gave the horse a reassuring pat on the neck. 'You've a decent home, Ginger Dick,' she said, 'and I'll see you again sometime, won't I?' she added, throwing Ambrose a trusting smile.

'Aye, I'll make that another promise.'

Florence paid Ambrose the amount they'd settled on for the colt. She gave him her address and he said she could expect delivery the following week.

Ambrose's eyes followed her until she disappeared from view and into Mena Hall's bow-top wagon. He was in no doubt that he was also being closely watched by the unseen, inquisitive eyes of fellow gypsies – and envious ones at that.

'There you are, me bonny lass,' Mena said, handing Florence a china cup and saucer. 'Our many pryin' eyes out there,' she said, nodding towards the little door, her small black eyes twinkling with amusement. 'I miss your mother, Florence. Tell me, where yer stoppin' nowadays?' she asked.

'I know I can trust you, Mena. But the thing is ...' Her voice trailed off.

'I know ... I know ... I understand ... You don't want yer father getting' wind of where you're stoppin', that's it, isn't it, eh? Can't say I blame yer either, lass. He's got a right nasty streak in him has that Benny Grainger.'

Florence nodded her agreement and the old woman continued. 'I told her, your mother, I said: "Don't you wed 'im, Esme. Marry in haste repent at leisure," I says to 'er! But she wouldn't listen to me.... Well, God rest her soul, she's at peace now ... aye ... God rest her soul....'

Old Mena gently closed her eyes and drifted off to sleep. Florence couldn't help but wonder about the old lady. She'd lived on her own all her life. She had no family that anybody knew of, but she was much loved and well respected in the gypsy community and, although she travelled the roads alone, she was never short of a stopping place, and was welcomed wherever she went.

Mena opened her eyes suddenly and sat up straight.

'I'm settled now. I've bought a place near Ryeburn, Mena. Hamer Bridge,' Florence said, continuing the conversation from where they left off. 'And it'd be a real pleasure to have you to stay sometime. You come and visit for as long as you want whenever you want. There's plenty of room to pull your wagon on ... or you're welcome to stay in the cottage with me.'

'That's kind of you, lass. I'll remember what you've said, and I thank you kindly for the invitation. You never know – I might just take you up on it one of these days.'

'Oh, I hope you do,' Florence replied sincerely. 'Well, I'd better be off now, Mena, I've a bus to catch to Thirsk, then another to Ryeburn.'

Florence held the frail old lady in her arms for a long time before leaving her and prayed she would see her again one day soon.

After Florence departed, Mena picked up the teacup the girl had used and was about to toss the dregs away when something caught her eye. She sat back down again and cradled the cup in both hands. Then looking intently at the tea leaves lying at the bottom of the cup, Mena closed her eyes and stilled her mind ... extinguishing all thoughts. The old woman's gnarled hands stroked the cup lightly that Florence had held only moments ago ... and allowed her spiritual energy to flow. It was an energy which held God's precious gift of foresight to pervade her being.

One moment the old fortune-teller's face was wreathed in smiles, and the next moment, sad tears slid down her weathered cheek. Whilst blessed with *the sight,* this was a heavy responsibility to bear: Mena bore it with profound humility.

Mena stepped down from the wagon and into the bright sunshine, then, sitting by her campfire, she closed her eyes.

God protect her and guide her safely through the difficulties before her, prayed the old lady.

Florence stood in the middle of the room admiring it. The holes in the roof had been repaired; the black range gleamed and the windows sparkled. All she needed now was for Dancer to be delivered and her family would be complete. The new horse would take up residence alongside the goat that provided milk and cheese. Any surplus would be sold at market along with jars of the bilberry jams and jellies she'd prepared. And by the time autumn arrived she would have sufficient rabbit skins to sell to bring in further income before the winter set in.

She walked across the room and looked out of the window. There was still time to go for a walk up to High Moor even though the sun was low.

'Moth!' she called, throwing a thin shawl about her shoulders. 'Come on, let's go, boy!'

Florence set off at a run for the first hundred yards with Moth at her heels before slowing into a steady stride. She carried on walking until they reached a high point on the moor and it was here that Florence stood motionless, gazing in wonder; she was entranced by a landscape which stretched out before her in a glorious haze of pink, her breath caught in her throat at its utter beauty. She strode the moorland which was criss-crossed by ancient pannier tracks; its rugged beauty never ceased to move her.

It had come as a great surprise to Florence, how easy she'd found it to relinquish the old way of life; and in the last few months, that old way of life was quickly becoming a distant memory. The people of Ryeburn had not exactly warmed to her and welcomed her into the bosom of the community, but she'd suffered worse and would get over it.

Moth's sudden barking interrupted her thoughts. She shielded her eyes against the lowering sun to see Moth racing back and forth where a huge outcrop of rock rose from ground behind which another dog emerged. Florence recognized the dog immediately.

'Moth! Moth!' she called sharply, slapping her thigh. 'Here boy!' Moth ignored her demand and scampered off through the heather with his friend. Florence ran towards the dogs and managed to grab Moth by his collar. Moth objected vehemently and started dragging her back to where the other dog was now standing.

'Bruno! Stay!' a loud voice yelled. 'Have you no control over that damned animal of yours?' he snapped rudely, having ridden to where Florence was hurriedly tying a piece of band to Moth's collar.

She turned and glared at Garrett Ferrensby who was seated on a fine grey hunter. How she loathed having to look up at him. Had he been a gypsy at a horse fair she'd not have minded one bit. But he wasn't a gypsy – he was a rude ignorant gorgio and Florence said nothing. She turned her back on him and walked away with her head held high, sensing his eyes following her every movement.

She'd only gone a few hundred yards when there was a sudden loud whinny accompanied by loud barking. Florence ignored the barking and didn't look back straightaway – not until Moth broke free from her grasp. He was racing back to Bruno, who was yapping and barking at something he'd found. Garrett Ferrensby was nowhere to be seen and his grey horse was trotting towards her. She slowly reached out her hand, speaking softly to the animal as it neared.

'Here, boy … steady, boy,' she said soothingly. The grey put his nose in her hand and she gathered up the reins, then walked to where the dogs stood barking. Garrett Ferrensby lay in the deep heather and his eyes were closed. She knelt down beside him and saw there was blood seeping from the back of his head. He opened his eyes slowly, then started to groan.

'It's all right,' she said softly, the harsh words he'd flung at her forgotten. 'You've had a fall … a nasty crack on yer head. If I help you, do you think you can manage to climb on your horse?'

Garrett nodded. 'I – I think so … thank you … I'm sorry …'

'Don't talk. We'll get you to my cottage where I've something to ease the pain and stop the bleeding … there … up you go!' Florence took his weight and helped heave him up onto the horse's back. The grey hunter was big and powerful and capable of carrying them both and Florence leapt up behind him to ensure he didn't slide off and do himself more harm.

The sun had set and it was growing dark by the time they arrived at the cottage.

Florence settled her patient into the comfortable leather armchair by the warm range before heating some milk laced with a shot of brandy and handing it to him. She disappeared into the larder, returning with a bottle of mixture then began bathing the wound on the back of his head.

Garrett flinched. 'What's that you're using?' he enquired, eyeing her beneath a quizzical brow. She had one hand pressed firmly against his forehead to steady him whilst gently cleaning the wound with the other. Garrett lowered his gaze, allowing his eyes to travel appreciatively over the simple navy-blue dress she wore. The rise and fall of her firm breasts against the thin fabric was only inches away and he was filled with desire … and longed to reach out and draw her close to him … and for a moment, a soft … untouched silence seemed to hang between them.

Florence felt the heat from his body make contact with her own. 'It … it's called shepherd's purse. I've used it many a time … it'll stop the bleeding,' she said, breaking the spell.

'It was a snake,' he said, looking at her, attempting to read her every nuance of expression, 'an adder, I recognized the markings … that's what scared my horse … is he all right, by the way?'

'Your horse is fine,' Florence assured him.

'I don't know what would have happened had you not been around … thank you …' Garrett said. Then all of a sudden he was overcome with dizziness and felt extremely tired.

'Hush, hush, you must stay still and quiet, mister, you've had a nasty bang to your head. I'll go and fetch someone from High Agra to take you …'

'No, no, please …' he protested, his eyes flying wide open. 'I couldn't bear it. Not Ivy Baxter's fussing … please … they'll think I'm staying in Ryeburn for the night – as I often do. That's if you don't mind my being in your home?'

But Florence did mind. 'I've nowhere for you to sleep, here…. look!' She waved her hand, indicating what precious little space there was.

'I'll be all right here … to sit quiet, by the fire …' he said, letting his head fall back and rest against the soft worn leather. 'I don't need to lie down … I won't bother you … just need to …' His words trailed off as the desire to sleep combined with the comforting warmth of the fire overpowered him.

Florence fetched a tartan wool blanket from her bed and draped it across his knees.

Garrett woke to the sound of Florence humming softly, standing by the kitchen sink. He'd slept through whilst she lit the fire before going out to milk the goat. He ran his hand through his hair and winced when he caught the wound on the back of his head, and Florence turned around. The early-morning sun burst through the tiny window, making her black hair glisten. She smiled at him and poured him a cup of tea.

'Porridge and toast?' she asked.

'Yes, thank you.' Garrett fumbled with his stick and made his way awkwardly to the dining table where she placed the food before him. 'Where's Bruno?' he enquired. 'I do hope he's not been making a nuisance of himself.' He'd forgotten all about the dog until now.

'He's fine; he's with Moth in the outhouse. I thought it best because they'd only yap an' keep you awake if I parted them.'

'I don't know how I'll ever be able to repay you f–for saving my life,' Garrett said.

'You don't need to repay me!' Her eyebrows shot up and her blue eyes widened as she looked at him. 'Good God, I wouldn't leave an injured animal! An' I didn't save your life,' she added, blushing, 'somebody would have come looking for you … you being important – an' all that.'

He was unprepared for the full impact when her eyes looked directly into his. They were the most incredible blue … with pupils as black as jet framed in thick dark lashes. He couldn't take his off her; she was breathing quickly and her face was flushed. She was not just attractive, he decided, but the most beautiful woman he'd ever laid eyes on. Was there any wonder her face had hardly been out of his mind since he'd first met her? And when he stayed with Daphne at the hotel and made love to her, it was Florence Grainger's eyes he gazed into, her lips he kissed, and her body he devoured.

'Err … I'm sorry,' Garrett apologized when he realized he was staring. 'What did you say?'

'I said Bruno is barking and making a din. Maybe you'd better get going now – I'm sure you can manage on your own – it isn't far.'

It was a dismissal. Garrett wiped his mouth with his handkerchief and stood up to leave.

There was an unexpected loud knock on the door which startled them both.

Florence walked over and opened it. 'Yes?'

A tall, immaculately dressed man stood unsmiling in the doorway. 'Is there something you want, mister?' she asked, frowning.

'There most certainly is. I am Robin Ferrensby – and *that*,' he was pointing to the outhouse, 'is my brother's horse!'

'Hello, Robin old boy! Where the devil did you spring from?' Garrett asked, making an appearance behind Florence, and placing his hands on her shoulders, he gently moved her to the side. Garrett stepped through the doorway before turning to address her.

'Thank you for your assistance and your hospitality, Miss Grainger,' he said, taking her hand gently and shaking it. 'I hope to see you again very soon.'

He then turned to his brother. 'I'll get my horse. Come, Robin, Miss Grainger is a busy lady and has other things to attend to.'

Florence stood at the kitchen window watching the two brothers.

Garrett's brother, Robin, was livid. Although she couldn't hear what he was saying, his face was red with anger as he shouted at Garrett. The angry brother mounted his horse, then waited whilst Garrett mounted his grey. Garrett pulled on a rein and turned the animal round to face the cottage. He saw her watching them from the kitchen window and raised his hand and smiled in her direction.

Back at High Agra, Garrett was still on the receiving end of Robin's wrath.

'Cavorting with a damned gypsy? Good God, man! Are you completely mad? Have you any idea what this could do to my reputation at Westminster? What it could do to the family name? Have you lost your mind *altogether*, Garrett?'

Garrett poured himself a large whisky from a decanter on the dresser.

'Want one?' he asked, ignoring the vicious onslaught.

'Bugger the bloody whisky, Garrett!' Robin blared. 'Are you listening to a word I'm saying?'

'I'm listening. How could I not? The entire household is listening to your unwarranted diatribe!'

'Unwarranted? Hah! Now that is a laugh!' Robin sneered.

'Florence ... Miss Grainger,' Garrett said, spurning Robin's disparagement, 'actually saved my life, I'll have you know – and *you* can believe what the hell you like. Why don't you get back to bloody London and your smart friends – who give a damn – because quite honestly, Robin, *I* don't give a damn!'

Garrett swigged the whisky back in one gulp and poured himself another.

'Felicity's coming up next week,' Robin said, '... and I don't want her upsetting.'

'Why's she coming? I thought she hated Yorkshire – and everybody in it, come to think of it,' Garrett mumbled sarcastically.

'Felicity does not hate *anybody*, Garrett; she's ... she's just not country, that's all.'

Garrett flopped down into an armchair. He cradled the glass of whisky in his hands, watching, but not listening, as Robin rambled on, listing Felicity's finer qualities. And his heart sank at the thought of her and Garrett's London set descending on High Agra for the grouse shoot.

Two weeks later Ambrose arrived at Ryeburn.

He followed the directions Florence had given him, and before long he was on the open moor road that led to Hamer Bridge.

Ambrose pulled the cart to a halt and climbed down to soak up the surroundings and stretch his legs. The weather had been oppressively hot down in the Vale of York with the air full of thunder – he could smell it. He looked back towards Ryeburn where the sky had grown black as ink and where quiet rumblings of thunder heralded fine veins of lightning against the black sky. A flock of lapwings suddenly took flight at the sound of the approaching storm. Their broad, rounded, black and white wings flashed brightly in the birds' wavering display; their distinctive, penetrating call caused the horses to shift restlessly.

'Whoa ... steady ... there, boy,' Ambrose said, his soothing tone calming the horses' fear. He placed a pail of water down for them, but first rinsed his face and tied a clean spotted neckerchief around his neck.

High Agra came into view as the heavens opened. Ambrose stopped the cart. He was awestruck at the stateliness and grandeur of the house rising into the sky from its elevated position.

The proud stone edifice seemed to look down on all who passed, informing them that the persons residing here were landed gentry. Not expecting to see anything as grand upon the moors, Ambrose couldn't help but wonder who would live in such a fine house.

The cart bumped along the rutted track, then over a narrow bridge that spanned a small stream. Ambrose relaxed his concentration when he recognized the fold in the hills and a single dwelling Florence had described perfectly.

He smiled when he saw someone standing in the doorway. It was Florence. She was beckoning him and she ran to greet the sopping bedraggled assemblage.

'Quick! In here!' Florence shouted above the noise of the storm. And running ahead of him she opened the double doors for Ambrose to guide the horses and cart inside.

'We'll see to the horses first,' Ambrose said, removing the wet heavy harness. 'You put those two where you want them,' he added, working quickly.

Florence didn't reply. She couldn't speak and stood speechless, tears flooding her eyes.

'Ginger Dick ... you've brought Ginger Dick. I-I can't believe it,' she sobbed, flinging her arms round the old horse's broad neck. 'Why? Why did you bring him with you, Ambrose?'

She turned to Ambrose, but he had his back to her and was rubbing down one of the horses with a straw wisp. He slowly turned and faced her. Through her tears she saw he was smiling softly at her; her heart skipped a beat and a hot flush swept up her cheeks.

'I couldn't keep him. Not after I saw what he meant to you ... so I fetched 'im for you,' he said, shrugging his shoulders and wanting to dismiss the matter.

'Oh, Ambrose,' tears filled her eyes again, 'how can I thank you? I'll pay you, of course, whatever you want ...'

'Nah, you owe me nix. He's yours by rights, anyway. Tell yer what, though, I'd love a cuppa!' he said, changing the subject. 'An' if I can get meself dried out, that'll be payment enough for the 'orse.'

The storm raged without respite for the remainder of the day.

'You'll have to stay, Ambrose, you can't leave in this weather and it'll soon be dark,' Florence said. She replenished his cup and adding milk and sugar, she stirred his tea before handing it back to him, aware of the lack of dexterity in his leather-bound left hand.

'Fell in a campfire when I was a kid,' he said, reading her thoughts.

'Does it hurt?'

'Nah, not much; only if I get over-hot or too cold. It stopped me going off to fight in the war, though. That hurt more than me 'and. They wouldn't 'ave me – so I trained horses for them instead. My brothers went to fight ... but they never came back. Like a lot of 'em didn't, eh?'

A coal moved in the grate, causing the flames to light up the room that had grown dark. He looked across at her. The ribbon holding back her hair had loosened; dark strands of hair escaped, touching her cheeks and softening her face. Her skin was a fresh creamy colour with a faint blush of pink to her cheeks although not dark brown as were most of the gypsy girls in the summertime. In fact, Ambrose thought, frowning, nobody would suspect she came from gypsy stock. In that moment he recalled something his mother had said about Florence's parentage. She'd told him Florence's mother was already pregnant when she married Benny Grainger. Maybe that was what he noticed and why he found her so attractive: she was different. And there was no denying it, he was very drawn to her. He wouldn't have made the journey with Dancer – nor handed Ginger Dick over so readily – had his attraction to her not been as strong as it was.

'Do you find it lonely up here on the moors with no one to talk to?' he asked.

'Haven't had time to think about whether it's lonely or not. I've the markets to do ... an' I'll keep the odd horse to break in and sell on ... I've got to make it work,' she said quietly to herself. Florence swallowed deeply, remembering Garrett Ferrensby's recent stopover. That had stemmed any feelings of loneliness, she thought.

Ambrose detected the uncertainty in her voice, and thought it sad – an attractive vibrant girl like her, forsaking her birth-right to roam her country's winding roads; roads created by her ancestors hundreds of years ago; simply because she was a young woman on her own with no family. In that moment, he was filled with the desire to sweep her into his arms and take her with him from this God-forsaken place – before the restless spirit he saw burning brightly in those sapphire-blue eyes was extinguished forever.

'Can't imagine it myself, staying put in one place for very long, d'you miss the open road?'

'No, not since my mother passed away. It's different for a woman on her own with no family to look out for her ...' Florence said with a trace of sadness in her voice.

Oh, how I would protect you, Ambrose mused. Protect you from men's lustful hungers. He'd seen the way their eyes had followed her at Topcliffe Fair, and now wondered what Ryeburn's townsfolk thought of this attractive raven-haired gypsy beauty living on their doorstep ... and what about her neighbour?

'Couldn't help but notice that grand 'ouse I passed on my way 'ere; friendly neighbours, are they?'

Florence turned quickly, her eyes searching his.

Ah, I see, so the neighbour *is* friendly. It must be a *mush* (man) to have that sort of effect on her. And her next words confirmed his thoughts.

'I've only met Mr Ferrensby once or twice,' Florence said, her cheeks flushing crimson and the tone in her voice rising an octave. 'He ... he wants to buy this place. It used to be part of his estate ... or ... or something like that.'

'You gonna sell it to him?' Ambrose enquired boldly.

'No, I'm not!' she said adamantly. 'This is my home now.'

'And a fine home it is too, Florence,' Ambrose said, rising from his chair. 'Now, if you don't mind, I'll bid you goodnight. Thank you kindly for the tea and shelter.'

Florence rose from her chair and went into the bedroom. She returned with a neatly folded blanket and placed it on a stool next to his chair. 'It can get chilly up here on the moors at night – even in high summer, you'll need this.'

'I'll sleep in the barn with the horses if it's all right with you,' Ambrose said. 'You know how it is…? I sort o' feel suffocated surrounded by four brick walls for too long … 'specially at this time of year.'

'No, that's fine … I understand. I'll see you in the morning.'

'G'night, Florence.'

'Goodnight, Ambrose.'

Florence went to the window. Her eyes followed him as he walked across the yard to the barn. He suddenly stopped and looked upwards at the swifts reeling high in the evening sky in aerodynamic fashion and feasting on swarms of midges. He turned to see her watching him and smiled at her.

Florence watched him disappear into the barn before going outside. The storm had passed, leaving the night air cool and fresh. The clean fragrance of moorland heather was carried on a gentle breeze and filled her nostrils. She looked towards High Agra where a tall chimney belched smoke into a darkening night sky, and she imagined Garrett Ferrensby and his brother sitting by their fireside making pleasant conversation.

She couldn't have been more wrong.

Chapter Six

THE TWELFTH OF August arrived with a platinum-grey sky. Garrett's horse chafed gently at the bit. He'd woken early and decided to ride out before Robin and his political London cronies shattered the peace of the moors. It's only for three days, Robin had promised, so do try to be polite, he'd pleaded. These chaps hold *my* political future in their hands. Then there was Felicity, who was driving the housekeeper mad with her incessant demands – while Garrett played pig in the middle having to mollify Ivy.

'It's either that woman or me!' Ivy had threatened.

'Just three more days and she'll be gone … I promise you. Try, please, for me, Ivy,' Garrett said.

'Three days. No more!'

Garrett looked back towards High Agra where evidence of Ivy at work in the kitchen was apparent as he eyed fresh smoke curling up and disappearing into a grey sky. His housekeeper and scullery maid would be making breakfast and packing picnic baskets in preparation for the shoot's luncheon party up on the moors. The food would be delivered by horse and cart at precisely 12:30 p.m. on Robin's strictest orders. Garrett checked his pocket watch. It's going to be a bloody long day, he thought, and sighed.

There was a sudden whinny and Bruno shot off over the heather. The dog had spotted his bedraggled-looking friend in the distance who was making a dash for him. Coming up a moorland track at a steady walk was what appeared to be a rider-less horse. It was a long few moments before she came into view. Florence

Grainger was striding confidently behind a black horse, holding the long reins.

Garrett climbed down from his horse and waited.

I'll have to stop: the track is too narrow, Florence thought nervously. Her heart raced at the very thought of seeing him again so soon. She observed from this distance he wore no jacket or hat, and his collarless shirt was tucked carelessly into his trousers.

'Morning, you're up and about early,' Garrett said. He regarded her with a bemused smile and noticed her sapphire-blue eyes sparkled with life. Her face was flushed with health and vitality, and her windswept black hair was loose and unrestrained; and Garrett imagined her and the black horse were as one – both beautiful ... and wild ... and free. And who shall tame you, my beauty ... I wonder?

Doesn't he ever smile? Florence thought, looking into his stern face.

'He's a fine animal.' Garrett stepped up close and ran his hand along Dancer's neck. 'Breaking him to drive, I see, eh?'

'Drive – and ride. Don't see any point in 'aving a horse if it's only used for sitting on. Horses are like humans, they enjoy working. How're you since your fall? Better, I hope?' she added quickly. That was thoughtless, Florence, she thought. People like Garrett Ferrensby didn't work. Well, not proper work like the rest of us.

'I'm fine, thanks to you.' At close quarters he saw the top button of her blouse was unfastened; and he saw the beat of her heart pulsing in her throat. She was wearing a pair of over-sized men's trousers and a blouse neatly tucked in; and all held together at her waist by a broad leather belt. She saw and felt his eyes devouring her. Her mouth was dry and her hand grasped the reins more tightly to stop them shaking. What was happening to her and why did she feel like this? Then their eyes met briefly and her heart did a nervous flip and she looked away.

'Can I come and see you again, Florence?' he was saying.

'No, you can't!' she said, shocked at his request. 'I ... I ... must go ... Dancer's getting restless,' she stammered.

'Please, I must see you,' Garrett pleaded.

'Don't ... please don't say things like that ... We're different, you and me; we're from different worlds....'

'No we're not... we're human beings with needs ... please ... I must see you. You're all I think about day and night.'

'No! I've got to go. Please, for your own sake and mine, leave me alone.' Florence clicked her tongue. 'Walk on, Dancer. Moth! Come on, boy!'

Garrett stood watching her disappear down the track behind the horse with the dog at her heels. Then he suddenly remembered he hadn't told her about the grouse shoot taking place today. She'll wonder at the sound of gunfire going off on the moor. 'Florence!' he shouted. She either didn't hear him or ignored his calling and carried on without glancing back.

Benny Grainger flopped down on the grass and removed the grimy neckerchief from about his neck and wetted it in the cool water of Hartoft Beck, which trickled noisily over the stones at the back of the house. From his position he'd not only a good view of Hamer Bridge, but also of the surrounding area should anyone call at the property. He took the last of the stale bread from his jacket pocket and softened it in the stream. Oh, how his belly ached for a decent meal – and his body for the comfort of a bed.

It was while stopping at Appleby he'd learned of Florence's whereabouts and her good fortune. And he wanted to know where she'd got the money to buy a house while he struggled to survive. Since Esme's death there was nobody left to do his bidding and his life had grown more and more wretched as time wore on; and the anger and hatred he carried in his heart for Florence over the last few months was all that had kept him going. She'd been the talk of the fairs – and him the laughing stock. *Esme had favoured Florence over her own husband!* they whispered among themselves at the annual horse fairs. If the money used to buy the cottage had come from Esme, then where the hell had *she* got it from? It was Ambrose Wilson's mother who'd told him where Florence lived. She'd seen her son was smitten with Florence and she didn't want him taking up with a fancy piece like that! Living in a house like some gorgio! No, he was needed at home. If he wanted a wife they'd find him one; and that someone would be to suit their needs too. *We'll find him a lass from amongst our own sort who'll travel the roads with us,* had been Mrs Wilson's parting words to Benny Grainger.

The sound of a horse whinnying brought him back to the present. From his crouched position he watched Florence return with the horse and lead him into the barn, and as his eyes followed her, the acid rose and burned in the back of his throat, knowing she could afford such an expensive colt.

Florence removed Dancer's harness and rubbed him down with a straw wisp then turned him into his stall where Moth lay in the corner chewing on a hoof-shaving. She slapped her thigh and the dog instantly got up and followed her.

Back at the cottage Florence was having a cup of tea at the table when Moth suddenly leapt to his feet and started barking loudly to be let out. Florence opened the door. She gasped and took a step back while Moth growled deeply at the unkempt stranger standing in the doorway.

'Get the bugger away from me, Florence! Tell it to back off!' Benny Granger yelled as he backed away quickly from the open door. Florence waited until Benny retreated to a safe distance before calling the dog to her side. Moth stood beside his mistress; his sharp intelligent eyes fixed on the unwelcome stranger.

'Does he bite?' Benny asked, keeping his distance.

'Yes. One word from me,' Florence assured him, 'and he'll tear you apart!' she lied, her legs turning to jelly.

'I've been walking for days, lass. At least give yer old dad a cup o'tea, eh?'

'You're not my dad! Remember?' The dog began to growl again as Florence raised her voice. She put her hand on his head to quieten him. 'Who told you where I lived, eh? There's nowt for you here an' I don't want you around. You did me a big favour that day you told me you weren't my father. I'm only sorry that my mam wasted her life marrying you because she was pregnant with me. You're nowt but a mean, rotten man, Benny Grainger; and she didn't deserve the likes of you.'

'Aye, you're mebbe right ... Florence. But I beg o' you, don't send me away wi'out summat to eat and drink ... me belly hurts for want of food ...' But the ache for food was nothing compared to the hatred he felt for her right now when she held the upper hand – forcing him to beg.

Florence wanted rid of him and thought if she gave him a decent meal then he would be on his way and out of her life for ever. She glanced at the clock on the mantel. It was only nine o'clock. If she fed him now he could walk to Ryeburn and beg a lift from there.

'I'll give you a good meal and pack you some food up and then be on yer way, d'you hear me?'

'Aye, I hear yer, Florence, that'll be grand,' he said, watching the dog who wandered away from Florence as she entered the house.

'Sit there.' Florence pointed to a chair by the table. She broke three eggs into a frying pan and sliced some bread and toasted it on the open fire. 'Here,' she said, placing a heaped plateful of food in front of him and a cup of heavily sweetened tea. She remembered he always had *his* tea extra sweet because there was never any sugar left for either herself or her mother. 'I'll pack you some food and fill a bottle with tea for you to take with you,' she said, disappearing into the little larder.

Benny Grainger paused and looked about the room, which was furnished with fine-quality oak furniture; even the plate he ate off was of the finest china. How the hell's she come with money to buy stuff like this? Times had been particularly hard since Esme died, and she'd been a good grafter; folk had been happy to employ her and he'd been only too glad to pocket her wages. Seems I made a mistake after all, leaving Florence at that there farm ... Hmm, now was that where she got the brass for all this, I wonder? He picked up a shive of bread and meticulously wiped his plate with it before cramming it into his mouth. He reached across the table and picked up a knife that lay on the breadboard and tucked it into the back of his belt. The dog was nowhere in sight.

Florence emerged from the larder carrying food wrapped in a cloth tied with string. 'That'll keep you going until you find somewhere,' she said dropping it on the table in front of him. 'Now get out and don't come back!'

Benny wiped his mouth with the back of his hand. 'That was a right kushti meal, Florence. Now, don't be getting all het up, like. I was thinkin' how I could help you round here for a while. I've nowhere else to go ... an' I could see to the 'orses and—'

'You what?' Florence snarled. 'You stay here? Huh! It's been bad enough having to look at your face again. You make me sick! Now take that food and get out or I'll ...'

The words died on her lips and the colour drained from her face as she stepped back slowly.

'Or you'll what?' Benny said, brandishing a breadknife and grinning cruelly.

Florence's eyes darted round the room looking for Moth, but he was nowhere to be seen. Benny might be stronger than me but I'm faster on my feet, she thought. Out of the corner of her eye she caught sight of the poker resting on the hearth not three feet away. There was an unexpected creak of the front door as a sudden wind got up. Florence made a dash for the poker, then screamed when Benny caught her tightly by the wrist.

'No! Please ... leave me alone!' she cried. He twisted her arm behind her back then flung her roughly into an armchair.

'You bloody bitch ... I'm gonna give you the hiding of your life! You've been asking for one since you were bloody born!' He held the knife inches from her face and with his free hand he unbuckled his black leather belt fastened about his waist.

'Arrrrrgh!' Florence screamed as he brought it down hard on her. The loud smacking sound pierced the air when the leather made contact with the bare flesh of her arms. She doubled over burying her face in her lap – and covered her head with her arms.

The wolfhound heard his mistress scream. Moth darted into the room and leapt through the air, landing on Benny's back. The weight of the dog brought him to the ground in an instant.

The room fell silent. Florence lifted her head and opened her eyes and sank back into the chair. Moth whined and came to her, nuzzling her hand with his nose. Florence burst into tears and buried her head in the dog's neck. 'Oh, Moth ... Moth, thank you....'

A few minutes later when her sobbing had subsided, Florence disentangled her arms from round the dog. She glanced down at the body of her stepfather lying on the floor in front of her. His head was turned away and she couldn't see his face. Florence frantically leapt to her feet in a sudden panic, realizing he might come to quite soon and she would need to be prepared. She picked up the poker on the hearth. 'Moth, stay close... there's a good boy.' Her body trembled with fear as she stood by watching and waiting for him to stir.

He didn't.

After what seemed an eternity, Florence stepped round the body to the other side. She gasped and covered her mouth with both hands when she saw his face. The poker fell from her hand and clattered noisily to the floor. Benny Grainger's eyes stared ahead wide open and unseeing. Blood seeped through the grubby old shirt and jacket he wore, forming a pool on the floor. Taking a deep breath, Florence crouched down beside him; and using all her strength, she heaved his body over onto his back. It was then she saw the knife he'd threatened her with buried in his own chest. 'You bastard!' she said, spitting at the upturned face.

With enormous struggle and determination, Florence managed to drag the dead body into the barn. She wrapped it in sacking, tying it at both ends, then covered it with straw. Florence needed time to think about what she was going to do ... because she couldn't go to the police. They would never believe it was an accident and she'd be convicted of murder, then hung.

Her heart hammered in her chest as Florence steadied herself, leaning against the wall of the barn. Oh, Mother, help me ... tell me what to do? But no answer came and Florence went back inside the house. She cleared away the table and scrubbed clean everything Benny had touched; including the cushion he'd sat on for a few minutes, which was stripped and dropped into a bucket of warm soapy water. She scrubbed the bloodstained floor until her hands were red raw but a dark shadow still remained. Once Florence had dragged the large rug from the bedroom to cover the mark, it wasn't long before any trace of Benny Grainger's visit had been eradicated.

Florence fell asleep at the dining table physically and mentally exhausted. She woke with a jolt to the sound of gunfire, knocking over her cup of tea that had gone cold. She flew from her chair and to the window, but couldn't see anything. In the next instant a bombardment of gunfire made her dive to the floor. Moth was barking and yapping.

'Here, boy,' she said, calling him to her side. The dog came obediently to where she'd crouched on the floor behind the bulky armchair.

And that was how Garrett discovered her.

The shooting party was on the last drive on High Moor and Garrett had had enough. His leg ached and he'd grown weary of the company of Robin's city friends. 'I'll make my way back down the moor now, Robin, if that's all right with you. My leg's giving me jip. I'll see you all back at Agra.'

'Oh, yes, of course ... of course, sorry about the old leg, Garrett, didn't think ... bloody thoughtless of me,' Robin said, breaking open his twelve-bore and ejecting the spent cartridges before reloading and snapping the gun shut. 'We'll see you back at the house, old boy.'

Garrett, making his way home, decided to call in at Hamer Bridge. There was no sign of Florence as he walked past the barn and to the house where the front door was slightly ajar. He stood a few moments waiting for signs of movement inside but heard nothing.

'Hello,' he called, and tapping gently on the door he stepped inside.

Florence was crouching on the floor at the side of the chair with Moth beside her. She held on tightly to the dog's collar as he whined and strained to be free from her grasp.

'What...? What the hell has happened?'

Garrett dropped his cane and was at her side in seconds. Moth broke free from Florence's hold and stood between her and the intruder – a deep low growl in his throat.

'It's all right ... it's me ... Bruno's master,' he said softly, calming the animal. Moth sniffed his proffered hand, recognizing the familiar scent, and relaxed. Garrett leaned down and gently helped Florence to her feet and she made no resistance. She resembled a frightened vulnerable child – and a great wave of pity flooded him. They stood silently for a few moments, their differences forgotten.

Another barrage of gunfire exploded in her ears, causing her to jump; Garrett swiftly gathered her into his arms, holding her close without objection. He felt her body tremble with fear next to his own and smoothed his hand across the back of her head, caressing her black hair.

'Shhh ... it's all right ... it's nothing ... they're only shooting grouse on the moor.... I tried to warn you about it when I saw you on the moor, but it was too late, you'd left.' He spoke softly as he continued to hold her; all else forgotten except the sheer pleasure of holding her in his arms.

He felt a sharp sting of disappointment when she pressed him away from her.

'I'm all right,' she said, flustered, the colour rising in her cheeks. 'I didn't know ... what it was ... what was happening. Daft of me really, being scared I mean, it's just ... I never expected to hear gunfire. Ca ... can I offer you a cup of tea, or ... or something?'

'Tell me, Florence, honestly, do I look like I want tea?' She couldn't help but smile at his remark, and Garrett, taking a step forward, closed the gap between them. He rested his hands on the curve of her hips and pulled her close against his aroused body. They stood quite still, their eyes locked, seeking one another's thoughts. Garrett leaned down and brushed her lips softly with his. Her pulse quickened – he both fascinated and frightened her. She couldn't help but wonder if he'd be kissing her if he knew of the dead body she had hidden in the barn. The thought brought her to her senses and she pushed him away from her.

'Stop, please, stop this. You must go now,' she said, disentangling from his arms and stepping out of reach.

'Bloody hell, woman, what are you playing at? You welcome my advances one minute, then you bloody well spurn them the next! '

'We're not good for each other – you and me! We both know it ... your brother knows it!' Then she added bitterly, 'And all of Ryeburn knows it too! You should see the way they look down their noses at me!'

'Hah, look down their noses at you? Hah. And don't you know why? It's because they're jealous of you ... Florence ... Please ...' He reached out to take her hand, but she pulled it away.

'Please leave ... and don't come back,' she said, her voice a mere whisper. 'I don't want any trouble, please try to understand; I came here to make a new life ... to get away from ... from ...'

From that dead man in the barn, she wanted to scream.

'Get away from what? And why here? C'mon, you can tell me, Florence. Who was it sold you Hamer Bridge?' His eyes had narrowed suddenly and his voice had deepened and hardened.

Florence looked into his eyes and froze. So that's what it's all about. He doesn't care about me! To him I'm nothing more than the low-born daughter of a gypsy. It's my cottage he's hell-bent on getting back.

Garrett limped across the floor to where he'd dropped his cane, and picked it up. 'Think about it,' he said in an abrasive tone.

'I don't need to *think* about it. You've already had my answer and it's still the same. Hamer Bridge is not for sale ... Not now, not ever! Goodbye.'

Ignoring her farewell, Garrett walked out of the door and banged it shut.

Twilight crept across the moor together with heavy dew dampening the morning air. Ginger Dick whinnied excitedly as Florence led him out from the barn and onto the moor. Tied to the traces was a rickety gate that had seen better days. And on the top of the gate wrapped in sacking was the body of Benny Grainger.

Florence had ventured out onto the moor last night at dusk in search for a suitable place to dump the body. She discovered a disused mineshaft partially covered by a boulder. The mineshaft was about two hundred yards from the rocky outcrop where Garrett Ferrensby had come a cropper on his horse, she noticed, and marked the spot with a small cairn of stones.

It was almost light by the time Florence reached the designated spot.

'Walk on, Ginger Dick,' she said, clicking her tongue while the boulder which covered the entrance was slowly dragged away, exposing a gaping hole. Then, using all the strength she could muster, Florence heaved the body over the edge; and the clattering sound of tumbling stones indicated it had plummeted to the bottom. Florence leaned over and peered into the dark cavern, but saw nothing.

Whilst riding home on the comfort of Ginger Dick's broad, steady back, Florence felt neither sadness nor regret for what had happened – only a sense of relief. 'Maybe now we can make a fresh start, eh?' she said. And bending forward she put her arms about the old gelding's neck and hugged him.

Garrett Ferrensby leaned back against the rocky outcrop with a menacing expression on his face and drew hard on his cigarette ...

He'd witnessed everything....

Garrett could hear laughter emanating from the drawing room when he entered the house and slipped into the room unnoticed. He helped himself to a large whisky from a serving table by the door and drank half the measure in one gulp before topping up his glass.

They'll be gone tomorrow, thank God, he thought, glancing round the room. Felicity gave a high-pitched laugh from the other end of the room and Garrett turned to look at her. His sister-in-law was in her element here at Agra playing lady of the manor to a bunch of bores.

He couldn't help but compare the differences between her and Florence in his own mind. Garrett smiled, thinking, Felicity couldn't hold a candle to her. He'd not had time yet to think through the implications of Florence's activities on the moor. Was it a body she'd dumped down that disused mineshaft? And if so, who and why? But, even more to the point was what should *he* do about it? Report the incident to the police? No ... no ... that wouldn't do at all.... Garrett quaffed the remainder of his whisky and lifting the decanter replenished his glass.

'Hey, steady on with the booze, old boy!' Robin was standing close to him with his back turned to the room full of people, and next time he spoke, he enunciated each word abrasively and quietly between clenched teeth. 'We have some important people here, Garrett, and believe me when I tell you, my political future rests in *their* hands,' he hissed. 'And that bloody Liberal, Lloyd George, will be out of the picture soon. So do *not* embarrass me, Garrett, not now ... *please*.'

Garrett looked at him and couldn't contain his laughter as the whisky surging through his bloodstream buoyed his self-confidence.

'Aw, for Christ's sake stop being so damned pompous, Robin! And all I can say is God help you if your future depends on this bunch of Tory twats, hic ...'

Garrett swayed unsteadily on his feet when making a sweeping gesture with his arm. Then, draining his glass he passed it to Robin. 'Top me up again, please, *dear brother*. Or ... would you rather I limp over there and ask our *very* kind hostess, *deeeear Felicity*? Oh ... talk of the Devil, here she is!'

'Get him out – *now!*' Felicity spoke in a loud whisper through gritted teeth. 'I don't care how – just do it!'

Robin gathered up the decanter from the table. 'C'mon, old boy, let's you and me have a quiet chat and a drink on our own, eh?' He placed his arm around his brother's shoulders and steered him from the drawing room and down the hall and into the study where he locked the door behind them. Robin threw a log onto the dying embers and raked the fire back into life. Garrett fell into the armchair. Robin replenished his brother's glass and filled it to the brim before handing it back and Garrett drank it straight down.

'Bloody woman ... sh–she ... she doesn't want *me!* Can you believe it? A–and she won't sell me Hamer back.' Garrett buried his face in his hands for a few moments, then raised his head. 'That place belongs to this estate, Robin. Why? Why did Father sell it? Do *you* know?' he asked, with much indignance. Garrett's coherent outburst was short-lived. 'Aw, Flo ... Florence ... ohhh ... hic ... Florennnce ...' he slurred, the power of speech escaping him. Robin sat quietly in his armchair opposite, watching and waiting as Garrett's eyelids grew heavy. It wasn't long before the empty glass slipped from his brother's hand onto the floor, and loud snoring signified his inevitable unconsciousness.

Robin swallowed the anger that stuck in his throat. He leant down and picked the glass up off the floor. He glared at his brother with blistering hatred in his eyes. 'You bloody bastard!' he said, his words oozing a bitter calmness. 'Why the hell couldn't you have been killed at Passchendaele? But oh, no ... that wouldn't do, would it, Garrett? No ... that would make life just a little too easy for the rest us.'

The handle on the locked door made a noise as someone tried to open it and Robin walked across the room and opened it slightly.

It was Ivy Baxter. She craned her neck to see who it was Robin had been talking to but he managed to block her view, stepping in front of her and from the room. He reached back in round the door and removed the key.

'This room remains locked until I say otherwise – *that* is an order, Ivy. Do you have the duplicate key?'

Ivy Baxter frowned. There was something afoot and she didn't like it. In fact, Ivy didn't like, nor did she give a fig for, high-and-mighty Master Robin; or that stuck-up interfering wife of his for that matter! They'd turned the place upside down these last few days with their continual demands for fancy London cuisine. And here was she, with only two extra pairs of hands to help her. Aye, she'd be glad to see the back of 'em.

"Aven't seen t'spare key in years ... never needed to use it.'

Bloody impertinent woman! Is there any wonder Felicity can't stand her? They're all the same, these ignorant hillsiders. He locked the door and placed the key in his pocket and strode off down the hallway with Ivy Baxter staring after him open-mouthed.

As soon as he was out of sight Ivy Baxter turned to the study door. She bent down and put her eye to the keyhole, and unable to see anything unusual, made her way back to the kitchen.

It was four o'clock in the morning and Garrett woke up cold and stiff with an almighty hangover. The room was very dark leaving Garrett disorientated for a few moments with no idea where he was. He felt down the side of the chair and found his walking cane and walked to the door, which was locked. Garrett sat back down again wondering what the hell had happened for him to be locked in his own study. There was no key in the door so he couldn't have done it himself … unless. He went to his desk and felt around for a key, but nothing.

He drew back the curtains and a faint morning light was breaking over the moor. It was only then Garrett realized he could climb out of the window.

He made his way round to the back of the house and let himself in. He washed, then changed into his riding clothes before calling in at the kitchen where he helped himself to a thick slice of ham and chunk of bread.

It was early with no groom in attendance at the stables so Garrett saddled up his horse and rode out of the courtyard.

Robin woke when he heard the clattering of hoofs on the cobbles and went to the window. He observed his brother pass through the high wrought-iron gates. And as he disappeared from view sincerely hoped he'd not return before he and his guests departed for London later that morning. In fact, he wouldn't mind if Garrett never returned or if he never laid eyes on him ever again. Robin wondered for a minute or two who had unlocked the study door. His brother hadn't called out or he'd have heard him. Probably that bloody Ivy Baxter. He felt sure that the woman had lied and had a key all along.

The sun was warm and by the time he arrived at the rocky outcrop, Garrett was thirsty. He climbed down from his horse, removed the water flask from the pannier and drank deeply before leading the grey hunter to where rainwater pooled in a large hollowed rock. Garrett tied the reins to a wooden stake sticking out of the ground from some fencing years before and removed his jacket; and placing it on top of the springy heather he lay down. The sky was high and blue and the sun hot on his face; and somewhere, in the bright blue distance, the strident song of a skylark pierced the air. He shielded his eyes and scanned the skies, but couldn't locate the little bird. After a few minutes the skylark's singing ceased and the moor fell silent – a buzzard had entered the blue arena. It glided slowly and smoothly; and as it soared in circular, methodical movements, its keen eyes scanned the moor for prey before it disappeared from view and glided eastward towards the coast.

Garrett looked at his watch and stood up. That bloody tiresome bunch will be heading back to London soon, thank God. And although he'd no recollection of what he'd said or done last night, neither did he wish to hear his brother's version of events. Might as well make myself scarce until they've left, he thought, and collecting his horse set out for Ryeburn market.

The temperature increased on his descent from the moors into Ryeburn. Garrett was parched and dry from the heat and from overimbibing the previous night. After depositing his horse at the livery stables he made his way through the busy market square to The Swan Hotel. He walked round the back where a young girl was hanging sheets out to dry. She eyed him suspiciously when he walked up to her. He was unshaven and scruffy.

'What do you want?' she asked bluntly.

'I'm looking for Miss Bowman, Daphne Bowman. Is she here?'

The girl's mouth fell open with complete surprise on hearing him speak. This must be the squire from High Agra she'd heard them talking about in the kitchen and looking like it must be true what they said – he was losing his bloody marbles. Don't know what she sees in him meself, though, she thought, scrutinizing him. He's nowt to look at … but he 'as a nice speaking voice, aye, I'll give 'im that.

'It's 'er day off. Is she expecting you?'

'No, she's not. But if you'd be so kind and let her know Mr Garrett Ferrensby is here, please. I'm sure she'll see me.'

The girl scurried off, and within a few minutes Daphne appeared. It was her day off and she was still in her night attire. And the expression on her face told him in no uncertain terms, he could at least have taken the time to shave and dress properly before calling on her.

'Come in,' Daphne said, ushering Garrett through the door, then said to the girl, 'Back to what you were doing, and oh, Mildred?'

'Yes?'

'Mind your tongue. Do I make myself clear?'

'Yes, Mrs Bowman.'

'What on earth has happened, Garrett? You look like you've been sleeping rough. Have you?' Daphne asked when they reached her quarters.

Garrett didn't reply. He flopped down on the settee and laid his head back. He sighed deeply and closed his eyes for a few brief moments. 'I'm parched, Daphne, may I have a glass of water, please?' His eyes followed her as she walked across the room to the kitchen. The cream silk robe she wore shimmered, accentuating her curves and the swell of her breasts. She reappeared with a tray and he stood up and relieved her of it, placing it on a side table. He smiled at her whilst loosening the tie around her waist. The silk robe fell open and Garrett gently slipped it from her shoulders and drew her into his arms. He placed his lips in the hollow of her throat where a pulse throbbed, and he noted her shallow breathing.

'Let's go to bed,' he whispered. His mouth covered hers, and a rush of sexual desire flooded her body as he led her through to the now familiar bedroom where they made love most weeks.

Garrett knew nothing would ever come of their relationship. He didn't love her. She was merely a substitute.... It was Florence's face he saw before him, and Florence's body he touched when making love ... not Daphne's.

The clock struck two and Garrett quietly slipped from the bed and was getting dressed.

'You leaving already?' she said with a touch of sadness in her voice. He's changed, she thought, watching him. There was a time when he'd stay when it was my day off work – and we'd go for a long drive over the moors; picnic ... dine out, but now ... now all he does is visit me, and we have sex.... He's using me.

'Yes, sorry, I have to go. I've things to see to. Try and see you next week – all right?' he added before leaning over the bed and dropping a kiss on her forehead.

Daphne nodded, finding it impossible to speak. Her throat was full and she gulped audibly as he left the room. She jumped out of bed and ran to the window. From here she had a clear view of the market square and she watched him criss-cross between the stalls before vanishing from sight.

She decided then not to see him again.

Chapter Seven

IT WAS LATE August and the weather was hot and sticky. Ambrose Wilson pulled his bow-top wagon to a halt on the wide grass verge beneath the shade of a large oak tree. The horses were tired and in need of rest and watering before setting out for the last three-mile leg to Thirsk.

He was pleased with the six young horses he'd bought at Lee Gap gypsy fair. They consisted of: two piebald, a skewbald, and three Welsh cobs. He'd paid handsomely for them; the plan being, he would winter them; and then come the spring he'd break them to the shafts. In June he'd sell them on at the annual Appleby horse fair and hope to make a sizable profit.

It wasn't long before Ambrose had a fire going. And whilst the horses drank their fill he brewed a pot of tea and toasted bread over the fire.

Oh, it felt good to be on the road without his mam and dad. They had stayed on at Lee Gap fair and were content to make their way to Yarm fair in a few weeks with relatives.

Ambrose sat on the grass and rested his back against the trunk of a tree and closed his eyes; and the munching sound of his horses cropping the grass was a comfort to his ears.

Yes, he'd make the most of this time alone – treat it as a bit of a holiday.

The stallholders were packing up their leftover goods and the shops were closing when Ambrose drove his wagon through Thirsk's cobbled square. The colourful group of six young horses tied to the rear of the gaudy wagon caused the townsfolk to stop whatever tasks they were about and watch. A handful of ragged children ran behind and tried to keep up with them, but fell away as Ambrose made his way down Mill Gate and Bridge Street after crossing the bridge that spanned the Cod Beck.

He was heading for Miss Wooten's place. Miss Wooten was a fellmonger who lived in Long Street on the east side of the town. Ambrose and his family had done business with her on numerous occasions over the years and always found her to be a fair businesswoman. Whenever he called with pelts to sell, Miss Wooten gave him the use of a small paddock she owned that was located at the back of her house next to her warehouse.

'Whoa there, me beauties,' Ambrose said, pulling the wagon up outside her abode. It was quite a large residence with two generous bay windows flanking a large oak front door. He lifted the heavy bronze knocker and gave two sharp raps. He saw a curtain twitch slightly out of the corner of his eye in one of the bay windows and it wasn't long before the heavy door slowly opened, groaning loudly on its hinges.

'Hello, Miss Wooten, it's me, Ambrose Wilson.' He wasn't sure whether she recognized him. She'd aged a great deal since he last saw her, he thought, and lost ground. 'I've some rabbit pelts for yer,' he said, raising his voice a little.

The old lady screwed her eyes up. 'Yes, I know. I can see who it is, I'm not blind!' she said abruptly. 'And I can hear you. Come away in, young Ambrose. Don't want the neighbours knowing our business now do we?'

Ambrose couldn't help but smile to himself. *Well that's you put in yer place, fella mi lad,* he thought, following her obediently down the hallway and into a front sitting room.

'Sit down, sit down,' she said, indicating a high-backed armchair that was upholstered in lemon velvet brocade.

'Better not, I'm a bit mucky with being on the road for a couple of days travelling down from Leeds.'

'Well, in that case, go pull your wagon round the back. You know where everything is and where to put your horses and suchlike. Then when you've done we'll take tea together ... and then talk business.' She stood up. 'C'mon on then, lad, get a move on Mrs Towler's not gone home yet. She's my housekeeper. I'll ask her to make up a few sandwiches for us and slice some fruit cake.' As she spoke Miss Wooten craned her neck back to look up at Ambrose.

'Thank you, Miss Wooten, that's real kind of you.'

Ambrose led his wagon and horses round the back. People stepped out of their front doors and into the street and, although carts were a common everyday sight, it wasn't often a colourful bow-top wagon presented itself in the street – visiting a gorgio's house.

Hidden from view of the main street behind the house was a tall, narrow, three-storey warehouse with two tiny cottages tacked onto the side of it. Miss Wooten's housekeeper occupied one, and a widower and his son lived in the other. The father and son were employed by the old lady and worked in the warehouse. Behind the two cottages was half an acre of paddock and a small orchard beyond, where the fruit trees were laden with apples, plums, and pears.

He released the six young horses into the paddock. They cantered off, bucking and kicking and tossing their heads, pleased to be free of their restraints. Ambrose leaned on the fence and watched them awhile. He waited for them to settle in their surroundings before the last horse pulled the wagon into the orchard where he'd spend the night. Ambrose turned his eyes and looked towards the hills. The lowering sun in the west set the sky ablaze in varying shades of crimson revealing detailed landmarks in the Hambleton Hills that lay in the east. Roulston Scar and Whitestone Cliffe loomed large in the setting sun standing guard at the entrance of the North York Moors above Sutton Bank. It was in those desolate moors he'd lost his heart. No matter how hard he tried, he couldn't get her out of his mind ... and his mind was controlled by the feelings he had for her. His poor mother, aware he was smitten, had expended a great deal of time and energy at Lee Gap fair welcoming traveller friends' unattached daughters to join them for tea round the campfire every evening. She'd been angry when he informed her he knew what she was about and that she was wasting her time – he'd find his own lass without any assistance from her.

Ambrose glanced back at the hills once again before going to the house and joining the old lady for supper.

Miss Wooten rose early the next morning. She drew back the curtains and put on her dressing gown, then sat in a high-backed leather chair at her desk positioned by the window where the day-light assisted her tired old eyes. She turned the pages of the heavy ledger and her index finger flew down the column of numbers; her quick-thinking brain as sharp as it ever was. She'd been in a business partnership with her elder bachelor brother who'd died twenty years ago and she couldn't see any sense in retiring. What on earth would she have done with her time with no husband or children to care for? And having arrived at the age of eighty she'd no intentions of stopping work.

From her bedroom window she looked towards the orchard. The bow-top caravan looked colourful and appealing tucked between the fruit trees, she thought. She could see smoke rising through the foliage, but didn't bat an eyelid. Ambrose would be boiling his kettle and frying eggs. The fire would be doused and the square sod of earth which had been removed to make the fire would be replaced, with no sign of encampment remaining. The old lady smiled to herself. The Wilson family had called in to do business with her many times over the past twenty years. She remembered the first day they called with a number of cured rabbit skins. A severe storm had suddenly got up, making it impossible for them to travel, and she invited them to spend the night in the orchard. Since then the Wilsons had been welcome to stop whenever they happened to be passing through.

Two hours later the old lady was in the warehouse counting and examining the rabbit skins Ambrose had brought.

'Fifty-two, Ambrose. Is that right?'

'You can pay me for fifty-two if yer want, Miss Wooten, but there's only fifty.'

'My mind must be going, lad, I can't even count right nowa-days.' She looked across at him and grinned cheekily before bringing her attention back to the rabbit skins. 'Hmm ... lovely pelts,' she mumbled, her expert hand stroking the soft clean fur.

'And no hard edges,' she said before lifting them up to the light. 'Flawless. You're the only man I know, Ambrose, who can clean a rabbit skin to absolute perfection.'

'Ah, that's kind of you to say so, I'm right glad you're pleased with 'em, Miss Wooten; I takes me time, that's why – it's the only way,' he said with pride in his voice. 'Skin tears that easily when you're scraping it – it takes just one teeny slip,' he said, holding out his thumb and forefinger, 'an' the next thing you know ... yer've ripped it – an' it's buggered ... Oh, pardon for swearing.'

'Well, your price is always fair, always has been, so we'll settle up, lad. Come over to the house.'

Before leaving, the old lady handed him an envelope containing the addresses of two farming friends of hers who told her they were looking to buy a horse. She also took it upon herself to write Ambrose a letter of introduction and character reference.

'Keep the letter safe, Ambrose. I know the settled folk are wary of doing business with gypsies. I can't promise anything, mind, but this letter might stand you in good stead. No guarantees of course. But good luck, lad. I'll see you next year, God willing ...' she said with a wave of her hand and walked back to the house.

It was midday. Ambrose flicked the reins on the horse's rump and clicked his tongue. 'Git up there, boy,' he said, with a smile of satisfaction spread across his face. Old Miss Wooten had indeed done him a very good turn. He'd sold four of his six horses to the two farmers, but only after showing them the letter of introduction.

A gentle breeze tempered the heat as he neared the ruins of Byland Abbey. The twelfth-century Cistercian monastery rose out of the ground against the backdrop of the Hambleton Hills in majestic splendour.

Ambrose pulled the wagon onto the grass verge and watered the horses. He looked at his pocket watch. He should be there tomorrow before dark, he thought, and lying back on the cool grass he closed his eyes. Would she be pleased to see me or not – or has she set her sights elsewhere, he wondered; maybe a bit closer to home ... Oh God, how I long to rest my eyes on her again ... and ease this ache in my heart.

The grassy hillside gave way to bracken and heather and the western sky blazed red in the setting sun. Ambrose paused at the top of the rise where the moors spread out before him, stirring something in his soul, and he was unexpectedly awestruck as the beauty of the untamed wilderness was revealed to him.

The horses shifted restlessly, eager to be on the move and settled for the night.

Florence padded barefoot across the floor. She was tired and her feet ached. It had been a long day at Ryeburn market. She'd been up since five o'clock that morning and not stopped for a minute since. It had been a successful day as she'd managed to sell virtually everything she'd packed on the cart. And apart from the besoms and rabbit pelts, to her astonishment, the people had shown considerable interest in her bottled tinctures of herbal remedies as well as her chutneys and jams. It hadn't escaped her attention that when people asked her about the remedies, they held up a jar of jam or examined a rabbit pelt at the same time. Florence smiled to herself recalling one surreptitious enquiry from an older lady who whispered in her ear, "Ee won't give over touching me ... if thee gets me meaning. 'As thee owt I can slip into his pot o' tea at night to quieten the owd bugger down?'

Florence threw her head back and laughed out loud at the memory. Moth leapt quickly from his bed and pricked his ears, his sharp eyes looking inquisitively at her. 'Aw, I'm sorry, Moth,' she said scratching him behind his ears. 'Come on ... let's go and watch the sun set!' Moth barked excitedly as Florence snatched the shawl hanging on a nail by the door.

The moor was ablaze with colour and stained with vivid reds and oranges. Florence inhaled deeply at the perfume of the heather still lingering in the air. She stood on the high moor and looked about her and experienced a deep contentment. She'd been standing gazing across the moor for a long time and the evening had turned cooler and she shivered. Moth disappeared into the heather but re-emerged when she called him. He dropped a grouse at her feet, then pushed his cold nose into her hand. The bird moved slightly and Florence picked it up to examine it. There was blood on one of its wings and she quickly pulled its neck and put it out of its misery.

'Well done, Moth, let's go.' Then with a last glance across the moor Florence and her dog headed for home.

It was as she drew closer to Hamer Bridge she saw him. Her pulse fluttered with excitement as the distance closed between them, and she smiled through trembling lips when he jumped down from the wagon.

Ambrose looked into the deep-violet eyes beneath her quizzical brow, and the unanswered question he'd locked away in his mind broke free. 'Are you sorry ... sorry I've come, Florence?' he asked hesitantly. 'Just say so ... an' if you are I'll go now and not bother you, not ever ...'

'Shh ... there's no need to say anything ... I ... I'm glad you're here, Ambrose.'

Chapter Eight

DAPHNE HAD HARDLY slept a wink and the evidence stared back at her in the dressing-table mirror; dark circles round her eyes accentuated in her ashen face.

There was no point denying it any longer. She was pregnant. The fact she hadn't seen her period for three months and her rapidly expanding waistline was proof enough. The important thing now was what was she going to do about it? She hadn't laid eyes on Garrett for weeks; he'd obviously grown tired of her. Daphne buried her head in her hands and inescapable tears rolled down her face. 'You bastard!' she yelled, picking up a hairbrush and flinging it across the room. 'I'm not good enough for the likes of you, eh? No ... but good enough to bed! Oh, I bloody hate you Garrett Ferrensby ... I hate you ...'

But even as she directed her anger at him Daphne knew she shared an equal responsibility for the situation she found herself in. He hadn't once forced himself upon her. She'd given herself to him willingly and shamelessly and at the same time delighted in their mutual, sexual pleasure.

It was on waking the next morning that a plan began to form in Daphne's mind. She knew what she must do and do it soon.

Her employer was not pleased by her request to take three days off work especially as it was a busy time of year, but being an astute businessman he recognized that Daphne would be snapped up by any hotelier in the country had she it in mind to up and leave his employ. There was precious little money in people's pockets to spend on staying in fancy hotels, and whereas other hotels failed and were closing down up and down the country, his hotel thrived, and he acknowledged this was due to Daphne Bowman's diligence.

It was mid-morning and Daphne was discovering a part of the moors she'd never seen before. The air was sweet and she breathed in deeply, filling her lungs. As far as the eye could see there was no sign of activity save a colony of bees buzzing lazily, harvesting the nectar-laden heather. She considered stopping and resting a while, but the road had deteriorated, and she had to concentrate hard; slowing the pony to walking pace, she steered the wheels around the countless potholes that had appeared.

Daphne drew the trap to a halt as her destination came into view. Her heart beat rapidly and her resolve began to crumble. She hadn't expected anything quite so grand and imposing even though she'd heard the staff say High Agra was a grand mansion sitting high on the moors. The wind-scoured structure exposed to the raw power of nature's elements was bathed in grace and beauty.

Daphne's shoulders slumped and tears dimmed her eyes. For a moment she considered turning the trap around and driving straight back home ... but the life growing inside her urged her on.

She flicked the reins and the pony moved forward. 'He's not God!' she said.

As she neared her destination Daphne noticed the small dwelling nestled in a fold of the moor nearby. A couple were in the garden and she stopped to study them. The man was grooming a horse tied to the back of a bow-top wagon. The woman was the same height as the man and she handed him a mug of something to drink. He ceased grooming and took the proffered mug. They were standing very close to one another, almost touching. He said something and she threw her head back and laughed and the cheerful laughter rang through the air. The woman's hair was black as jet and it suddenly dawned on Daphne who she was. It's the gypsy girl ... the one who's causing an almighty upset in Ryeburn. Hah! Well, no wonder the women aren't so keen on you, she thought, smiling; you're beautiful ... and they won't like that, not one little bit. It would have been a different matter had you been some ugly old crone doling out remedies and advice; they'd have sent their husbands along in droves to see you.

Daphne's smile melted away at her next thought. I wonder … could it be that you are the reason Garrett's been avoiding me of late?

The pony whinnied and the couple turned and looked towards her, shielding their eyes from the sun for a clearer view. Daphne had been caught red-handed snooping and she urged the pony on.

The hard chink of hoofs on stony ground brought a young lad scurrying from the stables and Daphne handed him the reins. She took a deep breath to calm herself, then walked up the wide stone steps to the front door.

Scarcely had she raised the large bronze knocker on the blackened oak when the door opened.

'Yes. Can I help you?' Ivy Baxter had watched the woman's approach from an upstairs window. She'd also seen her stop and stare across to Hamer Bridge. Ivy sensed the woman's uneasiness. She was wringing her hands nervously and there was anxiety etched on her face; and when she spoke Ivy noted her voice was common to the area.

'I'm here to see Mr Ferrensby; is he in, please?'

'Is he expecting you?' Ivy asked, knowing full well he wasn't or she'd have been informed. People of his station didn't *drop in* uninvited.

'No. But if you let him know that a Mrs Daphne Bowman is here, please, I'm sure he'll see me.'

'Well, come inside, then, an' I'll see if I can find him. He's somewhere 'ere about.…' the housekeeper muttered, abandoning Daphne in the grand entrance hall.

She glanced up to where an enormous stag's head stared down at her with glassy eyes from above the main door. Somewhere in the house a door banged shut causing her to jump. At the far end of the hall a sweeping staircase led to a long, galleried landing where huge framed paintings of fierce-looking people, whom she assumed were Garrett Ferrensby's ancestors, adorned the walls.

Daphne's hands cradled her abdomen ... telling her unborn child, this is *your* family. Her thoughts were abruptly interrupted by an indistinct voice echoing angrily through the vaulted rooms; a mumbled response ensued, and then much to her relief, the housekeeper reappeared.

'He'll see you shortly, Mrs Bowman. If you follow me to the drawing room, please, and I'll bring refreshments.'

The drawing room was the most magnificent room Daphne had ever seen. Above a white marble fireplace rested a large rococo mirror. In the grate an arrangement of freshly picked delphiniums and roses screened the fireback. Exquisite regency chairs were upholstered in the exact same shades of soft velvet as two large Chinese rugs that adorned the oak floor. She walked over to the French windows and looked out across manicured lawns which stretched into the distance, merging into the moor beyond.

Daphne coughed and cleared her throat at the sound of irregular footfalls on the stone-flagged floor. Garrett walked into the room, then without acknowledging her, he turned and barked through the doorway.

'Tea, Ivy ... anybody!'

He closed the door hard and looked at Daphne. 'What on earth are you doing here, for God's sake, Daphne? Sit down!'

Daphne sat down immediately. But before she could answer him, there was a knock on the door and a maid arrived and wheeled in a tea trolley. The maid lifted the teapot to pour but Garrett stopped her.

'We'll manage now. Leave us! Now, girl!' he said sharply.

Shocked at his unwarranted angry outburst Daphne caught the girl's eye and smiled sympathetically.

'Thank you,' Daphne said, in a deliberate conciliatory tone.

'Well?' he prompted when the maid had left and the door clicked shut. 'You come into my house, uninvited I might add, and then proceed to undermine me in front of my servant. I assume your presence here is a matter of great importance?' His calm voice betrayed the cold glint in his grey eyes. 'Will you pour, please?'

It was an order not a request.

Daphne picked up the silver teapot and filled both cups, dribbling tea over the crisp white tray cloth. She saw Garrett raise his eyebrows at her apparent incompetence.

'Well, I'm waiting,' he said.

Daphne suddenly felt trapped and wished she hadn't bothered to come. She could barely breathe and he was watching her closely, as if taking pleasure in her distress whilst drinking his tea. She looked down at her own untouched cup on the table. Her mouth was dry. I've come all this way so … it's now or never, she thought, taking a deep breath.

'I'm pregnant,' she said. Her voice didn't sound like it belonged to her, she thought. It was too steady and calm.

A heavy silence descended over the room and Garrett's jaw hung open with the teacup suspended a few inches from his mouth. Unnerved, he repositioned himself in his chair. What the hell am I going to do now? Pregnant! God knows I don't love her, couldn't possibly marry her … *Surely* she must know that. We merely satisfied a sexual hunger in one another. Blast! And I was sure we'd been careful … haven't been with her for bloody weeks now … ah, maybe that's the reason she's here. It's someone else's child and she wants me to pay for it …

A clock struck eleven from the far end of the room. Its sweet chime occupied the tense silence and resonated through the drawing room.

'Are you sure it's mine?' he asked abruptly.

Daphne had vowed to herself she wouldn't cry but his callous remark prompted tears to spring to her eyes. How could he think for a minute I'd sleep with someone else!

'Yes, the child's yours, Garrett. And to think I was foolish enough to come here in the hope you might do the decent thing a–and ask me to marry you! Hah, that's a laugh. I couldn't have been more wrong; I'm not even welcome in your house – never mind your life …'

He interrupted her. 'Are you absolutely certain? I mean, h–have you seen a doctor and had the pregnancy confirmed?'

'Yes, of course I'm certain! And no I haven't seen a doctor.'

Daphne stood up to leave and Garrett rose from his chair.

'Wait, please, sit back down. We need to talk about this.'

'What have we to talk about unless you're willing to marry me? Which you're not, are you?'

'No, Daphne, I'm not willing to marry you. But I am willing to fulfil my duties. And by that I will make the necessary arrangements for you to see a ... doctor or somebody of good repute to have the pregnancy terminated ... What? What's the matter? Oh, no ... For Christ's sake tell me it's not true ... Surely you don't intend to keep it....'

Daphne fled from the room and slammed the door behind her. She almost collided with Ivy Baxter, who rushed into the hall to see what all the commotion was about.

'I'll see myself out, thank you,' Daphne said.

The maid she'd smiled at appeared from somewhere and reached the front door before Daphne and opened it. Daphne dashed to where her pony and trap stood waiting and climbed up onto the seat and flicked the reins hard.

The pony and trap sped down the drive and raced through the tall iron gates. Tears blurred Daphne's vision as the pony galloped on and out of control. The rutted track she'd so wisely navigated on her way in she now followed blindly at high speed.

Florence took the hare she'd snared and fastened it with a length of string to the belt round her waist. She'd not eaten hare in a long time. Ambrose will enjoy that, she thought; a smile spreading across her face. He'd stayed longer than intended and she wasn't looking forward to his departure and being on her own again. In his brief time there Ambrose had carried out numerous repairs about the place: the barn door now swung freely on its new hinges, some broken windowpanes had been replaced, as well as lots of rabbit skins prepared for market. Florence had offered him the couch in the living room to sleep on, but he'd declined and insisted on sleeping in the wagon. Over the last few weeks their friendship had deepened and she'd not given a second thought to Garrett during Ambrose's stay. She and Ambrose spoke the same language, there was no struggle ... no cultural division to separate them. Would he settle down, though, she wondered? Could he give up his travelling and adopt a new way of life, as she had done? Settling down is one thing – freedom to roam another. The settled person's views change with the seasons, but the gypsy's with every new dawn.

Her reverie was broken by an incessant barking from Moth,who was bounding through the heather towards her. Florence rested her hand on the dog's head to quieten him. She stopped and listened. There was a clattering of hoofs and rumbling of wheels which grew louder by the second. It sounded like a runaway horse and cart to Florence's ears – nobody drove along that rutted track at that speed. She raced through the heather and towards the track. Within moments a pony pulling a small trap rounded the bend and was coming straight at her at a reckless pace. She stepped into the track and stood stock-still raising her hand.

'Whoa … whoa … steady … steady there.' Florence's voice was gentle but loud enough for the pony to hear. The pony slowed and stopped. Florence took the reins and held the pony still whilst speaking softly. The pony was sweating profusely. 'There … there … good boy …' she said, soothing the animal, before moving her attention to the woman in the trap.

'You all right, missus?'

'Yes, I … I … honestly didn't know he'd take off like that … I lost control.'

'You sure you're all right? You don't look too well to me,' Florence said. Then she went up to the woman and saw she was crying. 'Come with me. We'll see to your horse and make you a cup of tea. You've had a nasty shock. I only live over there,' she added, pointing to the cottage. 'Think you'd be better walking? Bring a bit of colour back into your cheeks.'

'Yes, thank you. You're very kind … and you're right, the poor horse needs to settle down.'

'Where're you heading for?' asked Florence.

'Ryeburn. I … I've seen you there before … at the market. I believe you sell herbal remedies and such?'

'Yes I do.'

Walking back to the cottage, Florence led the pony and cart

with one hand while her other hand remained under the woman's elbow. Daphne felt calmed by the woman's physical touch and presence. She hadn't realized how tall the gypsy woman was, having only seen her from a distance. And she was strikingly good-looking, not pretty – she was beyond pretty. Her black hair and incredible blue eyes claimed one's complete attention. And when Florence smiled Daphne felt certain this girl could be the only reason for Garrett's avoidance of her over the past weeks.

At the same time, Ambrose heard the loud crashing of wheels and hurried up the lane to meet them and to relieve Florence of the pony and trap. He was just on the point of asking Florence what had happened when he noticed Daphne sway and close her eyes. Ambrose dropped the reins and caught her in his arms before she hit the ground.

'Good grief, Ambrose! Let's get her inside quickly and put her in my bed,' Florence said, dashing through the front door.

Daphne lay there for a good few minutes before she came round propped up on pillows in a strange bed. The lady with black hair was sitting in a chair beside the bed holding a cup of tea out to her. She was smiling at her and saying something … it seemed all very dreamlike and unreal.

'I'm sorry … what did you say?'

'There … now … I said, and take a sip of tea, c'mon now … I'll help you. Have you eaten anything today? And what's your name? I can't keep calling you missus. Mine's Florence … and my friend, the man who carried you in, his name's Ambrose. Can you hear me now?'

'Yes, I can hear you all right,' Daphne said weakly. 'My name's Daphne Bowman and I … I've never fainted in my life before, never.'

'Have you eaten anything today?' Florence asked again.

Daphne frowned. 'No, I haven't. Stupid of me I know … but … I just couldn't,' she said, sobbing loudly, holding her head in her hands.

Florence put her arms about the distressed woman and rocked her. You poor soul … I wonder what happened to you up at High Agra to bring you to this sorry state …

Chapter Nine

A COLD NORTH-EASTERLY WHIPPED across the moors announcing autumn had arrived prematurely for the people at Ryeburn market. Traders packed up their unsold wares and wrestled with the wind, struggling to fold up tarpaulins and dismantle the wooden stalls. Most of the shoppers had departed apart from the odd opportunist on the lookout for last-minute bargains.

Florence's eyes watered and stung from grit and sand blown into them. It was early afternoon and, if the weather didn't improve, she'd be lucky if she saw another market this year. Business had been good so far for Florence and she'd made enough to put aside money to see her through to the following spring. And if necessary, she still had a few sovereigns from her mother stashed away.

After packing up her stall, Florence made her way over the bridge to the café she frequented most Fridays when finishing work. Some of the locals remained wary of her whilst at the same time treated her with a quiet respect. There were also those among them with little money to spare who sometimes sought Florence out to ask her for advice rather than pay for a doctor.

Daphne pulled the voluminous brown cape around herself to hide her enlarged stomach and strode briskly across the market square. She had paid a visit to Thirsk recently – to avoid suspicion – where she bought one or two items of clothing for herself. It wouldn't be long now before she would have to relinquish her job at the hotel as it was almost impossible to conceal her condition any longer. It was imperative Daphne saw Florence that day. She'd heard the farmers saying in the hotel snow was on the way and it would only take a few light falls to drift and the road to the moors could be blocked for weeks.

Daphne spotted Florence through the café window and waved. Florence had saved a table by the fire and ordered tea and toasted teacakes for them both. Since that day on the moor when Florence rescued Daphne from a near-fatal accident, a bond of friendship had developed between them, and they now met in the little café every Friday after market.

'Here, let me take your cape,' Florence said, rising from her chair.

'No! No thank you … it's all right, I'll leave it on.' Daphne's sharp response caused people to look in their direction and she sat down quickly. 'Thanks for ordering,' she said, forcing a smile.

'Are you all right?' Florence reached across the table and clasped her hand and Daphne's eyes welled. 'You're worried about something … come on, you can tell me … and I might be able to help.'

'You must be away soon, Florence,' Daphne said, changing the subject. 'I heard the men talking in the hotel earlier and they said it looked like snow was on the way.'

'I've slept through worse weather with only a canvas roof for shelter, remember? So don't worry about me, I'll get home all right.'

Daphne was looking at her, but didn't hear a word she said. Her head was all over the place and she couldn't gather her thoughts.

Florence leaned forward, saying quietly, 'Come on, we can't talk here, let's go.'

Florence paid the bill and asked the waitress to put the teacakes in a bag for them to take away. They walked back to the hotel and up the back staircase to Daphne's sitting room. Daphne put the kettle on to boil and set a tray before removing her cape. Florence stood gazing out of the window which overlooked the market place and a familiar figure appeared from the doorway of the Three Feathers Hotel. She'd recognize that walk anywhere. Garrett Ferrensby pulled his coat collar up and made his way unsteadily to where his car was parked. He opened the door, then, sensing he was being watched, turned quickly and looked directly up at her window. He continued to stare and Florence stepped back, but it was not soon enough. Daphne walked to the window. She gasped and placed her hand to her throat to stem any further sound, when she saw him. Florence watched her friend's face contort with pain. Then her eyes lowered ... following Daphne's physical shape. She hadn't seen her without a coat for a few weeks.... *Oh, no! My God! She's pregnant! That's why she was distressed that day on the moor ... Garrett Ferrensby. Good grief ... is it his child?*

Daphne turned slowly to face Florence. 'You've guessed, haven't you?'

'Yes, b-but why didn't you tell me? Don't you know I care about you? Don't you trust me?'

'I know ... I know ...' Daphne said, sobbing. 'What a bloody mess I've made of my life. Garrett Ferrensby wanted me to have an abortion, but I couldn't ... Florence, I just couldn't ...'

Florence led her to the sofa and drew her arms about her.

'C'mon, it'll be all right. Look, you can come and live with me. Ambrose won't be back till spring – not that he'd mind anyway. It'll give you time to get back on your feet...'

'I know you mean well, Florence, but I don't want to impose ...' Florence opened her mouth to object, but Daphne silenced her. 'I'm going to make a new life for myself and my child. I've already decided what I'm going to do. I'm going to move somewhere where nobody knows me. I've a bit of money put by and I can manage on that if I'm careful. And when the baby's born I'll find work again.'

'When's the baby due?' Florence asked.

'I couldn't say ... not for certain. I'll see a doctor when I'm settled. By my reckoning middle to late January – couldn't be a worse time than the middle of winter ...' she added solemnly. 'Is it so obvious, Florence, m–my condition?'

There was no point lying. Florence thought she'd done well to hide it this long. 'I'm afraid it is. But I've not seen you without you being covered up.'

The clock on the mantelpiece struck five o'clock and Florence rose and put her coat on to leave. 'I have to go now, Daphne, it's getting dark. But will you think on about what I said about coming to stay at my place? Promise me?'

'Yes, I promise to give it some thought. And Florence, thanks … thank you for your friendship.'

Florence felt a lump rise in her throat. She hugged Daphne goodbye, saying she'd see her next Friday as usual, if not before.

The wind had abated when she stepped outside. Florence scanned the darkening skies. They're right, she thought, snow is on the way. There was the goat to milk and the horses to see to. Ambrose sprung to mind. He'd helped her with all the daily tasks – including peeling vegetables and making her cups of tea; she was already missing him. Perhaps it was blood calling blood – the gypsy bond between them. The days were shorter and the nights long and lonely. He'd be back in Cumbria by now. He said he'd be back in spring, if not sooner, for an answer to the proposal of marriage he'd left with her. He said he'd loved her from the moment he'd set eyes on her at Topcliffe Fair. Florence said she was flattered and very fond of him, but she needed time to consider his offer.

Daylight was fading swiftly and low cloud obscured the moors. Florence congratulated herself on her decision to use Ginger Dick that morning for market. He pulled the empty cart effortlessly along the narrow rutted track, and gathered pace when they rounded the last bend for home. Florence didn't see the man waving his arms from the roadside; she was lost in thought, contemplating her friend's predicament.

Ginger Dick slowed to a walk and whinnied loudly.

'I guessed you'd be passing by at some point, Florence. As you can see I've had a bit of an accident.' He gestured to where his car was laid on its side twenty yards away. 'Skidded off the bloody road and landed in the heather.'

'Can't you walk?' she said in a clipped voice.

'Do you honestly think I'd be sitting here if I could walk?'

She heard a smile in his voice as he replied and wanted to jump down from the cart and slap him hard across the face. He was perched on a clump of heather with his arms around his knees, eyeing her intently.

Any exchanges with her raised a level of intensity in him. She was like a drug to his senses and he couldn't get her out of his mind.

'If you wouldn't mind just reaching into the car to fetch my walking stick I can get up … and I'd be very grateful.' He smiled, waiting for a response – none came.

Ginger Dick took a step forward and the sudden jolt of the cart almost toppled Florence backwards. She secured the reins and climbed down. As she walked past him towards the car he reached out and grabbed her hand and she snatched it away.

'Can't we at least be friends?' he said.

She was close enough to smell the whisky on his breath and looked at him with unconcealed contempt. 'It's getting dark, I'll get your stick for you, but only because I wouldn't leave a dog defenceless out here on the moors!'

She strode across the heather to the upturned car and rummaged around through an open window until she located the cane.

'Here,' Florence said, throwing the cane down beside him. 'Can you stand? If not I'll go to the house and tell them to come and help you.' There was no way she was going to assist him.

'Are you going to tell me what I'm supposed to have done?'

She stared incredulously at him. 'Are you telling me you don't know? I don't believe it … You people with your damn money and your so-called *position in life* think you can trample over others …'

Garrett suddenly grabbed her by the ankle and brought Florence down on the heather beside him. His grip tightened as she struggled to be free.

'I have to go,' she heard herself say more calmly than she felt.

Their faces were almost touching. 'I love you, Florence, do you hear me? I love you.' The unexpected announcement left her lost for words. He crushed her against him and his mouth covered hers. Her arms slipped around his neck and kissing him back she melted in his arms. Their kiss deepened and he slid his hand hungrily down the curve of her waist; she gasped with pleasure when his hand stole beneath her blouse and caressed her breasts, and his gentle touch induced a powerful sexual response in her.

She opened her eyes which were moist with tears and looked into his; he smiled down at her. 'I have to go,' she said softly, her voice choked with emotion.

'Before I let you go, tell me … is there a chance for me … for us?'

In the momentary silence that followed Daphne's face swam before her eyes, and Florence was immediately filled with an over-whelming shame. Daphne was her friend and the poor woman was pregnant to this … this so-called *gentleman* who'd pulled her to the ground and kissed her; but she had kissed him back with a passion she didn't know she possessed and was equally at fault.

I must go at once – and quickly!

'This is wrong,' Florence said, pushing him from her, 'let me go.'

'No, it isn't wrong. How can it be wrong when it feels so right between us? And I know you feel the same, Florence, so don't deny it, because I'll not give up on you … never.'

Their faces were almost touching and their eyes locked and Florence spoke. 'And what about Daphne and your child she's carrying? Did you tell her you loved her *too*? I can't believe I've let you … let you kiss me. I'm ashamed of myself. Daphne is my friend – and a good friend at that!'

Florence saw the disbelief in Garrett's face and although she imagined there was a brief flash of apology in his eyes – it was gone in an instant.

'How dare you stand in judgement of me?' The calm clipped tone of his voice barely concealed his anger. 'I had consensual sexual relations with the woman.'

Florence blushed and averted her eyes. He placed a finger on her chin and turned her head to look at him. 'But I didn't kill her and throw her body down some disused mineshaft … did I?' He watched her gulp and her eyes widen in horror; and for a moment he was tempted to smile. 'Ah, so I am right. I saw you that day on the moor, you know. I was out riding and rested my horse by the rocky outcrop.' His eyes were cold and he gave a humourless laugh. 'Now, I'd like to bet the police would be interested to know who's down there. Hmm … what do you think, Florence?'

Florence yanked herself free from his grasp and rising strode to where Ginger Dick was growing restless and ready for home. She climbed up onto the cart and flicked the reins hard. 'Walk on, boy,' she said, without glancing back, her vision clouded with tears of rage. And as nightfall descended she relied on her trusty horse alone to guide them safely home.

Garrett watched Florence depart into the darkness. A sense of foreboding began to settle on him at the harsh bitter truth of words spoken by them both and he realized he'd lost the one and only woman he would ever love. His thoughts drifted to the gypsy who was staying at Hamer Bridge. He'd come across him on the moor one day while out riding. The man had introduced himself to Garrett as if he were his equal! 'Ambrose Wilson is my name, sir; and you … you must be the neighbour Florence mentioned?' He'd held out his hand which Garrett declined. This amused the gypsy, who had laughed aloud at Garrett's child-ish display and simply bid him good day before walking away leaving him looking the fool. Garrett's eyes narrowed at the memory as he made his way home and the ache in his heart was traded for anger. Oh, no, Florence hadn't heard the last from him. If he couldn't have her he'd make damn sure nobody else would – especially that bloody arrogant gypsy!

Chapter Ten

EVERY WAKING MOMENT for the next few weeks Florence had waited in fear of the police landing on her doorstop to arrest her for the murder of Benny Grainger. She hadn't dared venture into Ryeburn and was getting low on provisions now and urgently needed to stock up, for winter was fast approaching.

Florence dashed across the market square to the hotel. She'd been so wrapped up in concern for herself she'd not given any thought to Daphne's problem.

'Gone?' Florence asked in disbelief. 'What do you mean, gone? Gone where?'

The stony-faced receptionist glowered at Florence from behind the counter. 'Like I've just said, she's gone – and it's not my business to ask where to. Now, if you'll leave, please, I've work to do.'

Florence didn't move. 'I want to see the manager,' she said. And stretching to her full height, folded her arms across her chest in an act of defiance.

The receptionist sighed impatiently. 'Look, the manager's away for a few days. All I can tell you is that she left in a hurry. Be about three weeks ago. She didn't tell anyone where she was going. But ... from what I can gather by all accounts, she was in a bit of bother.' Then leaning forward the woman said to Florence in a loud whisper, 'In the family way, they said, and ... to that Mister Ferrensby or *his nibs* as the staff call him ... him who lives on the moor. Well, he comes to see her one day and *she* skedaddles the next. No, you can't get away with anything living in these parts,' she said, pursing her lips and shaking her head, 'everybody knows everybody's business. I'm from Hull myself. Nobody's interested in anybody but themselves there ... Hmm, has its drawbacks living in a small town ... makes you wonder which is the lesser of the two evils, doesn't it? Well, I can't stand here talking all day!' she concluded brusquely. 'Come back in a few days if you want to see the manager, but he won't be able to tell you any more than I have.'

Florence heard all she needed to know and thanking the woman, she left.

The bell above the door tinkled and Ivy Baxter glanced up to see Florence enter the café. She smiled and beckoned her over to join her.

'Thank you, Mrs Baxter,' Florence said, sitting down next to her. 'Haven't seen you in here before, what a nice surprise.'

'Oh, I come into Ryeburn now and again. Thought I'd treat myself today, what with snow round the corner you never know how long it'll be before you can get into town again. And, it makes a pleasant change to have someone make a cup o' tea for me,' she chuckled. 'Anyway, how are you, lass? Call me a nosy beggar but I couldn't help but notice you across the square just now coming out of the The Swan. How ... how is she ... the woman? Mrs Bowman's her name, I believe? Folks' tongues wag ... Eeh, but I can't help feel sorry for the woman myself.'

Had she not felt as anxious for Daphne's whereabouts and well-being at that minute Florence would have burst into laughter. Good God, has this town nothing else to talk about? And if not, can't they see it isn't *all* Daphne's fault; *he* was just as responsible for the pregnancy!

'What can I fetch you, Miss Grainger, Mrs Baxter?' the waitress asked, interrupting her thoughts and smiling at both in turn.

Well, well, Miss Grainger, indeed! Florence recalled the first day she stepped over the threshold and the unwelcome glares from the locals. Now she could lay claim to having earned the respect of many since her arrival here in Ryeburn, but there were still some in the community who continued to be wary of her.

'It's my treat, Florence. We'll have tea and scones for two please.'

After ordering, Ivy looked at Florence, giving her her undivided attention.

'In answer to your question, Mrs Baxter, I don't know where Daphne is, I only wish I did. Can't believe she's just up and gone without a word ... left her job ... I told her she could come and stay with me – oh, Mrs Baxter, if I only knew where she was ... I'd go and find her ... fetch her back ... a–an' look after her, make sure she was all right. Can't believe she's left without a word ...' Florence repeated.

Florence's eyes welled and the elderly housekeeper reached across and took her hand in hers; and beholding those huge, tear-filled sapphire-blue eyes she concluded Ryeburn had never seen the likes of such beauty – not in her lifetime anyway. And it was a beauty which appeared to have unhinged her boss.

Ivy was still holding the girl's hand and staring into her eyes.... 'I'm sorry, lass ... me thoughts are wandering ... what was that you just said?'

'I said, you do know who the father is? Don't you?'

Ivy withdrew her hands and released her hold. 'No, of course I don't know who the father is! Should I know? Do you know who it is?'

I'm too old for all this excitement, Ivy thought.

Florence's voice wavered. 'Well, maybe it's not my place to tell you if you don't know already ... I–I mebbe shouldn't have mentioned it ...'

'Well, you'll have to tell me now, lass, 'cos if you don't someone else will, and they'll likely not be as tactful as yourself.'

There was a momentary pause in which they regarded one another.

'The father of the child is Garrett Ferrensby.'

Ivy gasped at the news and sat back in her chair; her hands clasped prayer-like on her mouth and the colour draining from the woman's face.

Surely she'd some idea? Florence thought. Daphne mentioned to her that Ivy Baxter was there the day she'd gone to see him and tell him she was pregnant.

An uncomfortable silence settled between them; it was getting late and the café was beginning to empty.

'Have you lost your senses?' Ivy said, sitting bolt upright, knowing the girl sitting opposite hadn't, and that she was not the type to tell lies ... or make up stories.

Florence picked up on Ivy's thinly veiled hostility whilst at the same time appreciating the news must have come as a terrible shock to the housekeeper. 'No, I've not lost my senses. You recall the day Daphne went to High Agra to see Mr Ferrensby? Well, when she left there she was almost killed. The horse and trap bolted an' she was that upset when I saw her. I was walking home from the moor that day and luckily was able to pull the horse up ... Ambrose, he's a friend of mine, an' he was stopping at Hamer an' he carried her back to my place ... and she ... she fainted.'

There was a pause. 'Dear God,' Ivy said, 'if only I'd known ... I ...'

'You'd what? Make him marry her, huh, I doubt it! Daphne more or less begged him to marry her ... but he wanted her to have an abortion.'

'We're closing now, ladies.' The waitress who'd welcomed them with a smile scowled at them because they were holding her up.

Once outside the café Florence said, 'I'm sorry to be the one to tell you of this ... I realize you must be very fond of Mr Ferrensby ...'

'Oh, that I am, that I am ... but look, promise me something, will yer? If you hear from Mrs Bowman let me know. Maybe I can help ... I've a bit of money put aside ... and the bairn will be needing things ... Oh, what a to-do,' she said anxiously. 'An' you know what? To have had a bairn running about the place would've given Agra what it desperately needs ... fresh new life ...' she added pensively, exposing her loneliness.

'Come and visit me at the cottage whenever you want,' Florence said, clasping Ivy's ungloved hand which was as cold as ice. 'It'll be a long winter ... for the pair of us up there.'

'Aye, true enough, an' it'll be your first ... I pray it won't be too harsh a one for you.'

'You sure you'll be all right now, Mrs Baxter?' Florence asked, feeling guilty at upsetting the woman. 'I've to be away home, I've the animals to see to. But I can stay with you until you leave if ...'

Neither woman had seen Garrett Ferrensby approach. 'That will not be necessary, Miss Grainger; Mrs Baxter will be perfectly all right. I shall see she gets home safely.' A thin smile touched his lips. 'Perhaps,' he said softly, 'I can also offer you a lift. I have my car.'

He leaned his face close to hers and grinned infuriatingly and she could smell strong drink on his breath.

'Thank you, no, I've ridden here. Goodbye,' Florence said. The sweetness of her tone didn't conceal the sneer she intended as she made a hasty retreat.

'Well, well, now, Ivy, I didn't realize you and Miss Grainger were such good friends. What did you find to talk about?'

'We're not *good* friends!' she snapped back. 'We just happened to bump into one another in the café, that's all ... an' anyway I like her, she's a decent enough lass in spite of being a gypsy. Come on, then, if you intend taking me home; snow's on its way – I can smell it,' she added, thinking at the same time, just as sure as I can smell the booze on your breath! On the drive home Ivy felt vexed by her employer. He wanted to know everything about what she and Florence had discussed – yet, here he was, prepared to disown his kith and kin! But it wasn't only that; he'd robbed her of a child to indulge in her latter years at Agra; by-blow or not, Ivy thought, she didn't care; she'd love the child enough for it not to make any difference.

Garrett drew back the bedroom curtains. Christmas Day arrived at High Agra accompanied with an icy blast from the north; and during the night heavy snow had fallen, transforming the moors into a white virginal landscape. Robin and his wife had arrived from London for a few days and Garrett was wondering how the hell he was going to get through their visit without anaesthetizing himself from morning till night. Pity this bloody snow hadn't arrived two days ago – that would have put the kybosh on it.

His thoughts were temporarily distracted when he saw smoke coming from the chimney at Hamer Bridge. In the stark white backdrop he could also see her dog scooting about excitedly in the snow. Hmm, now there's a good diversion ... he thought, smiling to himself. Bruno and I might drop in to wish you a happy Christmas. He was about to turn away from the window when some other movement caught his eye – it was her, Florence ... she was running like a young schoolgirl playing in the snow. He knew it wasn't possible, but he imagined he could hear her laughter and see her clear blue eyes sparkling beneath the fur hat she was wearing.

Florence cracked the ice on top of the water barrel and filled her pail. The pump in the yard was frozen solid and she was pleased with herself for having the sense to fill the water troughs for the animals yesterday. She looked to where Moth was playing in the snow and smiled. Florence then rushed indoors and re-emerged wearing a rabbit-skin hat pulled down over her ears and a pair of leather gloves. She ran laughing to where Moth was and made snowballs which she threw for him. Instantly sensing a game was going on Moth stuck his nose into the deep snow, and waiting cautiously, his eyes not leaving Florence for a second, when she ventured close enough he quickly brought his nose up, showering her in snow.

'We're a good team, you and me, Moth,' she said rubbing his ears and kissing his head. In the short time she and the dog had been together she couldn't imagine life without him now. 'Happy Christmas, Moth, my friend. C'mon, let's go get warm,' she said. And the playful pair, oblivious to Garrett watching them, abandoned the cold outdoors and rushed inside.

Florence mashed the tea and sat by the fire and prepared vegetables which she then added to the rabbit stew already simmering on the range. She looked about the little cottage. It was her second Christmas without her mother and she still missed her very much. You'd have loved this little house, Mam; me and you, we'd 'ave been happy here without *him*, Florence thought, feeling very lonely all of a sudden. And her thoughts drifted to Daphne whom she prayed was safe and well and would contact her soon. Then a lump rose in her throat when she thought of Ambrose ... *Do you miss me as much as I miss you?* she wondered. He would be sharing Christmas with his mam and dad, family and friends. The groups of gypsies would be in and out of each other's wagons exchanging hand-made gifts, clearing snow, and keeping the campfires burning dotted about the campsite; and the little stoves would be permanently lit inside the wagons to keep them warm, but none the less winter would be tough for them.

Florence sighed deeply. He said he'd come back in spring … and Ambrose is a man of his word. Florence's ponderings were interrupted when the pan boiled over causing an ear-splitting hiss and Moth to bark.

'Oh, Moth, be quiet!' Florence yelled, and set about cleaning the mess on the range and setting the table for Christmas Day.

Garrett adopted his well-rehearsed smile when his sister-in-law entered the drawing room. 'I understand congratulations are in order, Felicity?' he said sweetly, and dropped a kiss on her cheek. 'When is it due exactly, Robin didn't say?'

'Yes I did,' Robin said, slipping into the room unnoticed. 'But you were too bloody inebriated to remember!'

'Oh, please!' Felicity cut in. 'Promise me you won't argue – not today, on Christmas Day of all days. And Garrett was being very sweet by the way, Robin, asking when the baby's due. He will be his or her uncle after all. Now come you two, let's enjoy ourselves. Mrs Baxter's been in the kitchen slaving away all morning on our behalf.'

'You're quite right, my darling,' Robin said apologetically to his wife. 'I'm sorry, old boy, forgive me, eh?' He looked to where Garrett was filling two glasses.

'Here, brother,' Garrett said, handing him a glass. 'Get that down you and consider yourself forgiven. Cheers, and a very happy Christmas to you both … oh, and not forgetting you, young fellow, my girl,' Garrett chuckled, acknowledging the small bulge beneath Felicity's tight-fitting dress.

During the first course of dinner Felicity announced they would be leaving early to visit her parents before going back to London. The welcome news of their early departure lifted Garrett's spirits; surely, he told himself, he could manage to bite his tongue for just two more days? He glanced out of the window.

There'd been no more snow … God, please, spare my sanity … don't let them get snowed in here …

'That's if the snow clears,' Robin said, as if reading his thoughts.

'Oh, I think we'll manage to get you to the station. The snow's not too bad, I hear, once you get off the moor. Isn't that so, Ivy?' he said, addressing the housekeeper, who'd entered with a kitchen maid who was clearing away their plates to make way for the main course.

'Aye, Wass and Byland's clear and only Sutton Bank's closed.'

Felicity cringed at her brother-in-law's familiarity with a member of staff. Robin was right; Garrett would drag the family into the gutter given half a chance. But the child she was carrying, should it be a boy, would one day be heir to High Agra … she had it all planned; Felicity's eyes narrowed as she surveyed Garrett draining his glass. *He'll* drink himself to an early death with a bit of luck; and Robin shall take up his position as head of the family at Agra. And I'll insist we keep the house in London. I could not abide living here all year round.…

'More wine, darling?' Robin asked.

'Er … pardon? Oh, I'm sorry, what was that you said?' Both men frowned, wearing puzzled expressions. 'Are you sure you're all right, Felicity, you were miles away.'

'Yes, I'm fine, honestly.…' She gave a strained laugh, saying, 'Put it down to impending motherhood.'

Back in the kitchen Ivy took her seat at the head of the table. She was flanked by Enid the scullery maid on one side, and Janet the housemaid on the other. Both had been more than willing to forgo time off over the Christmas period. They hailed from the remote hamlet of Urra in Bilsdale, where, when the snow arrived, it stayed, and was usually knee-deep, frequently cutting off the villagers for weeks at a time. While living at Agra, the girls could go into Ryeburn where they'd meet other young people from neighbouring villages; and besides, the food was good in the Agra kitchen and Mrs Baxter was a generous and kind woman. But neither girl had taken a shine to Mr Robin's wife and they wouldn't be sorry to see the back of her.

'They're off t'day after tomorro', aren't they, Mrs B?' Enid said, grinning at Janet. 'That's if t'snow's gone and they can get out. Bah gum, we'll be on our 'ands an' knees tonight prayin' like mad for a quick thaw, won't we, Janet?'

Both girls burst out laughing, but Ivy kept a straight face. For no matter how much she disliked Robin's wife she would never betray the Ferrensby family, nor stoop to gossiping about them, especially with her staff.

'Just remember who pays your wages, girls!' Ivy cautioned them, bringing the laughter to a sudden halt.

'Yes, I'm very sorry, Mrs B,' the girls chorused. Tonight they'd laugh and gossip between themselves snuggled up in their warm beds in the icy attic.

Chapter Eleven

IT WAS PAST midnight. The night was still and silent when Garrett stepped outside and walked along the drive. His mouth was dry and his head ached from drinking too much wine. He'd gone to bed early, sleeping solidly until a bright moon rose and spilled through the window illuminating the bedroom.

The snow glittered in the moonlight creating a magical scene spreading for miles across the snow-swathed moorland. Garrett slowed his pace. He was only a short distance from the cottage when he saw her. Florence was standing with her back to him gazing out at the same snow-covered landscape and hadn't heard the approach of his footfalls in the virgin snow.

'Flawless … isn't it?' He'd reached her side and spoke in a soft broken murmur.

'Yes … it is,' she said; and for some inexplicable reason was unperturbed by his arrival. She'd dreamt about him earlier tonight and when she woke suddenly was unable to get back to sleep. So it was of no surprise to her to find him here … in her presence; it was fate.

'You couldn't sleep either, eh?' He was watching her and smiling. She turned to face him and smiled back. Their breath smoked in the cold air.

'You must be frozen?' Florence said, looking concerned at the thin white shirt he wore without a jacket. When she looked up at him, she was smiling her glorious smile again causing warmth to flood his body. He pulled her into his arms before she could protest and kissed her. Florence melted into his embrace and returned his kiss with a passion to equal his own.

'Please … don't be afraid of me, Florence …'

'I–I'm not … I'm afraid of how you make me feel,' she said, her eyes meeting his.

He felt the tension ease, his face relaxed, and he smiled.

'Here, hold that,' Garrett said, handing her his walking stick, 'don't know about you but I'm cold.' He swept her up into his arms and they both laughed as he carried her unceremoniously into the cottage.

The fire in the range was still alight, and Garrett sat down on the rug before it and gently drew Florence down beside him. He kissed her … allowing his lips to linger whilst keeping his eyes wide open and perceived the stirrings of sexual desire in her grow stronger, experience conveying to him that she desired him as much as he did her. He smiled down at her when she gazed at him from deep-blue eyes. Then his hungry gaze settled on her nightdress outlining the shape of her body beneath and he slowly but gently slipped it over her head, revealing her nakedness. His heart contracted and he could barely swallow; she was more beautiful than he ever possibly imagined and hot passion flooded his mind and body.

'You're mine, Florence … and always will be … I love you,' he decreed softly, as his body enveloped hers. 'Nobody will ever love you … not as I love you … never …'

Before dawn broke, Garrett woke and reluctantly crept from Florence's bed unseen.

Florence woke at the sudden cold blast of air and the sound of a door closing. A tear trickled down her cheek when she saw the empty space beside her … and she knew beyond doubt she loved Garrett Ferrensby with all her heart. She lay still and quiet recalling the exquisite night of passion and his declaration of love for her … Did he mean it? Will he marry me? Then gripped by a sudden panic she sat bolt upright. 'Oh, no … Daphne … my God! What have I done?' she cried out loud, burying her head in her hands.

Any thought of love was instantly eclipsed by guilt.

Through the night a thaw had set in, softening the snow into brown slush. Garrett walked back to High Agra in a dream. If ten foot of snow had fallen through the night he would have neither noticed nor cared ... for he'd fallen madly in love; he decided whilst walking back to High Agra that he was going to marry Florence Grainger.

The girls looked up in surprise when their employer entered the kitchen by the back door half-attired.

'Cup of tea on the go, girls?' he asked, walking to the range to get warm. The girls nodded in unison and scurried to fetch a cup and saucer. As one girl poured the tea the other girl stood gaping at Garrett, dumbfounded.

'Ivy's not here then yet?'

'Mrs Baxter starts at seven and we starts at six,' said the non-dumbfounded girl.

'Tell her I wish to speak to her later in my study,' Garrett said and left.

As soon as he was out of earshot the girls burst out laughing.

'What the 'ell was all that about, eh?' one said.

"Ow would I know? The gentry are all queer buggers, me mam says – and she's bloody right too!'

The breakfast gong sounded and before going downstairs Garrett inspected himself in the long mirror. He'd dressed in warm tweeds ready to drive Robin and his wife to Thirsk to catch the train to London. Thankfully last night's thaw meant the roads were passable.

In the hallway Garrett saw Felicity giving instructions to a stable hand regarding their suitcases and he sighed with relief. It meant he didn't have to convince them the road was clear and that it was all right to go.

'Morning, Felicity.'

'Morning.... My, you're cheery this morning,' Felicity said, her tone inquisitive.

'Come – let's go in to breakfast before Robin starts without us.' Garrett cupped Felicity's elbow and steered her down the hall into the dining room.

With breakfast eaten and coffee cups refilled, Garrett walked over to the fireplace. He stood with his back to the flames, allow-ing the heat to ease the ache in his leg.

'Something happened that I should know about, old boy?' Robin said, looking at his brother and frowning. 'Thing is ... I'm a little uncertain as to whether the look on your face is one of delight ... or ... or, disaster. Hopefully it is not the latter,' he added.

Robin's cutting words produced an uncomfortable silence. Then Robin and Felicity both looked at Garrett and waited.

A clock chimed somewhere in the room.

'I'm not answerable to either of you, Robin, or anybody else. I'd hoped to give you my good news and we'd part on friendly terms. But that's never happened in the past ... and I don't expect you to change the habit of a lifetime, dear brother.' Garrett looked at his pocket watch. 'It's 10.30; we need to be leaving soon. I'll bring the car round.'

'OK, OK, I'm sorry, Garrett – that was rude of me ... please sit down and share your news with us.' Robin had risen from his chair and reached the door before Garrett and put his hands up in a gesture of surrender. 'Let's not part like this,' he pleaded.

Garrett eyed his brother warily. He was going to find out anyway eventually.

'I'm in love. And I hope to marry the woman very soon – that's if she'll have me. There. I've told you. Now let's get you both to Thirsk.'

'That's wonderful ... wonderful news,' Felicity said half-heart-edly, donning a smile. 'W-who is she? Do we know her ... her family?'

Garrett said nothing.

Robin looked into his brother's face, then sat down in the nearest armchair and as the nightmare of what he was about to hear dawned on him, he was shaking his head from side to side with a look of horror on his face.

'It's the gypsy, isn't it?' Robin said. His voice was a mere whisper before the anger welled up inside and he was fuming and glared at Garrett. 'Isn't it?' he yelled. 'Answer me! Isn't it?'

'There's no reasoning with you, Robin. Never has been. I'll

fetch the car and take you to the station. It's best we say nothing more on the matter.'

Garrett walked to the door and halted. He turned to where an astounded Felicity had joined her husband and perched on the arm of his chair; her face wreathed with worry. 'Florence is her name by the way, Florence Grainger, and I intend to bring her here to live once we're married,' he said before closing the door behind him.

'Your brother will ruin us, Robin, he'll ruin us! It will be nothing less than political suicide while you remain a Member of Parliament.' Felicity stood wringing her hands and tears swam uncontrollably down her face. 'Is there nothing, *nothing*, you can do? Surely ... surely there must be *something!*'

'Stop blubbering and pull yourself together, woman!'

Felicity gasped. Robin had never raised his voice to his wife ever before – but having done so on this occasion it had the desired effect.

'Right, now I need to be back in London. We say nothing of this to anyone. Do you understand? Nobody must get wind of it.' He took Felicity's hand and turning it over, kissed its palm ... 'I'm sorry I shouted, my darling ... everything will be all right, you'll see. He hasn't even asked her to marry him yet. And something tells me she'll know her limitations, and their incompatibility will become apparent – even to her. You see, Felicity, the gentry and gypsies have different natures; they can't be combined ... like oil and water.'

The drive to Thirsk had been tense and silent with neither brother giving way to the other. When they reached the station Robin located a porter. He then retrieved his wife from the back seat and marched off.

'Bye, Garrett,' Felicity called, looking over her shoulder to him, and then mouthed, '*Sorry*,' as Robin pulled her along to keep up with his long strides.

Garrett stood on the platform and watched the train disappear down the track through a haze of steam and smoke. To have parted on good terms with his brother was too much to ask. Maybe he'll come round in time, he thought. Who could not fall in love with Florence? She was everything any man in his right mind desired ... Then quite out of the blue something his father had once said sprung to mind: *To desire a woman is one thing, Garrett, but to marry one is a whole different kettle of fish!*

Garrett abruptly discounted this recollection and walked back to his car.

The office boy felt sorry for the heavily pregnant woman and held the door wide open for Daphne to pass through as she left Hyde & Wade solicitor's in Thirsk and into the cold morning air. Embarrassed by his staring, she sought to pull her coat across her swollen abdomen, but it wouldn't reach. The baby was due in two or three weeks and she didn't want to spend any of the little money she had left on clothes she'd never wear again.

Hyde & Wade had come highly recommended by Daphne's landlady. The woman had been startled; wondering what on earth someone living in humble, rented accommodation, could possibly want with a solicitor? Mrs Bowman had told her she was a widow and that her husband had died recently from injuries sustained when fighting at the front.

Daphne walked down Finkle Street and into the cobbled market square. She'd call at the butcher's before going home and buy something nourishing for tea – keep her strength up for the sake of the baby.

It was while crossing the road she saw him. The approaching inharmonious sound of a motor-car engine amid the clatter of cart wheels made her look up. She found herself staring at a yellow car with Garrett at the wheel. Their eyes met and Daphne's mouth fell open. The driver slammed on the brakes and stopped the car in the middle of the road and jumped out.

'Daphne! Daphne ... Wait! Please!'

Daphne shot down a ginnel and out of sight.

Garrett scoured the market square, but couldn't see her.

'Get that bloody motor outa me way!' a man yelled. He was driving a brewer's dray pulled by two carthorses and his attempt to wend his way round the stopped motor car had failed.

'All right, all right, I'm moving!' Garrett snapped back.

'Bloody motor cars ... nowt but a bloody nuisance – 'olding every bugger up!' he said gruffly. 'An' they mek enough racket to bloody deafen a man!' came his parting shot as he flicked the reins on the horse's rumps.

Garrett parked the car and walked across the cobbled square and into the Golden Fleece and ordered a drink. He found a seat in the window which overlooked the market square and ordered a drink. From this position he would spot her should she show up in the square again and he'd rush out to her.

After a couple of whiskies his mind relaxed a little. He'd been shocked to see Daphne in that state; ready to give birth at any minute ... her distended stomach appearing grotesque to him. Why the hell hadn't she got rid of it while she had the chance, for Christ's sake? Garrett wondered. Shortly after Daphne had visited him at High Agra he'd had a pang of conscience and felt sorry for her, for he had no qualms the child was his. Subsequently, he'd met his solicitor, instructing him to make contact with Daphne and Garrett arranged for a sum of £500 to be paid into an account for her. Clive Hatch, his solicitor, accused him of being *over-generous* – stating fifty pounds would suffice for an abortion with ample funds left over to give her time to decide what she wanted to do with her life. The solicitor's attitude had greatly annoyed Garrett, who reminded Clive curtly that Daphne Bowman had been a good friend to him during the last few months – and to also remember she was a war widow with little money.

The day was drawing to a close and Daphne was unlikely to put in an appearance again. Garrett threw his head back and emptied his glass and set out for home. It was an entirely different climate down in the fertile Vale of Mowbray lying between the Hambleton Hills and the uplands of the Dales from that of the North York Moors. The weather was unpredictable and could change at the drop of a hat on the moors.

Chapter Twelve

Daphne hurried across the cobbled square, her heart beating rapidly in her chest. She darted into an alley next to the butcher's and through the front door of a tiny one-up one-down cottage. The cottage was jammed between the butcher's shop and the slaughterhouse. Inside the cottage was dark and smelled stale, and Daphne couldn't decide which was worse, that, or the stench of rank, fetid animal flesh outside. The fire she'd built up an hour ago had gone out and the room was already growing cold. She relit the fire and put the kettle on before easing her aching body into a large grubby armchair at the side of the hearth.

I wish he'd not seen me in this state, Daphne sobbed, burying her head in her hands. He obviously thought I'd got rid of it ... the look of horror on his face confirmed that. Had he called out her name ... or was that just her imagination? She jolted suddenly at a loud rap on the door accompanied by the piercing hissing of the kettle boiling.

Daphne opened the door to find Agnes Jones standing on the step. 'Yes?'

'I've been looking out for you comin' home. I–I was wondering if I could have a word with you ... if you 'ave a minute. Ooh, is that your kettle boiling?' Agnes Jones said, rubbing her hands together. 'I could murder a cuppa!'

'Please, do come in,' Daphne said. 'I was just about to have one myself,' she said politely, forcing a smile. After all this was her landlady and she could hardly refuse her.

Agnes and Edgar Jones were brother and sister who owned

the butcher's shop and much of the property adjoining it; including a fishmonger and greengrocer situated at the other side of the market square.

Daphne poured the tea and sat down.

'Ah've brought yer this.' Agnes Jones dropped a package of bloodstained newspaper onto the little table set between them. 'Pig's liver. Iron. It'll help keep your strength up. Not long to go now, Mrs Bowman, 'ave yer? And 'ow are yer keeping?'

'No, not long to go now … and thank you for the liver, Miss Jones, that's very kind and thoughtful of you.'

Agnes studied the room. The smell of dampness crept into her nostrils; the heat from the fire powerless to conceal it. This was no fit place for a child to be brought up in.

'You wanted to see me about something, Miss Jones?' Daphne said.

'A-hem …' Agnes coughed and cleared her throat. ''Ave you thought about how you're going to manage … like? After the bairn's born, I mean?'

'What do you mean? I don't understand … How will I manage?'

'Working and suchlike … bringing a bairn up on your own won't be easy.' Agnes Jones moved uncomfortably in her chair before continuing. 'Thing is, I've a proposition to put to yer … well, not just me … but our Edgar as well. That's if you're in agreement. Eeh, is that tea mashed yet? 'Ere, you sit yourself down and I'll see to it.'

It wasn't long before both women sat facing one another.

'Well, I may as well not beat about the bush. As you know me and my brother 'ave never wed. We've no family … and neither of us is likely to, not now, I'm too old, and Edgar? Well, Edgar's too wrapped up in making money. Not that there's owt wrong wi' making money!' she added in her brother's defence. 'Now, hear me out before you say owt – and give it some thought before you decide. The thing is, we'd like to adopt the bairn you're carrying and bring it up as our niece or nephew. The child would have the best of everything and want for nowt. It'd have a good home, a private education … and when we're gone, well, we're not badly off, and the bairn would inherit the lot.'

Daphne's cup remained suspended between the table and her mouth whilst she listened to the ludicrous proposal. And when the woman stopped speaking, Daphne slowly replaced her cup back on the saucer. Her mouth was dry and when she spoke her voice was croaky.

'Are you being serious? Did you just ask if I would give my child away?' she asked, wondering whether she'd misheard.

'Yes, I did, and I'm being very serious. Anyway, there you have it. Think about it,' Agnes Jones said, rising to her feet. 'Don't give your answer right now. I'll come back in a week or so when you've had time to think it through, properly – and sensible, like. I'm sure you'll do what's right for the bairn.' The woman readjusted the shawl about her shoulders and on reaching the door, said, 'Because, Miss Bowman ... a mother *always* does what's best for her children.'

Agnes Jones closed the door quietly behind her.

Daphne sipped her tea which had now gone cold and rested her head on the back of the armchair. It was like a terrible dream ... no, a nightmare. Had that woman truly sat here at her table suggesting she give her and her brother her baby? Give her child away to strangers ... or to anybody for that matter. Reflecting on her situation made her feel more alone than ever before and dreadfully sad. Her personal savings were vastly depleted with only a few pounds left. She hadn't touched a single penny of Garrett Ferrensby's money. In Daphne's mind that was *their* child's inheritance which her son or daughter would come into when they came of age.

Daphne slept fitfully that night and woke in the early hours with a nagging pain in her lower abdomen. The pain gradually subsided after drinking a cup of chamomile tea. A warm smile played on Daphne's mouth as she thought of Florence, who on occasions presented her with gifts of specially prepared herbal teas. Daphne recollected those intelligent blue eyes looking into hers whilst meticulously explaining the medicinal usefulness of each packet and that chamomile would help her relax.

I hope you've forgiven me, Florence ... for disappearing from your life without a word. That was very wrong of me; you were the only true friend I ever had.

It was the next morning. Daphne was filling the coal scuttle, and while doing so, she slipped on a patch of ice – and fell full length. She cried out for help but nobody heard her; and clutching her stomach in great pain she struggled to her feet and slowly edged her way back inside the cottage. Once indoors it took every ounce of strength she had left to drag herself up the stairs on her hands and knees and climb into bed.

Daphne lay there … her face was ashen from cold and shock. 'Rest …' she told herself. 'I must rest … rest … then I'll be all right …'

Daphne didn't hear the loud hammering on the front door that same night. Nor did she hear Agnes Jones's voice bellowing through the letterbox.

'Mrs Bowman, it's me, Agnes, Agnes Jones!' Agnes had been concerned since lunchtime when it came to her attention there was no fire lit in the cottage and the day was bitterly cold. 'Are you all right cos I see you've no fire lit. There's no smoke comin' out of yer chimney. Mrs Bowman! Look, I'm comin' in with me spare key, all right?'

Agnes Jones turned the key and pushed open the door. She stepped into the cottage where the iciness greeting her equalled that of the wintry outside. She held a lantern high and glanced round the room; there was no visible sign of life anywhere. It was when she was about to leave that she heard a groan coming from the upstairs. She hurried up the stairs taking two at a time.

'Aw, lass, lass … what's happened to yer? Is the bairn on its way?' Agnes placed a cool hand on Daphne's forehead. It was hot and damp with perspiration. 'I'm off to get a doctor for you, luv … I won't be long.'

The moors were lovely, despite the snow that had fallen covering the landscape in mountainous drifts, and Florence walked under empty, grey skies, hugging a well-trodden path visible only to those who knew the area.

She'd been cooped up for two whole weeks now because of

the harsh weather and the gypsy in her couldn't endure one more day indoors. Florence needed space to breathe and to cast off the fetters that the gorgio coveted – living within four walls. She had received a letter from Ambrose prior to the snow arriving and wanted to give it some serious thought before replying. The letter was a proposal of marriage and was written in an exquisite hand that must have necessitated Ambrose entrusting someone else to write to Florence on his behalf.

Florence's heart and mind were in turmoil. She hadn't heard anything from Garrett since that unforgettable night he'd made love to her ... but her mind had been full of nothing else since. She'd seen him in the distance riding out on the moor a few times, but he was never alone, and it was difficult to make out who his companion was; maybe it was his brother visiting from London ... and Florence supposed Garrett wouldn't wish her to be on the receiving end of Robin's hateful conduct. But she must see him before giving Ambrose her answer ... especially after what they'd done together. Cold air stung her cheeks as her tears fell as she recalled vividly what her mother said to her on her sixteenth birthday. Don't allow any man to *have his wicked way with you* before marriage, Florence. He'll desert you. Always remember this; mark my words. A man will say anything to get you into his bed.

Florence was tidying away the supper dishes when Moth jumped up from where he lay in front of the fire and ran to the door barking. Florence peered out through the window and saw someone nearing the cottage. It was Garrett. Her heart leapt with delight.

'Come in. I was hoping you'd come,' she said. 'We need to talk.'

'Oh, is that really necessary?' Garrett said disappointedly. 'I'd rather hoped you'd join me in a glass of wine instead ...' he said, grinning and brandishing a bottle of wine.

Florence looked at him and saw he'd been drinking. She glanced at the clock on the mantelpiece: it was only 6.30 p.m.

He flopped into one of the armchairs and smiled at her. 'Bring a couple of glasses ... there's a good girl, Florence.'

'No! Out! Get out! Now! How dare you come here in that drunken state? You ... we ... you, you made love to me and ... told me you loved me. I thought you'd come here tonight to ask me to marry you!'

He was staring at her incredulously.

'What?'

'You heard me well enough, Garrett Ferrensby! Oh, I see, that's what you do, isn't it, eh? Charm the ladies into bed with your fine words and empty promises, then dump 'em? Just like that! Eh?' she said, clicking her fingers loudly in his face. 'Just like you did my friend Daphne?'

As soon as the words were out she regretted them, wishing she could take them back. The voice inside her head screamed, Why, oh ... why do we always end up fighting Garrett? I'm so sorry ...

Garrett rose to his feet slowly and brought his face close to hers – his mouth twisting with contempt before he spoke. 'You know what, Florence? You were quite right in what you said when we first met.' His voice was low and without emotion. 'There could never be anything between us – you and me – and that it wouldn't work? You remember saying that? Well, I think you hit upon a truth that day. And it would be impossible for us because I now know that I could never *ever* trust you.'

'*You*, not trust *me*? Hah, that's a laugh! Don't you mean the other way round – that I could never trust you?'

'You misunderstand me, Florence ...' There was a slight hesitation in his voice before he continued. 'Of course I realize I could trust you to be always faithful,' he said, throwing his arms wide. 'That goes without question ... but ... and more importantly ... I could never completely trust you *not* to revert to your ignorant gypsy habits.'

Florence wasn't prepared for the pain that hit her. To be kicked in the chest by a carthorse would have hurt less. In the next few moments as they regarded one another a chasm so wide and deep sprang up between them ... one which would prove impossible to cross. And tears of sorrow shone in both their eyes, but it was too late ... a line had been crossed.

Garrett walked to the door. His voice cracked, betraying the sorrow in his heart. 'Goodbye, Florence,' he said softly without looking back – and was gone.

Chapter Thirteen

THE SCENT OF lavender lingered in her nostrils ... invading the foggy stillness of her mind. Her eyelids felt heavy but Daphne slowly forced them open. She was in some strange bedroom ... or was it a hospital? No, it was far too beautiful. For there were two large casement windows draped in exquisite cream silk curtains; embroidered in brightly coloured flowers as was the matching bedspread covering the large brass bedstead she lay in.

As her head began to clear Daphne looked down at her body which lay beneath the covers and she suddenly flung them aside. She stared down at her stomach, which was no longer swollen with child!

'No! My baby! Where's my baby gone? W–what's happened?'

Disorientated by the force of emotion, Daphne heaved her leaden legs over the side of the bed, and holding onto a spindly bedside table, hauled herself on to her feet. She took a step forward but her legs were too weak and unable to hold her; and when the bedside table toppled under the strain, Daphne collapsed to the floor.

'Mrs Bowman ... can you hear me...?'

The tall thin doctor hovered above his patient, who was as white as the bleached sheet she lay upon. Little did the doctor realize what a terrible fright he gave each of his patients when opening their eyes and seeing him for the very first time. His long, thin, dark beard tapered to touch the waist of his trousers while his skeletal body didn't inspire confidence in the sick.

He held the smelling salts beneath Daphne's nose. 'Come, Mrs

Bowman ... wake up.'

Daphne tossed her head from side to side trying to avoid the smelling salts, but the doctor held her fast and spoke sternly.

'No, young lady, breathe in deeply, I want you awake; I've other patients to see to today!'

Daphne opened her eyes. 'Where's my baby?' she cried. 'I want my baby ...'

'Ssh ... sh ... your baby is fine, Mrs Bowman ... you'll see him soon. A wet nurse has been employed and is feeding him at present.'

'A wet nurse? Why on earth would I need a wet nurse? I'll feed my own baby ... bring him ... did you say I had a son? W-what am I doing in this place ... where am I?'

'Ah, here she is.' The doctor smiled broadly at the woman who entered the room; grateful to be relieved of the task of explaining to her the past events that had brought her here. 'Miss Jones. She will explain everything. And ... you have this lady and her brother to thank for saving your life – and the life of your child. You're a very fortunate young woman, believe me. Now, lots of rest along with a little daily exercise, and you should be good as new in no time. I'll call in again soon,' he said brusquely. 'You know where to find me, Agnes, should you need me.'

Agnes saw the doctor to the door. 'Thank you, doctor. Now, call and see our Edgar at the shop before you leave, he's put summat aside for you ... *a bit of best steak,*' she whispered.

'Thank you, that's most kind of you Agnes.'

Agnes...? Agnes Jones. Daphne's memory came flooding back. This was the woman who wanted her baby ... her and her brother.

Agnes Jones pulled a chair up to the side of the bed and sat down facing Daphne.

'When can I see my son, please...?' Daphne asked.

'As soon as he's finished feeding I'll bring him to you myself. You've been very ill, Mrs Bowman ... Can I call you Daphne?'

'Yes, all right,' Daphne said. I'll agree to anything, anything, she thought, just to hold my son in my arms.

'Good. And you can call me Agnes. Your son was born two weeks ago on the tenth of January. One morning I couldn't help but notice you hadn't lit your fire and it was a bitter cold day. By evening I was getting worried cos it still wasn't lit – and that wasn't like you. Anyway, knowing the condition you were in,' she said, looking at Daphne's flattened stomach, 'I knocked on your door and shouted through the letterbox, but there was no reply, so then I took it upon myself to use my own key. I found you in bed. You looked very sick indeed and had a high fever. So I got our Edgar and some fellas to carry you to our place.' Agnes couldn't help but chuckle when she added, 'They carried you here on an old door. I hope we did right by you. The doctor who's just left delivered the bairn ... Well, that's it ... And here you are. I promised the doctor we'd take good care of you and the child – and no expense spared, mind.' Agnes rose from her seat. 'Bet you could murder a cup of tea, luv – I'll fetch you one along soon ... with your baby.'

Daphne grabbed her hand before she left and squeezed it softly.

'Thank you ... thank you for all you've done ...' she said. And choked with emotion, Daphne smiled feebly through her tears of gratitude at this woman who'd saved their lives. 'I'll be forever in your debt ...'

''Ow is she, then?' Edgar Jones enquired. His large frame filled the drawing-room doorway; and his bloodstained hands and apron denoted his trade.

'Aw ... Edgar!' Agnes said, abandoning the baby jacket she was knitting. 'Don't come in 'ere dripping in blood! An' who's looking after the shop?'

'There's no customer in at the minute an' I was just wondering, 'ow she was?' he asked, gesturing toward the staircase. 'Has she asked for the bairn yet?'

Agnes didn't reply, but walked through to the kitchen and Edgar followed her.

'Take a tray of tea for Mrs Bowman, please, Kitty, and tell her I'll be up in a few minutes.'

After the maid had left, Agnes spoke. 'Yes, Edgar, she wants to see her son. I'll take him up when you've gone back to the shop. I, we ... we're going to 'ave to be patient. When she sees what *we're* offering the lad, what mother in her right mind would deprive her child of that, eh? When she's got nowt else to offer him but the workhouse ... pain and poverty ...'

Edgar felt sorely sorry for his sister. She hadn't experienced what he had; which was a lifetime of slaughtering and butchering animals. He'd spent the best part of forty years watching lambs and calves being taken from their mother's side and witnessed the mother's distress, bleating in vain, and helpless to save her young.

'Well, maybe it's best not to get your hopes up too much, our Agnes,' he said gently.

'What d'yer mean, not get my hopes up?' she snapped sharply.

'You know what I mean, Agnes. It's her bairn, for Christ's sake – not yours!'

The black look she threw him communicated he'd said enough and an awkward silence descended.

'I'd better be getting back to t'shop,' Edgar said. 'I'll see you later.'

Agnes watched Daphne as she sat up in bed holding her baby. Her face was wreathed in smiles; she was bursting with the love only a mother could appreciate. The transformation had been instantaneous. Daphne's eyes shone with elation and her ashen face was instantly transformed with a rosy glow of well-being.

'You're perfect ... my own dear son ... just perfect ...' Daphne had removed the baby's shawl and was examining his tiny fingers and feet. Her finger softly stroked the side of his face ... 'So like your father,' she said quietly, gently running her finger over the arched eyebrow. The pale-blue eyes she knew would turn grey in time looked into hers – and her heart leapt with pure joy.

'Have you thought of a name for him yet?' Agnes said, interrupting Daphne's inspection of her son. The lump in her chest grew stronger observing mother and child, and Edgar's words rang in her ears ... 'Don't get your hopes up too high ...'

'Yes, yes I have. It's going be Joseph. Joseph Garrett Bowman. Do you like the name Joseph?' she said, looking down tenderly at her son. 'Joseph was my father's name ... yes, that's your grandfather. Heavens above, Agnes ... look, look! Can you see that he's looking at me?' Daphne squealed in delight. 'I mean really looking at me! He knows I'm his mother, I'm sure of it. I'd like his cot next to the side of my bed if that's all right with you. I'll help carry it in – I'm feeling so much stronger now.'

'No, no, you stay where you are and I'll get someone to bring it along ...'

When Agnes left Daphne carefully placed Joseph on the bed and dragged her legs over the side. She must exercise and get her strength back for the sake and welfare of her child. He needed her more than ever now. Daphne stood upright and slowly allowed her legs to take her weight, and when she felt them weaken she sat down again quickly. Later in the evening when everyone was asleep she would do the same again. For the sake of her son and her health, it would be foolish not to take advantage of all that was currently on offer: nourishing food and a warm home for them both. And as soon as she was strong enough she would make plans for their departure; for as kind as they were, she would never hand over her son to them.

She smiled down at the sleeping child. 'We'll manage somehow, Joseph, won't we ... my son?'

It would be two weeks later when Daphne was in the news-agent's that she saw the advert: a vacancy for temporary help assisting an elderly lady recovering from a bout of sickness. Apply within for particulars.

Dear Ambrose, Florence wrote,

I'm writing to thank you for asking me to marry you and to let you know that my answer is yes. I'm more than willing to leave Hamer Bridge and take up the travelling way of life once again, only this time as your wife.

I realize this letter is being read to you by someone else so won't write too much.

Affectionately yours,
Florence.

Florence addressed the envelope to: The Post Office, Topcliffe, as requested by Ambrose, before sealing it. She'd been surprised to hear he was stopping at Topcliffe, assuming he'd travelled northward to Appleby to be with his parents for the winter. This meant he could be with her in a week after receiving her letter if the break in the weather held.

The break in the weather also presented Florence with the opportunity of satisfying her desire to ride out on Dancer. The gelding was young and in need of exercise – just as she needed the wide open moorland to breathe in the cool air, and to be free of winter's cobwebs that choked up her mind....

Dancer pricked his ears and Florence altered her stride and broke into a smooth canter. Then the urge to race along with the wind was too great for her and she kicked him into a wind-whistling gallop across the open moor and the cold air stung her face. After covering some distance she slowed him down to walking pace. They passed by the large boulder covering the hole where she'd disposed of Benny Grainger and a cold shiver ran up her spine. That was another good reason to get away from this place ... Garrett will never let me forget ... he'll hold it over me to my dying day, she reasoned.

Dancer whinnied loudly and skipped sideways almost unseating her. A familiar-looking dog appeared from nowhere and began bounding round Dancer's legs.

'Bruno! Heel!'

She recognized his voice immediately. Florence stared in disbelief at the man and woman who'd reined their horses to a halt in front of her.

An elegant woman was seated side-saddle on a grey horse; and she was one of the most beautiful-looking creatures Florence had seen in her life. She wore an elegant, and very stylish, bottle-green velvet riding habit with matching hat. Beneath her hat wisps of golden hair escaped onto her soft cream cheeks. Her eyes sparkled and her wide generous mouth smiled warmly at Florence.

'Do you two know each other?' she was asking Garrett, a puzzled expression on her face. 'If so, do introduce me. And *that*,' she said, her eyes surveying Dancer, 'by the way, if you don't mind my saying so, is a magnificent horse. Garrett?'

Garrett's face was ashen.

'Are you all right, my dear?' she asked with genuine concern. 'Is it the cold? We really ought to be getting back, you haven't been yourself of late ...'

'W-what? Oh, I'm fine. And yes ... we are acquainted. I'm sorry, I do apologize, this ... this is my neighbour ... Miss Grainger. Florence ... this is Miss Denby...'

'How do you do, Miss Grainger. You must live at that sweet little cottage, Hamer Bridge?' She removed a fine kid glove and reaching across took Florence's hand and shook it firmly. 'Garrett and I have been friends for years, haven't we, darling? Then ... only last week when I came up from London with Robin and his wife – Garrett popped the question.'

Florence watched as the woman's face lit up with the adoration only a woman in love can own when she glanced across at Garrett.

'We got engaged yesterday ... didn't we, darling? My parents know of course, but no one else as yet ...'

The uncomfortable silence suddenly became glaringly obvious to her. Why didn't Garrett say his neighbour at Hamer was a woman – and a very attractive one at that? Over the years he'd often spoken of wishing to buy Hamer Bridge back – banging on about how it belonged to the estate ... then why hadn't he bought it when it came up for sale, she wondered? Then not wanting the wonderful time she was enjoying clouding with undesirable thoughts, she immediately discarded them from her mind. The only important thing she cared about was that she and Garrett were in love. They were engaged to be married and nothing else mattered. Garrett had told her one night that he'd always loved her ... and as neither of them was getting any younger they'd make a good match. It had all happened very quickly – too quickly for her parents. The Denbys of course had known Garrett's family for years and owned a large country residence in Rosedale which they used to escape the busy-ness of London and its relentless smog; as well as delighting in the country pursuits of hunting and shooting.

'My congratulations to you both,' Florence said, remembering her manners and breaking the embarrassing silence.

'Please, you must come to tea one day soon, Miss Grainger. We'd like that very much, wouldn't we, Garrett – especially since we're to be neighbours. Neighbours are like gold dust on these moors – as I'm sure you've discovered,' she added with a light laugh.

'Yes, do come.' Garrett's voice was tainted with sarcasm; and gathering up the reins he wheeled his horse round and walked away from the two women. 'Good day to you, Florence.'

'Bye, Miss Grainger … I hope we meet again, and very soon.'

'Goodbye, Miss Denby,' Florence replied, forcing a smile. *And good luck to you!* she wanted to call out after her – *you'll need it, cos you're far too nice for the likes of him!*

Strange, Florence thought, watching the newly engaged couple ride away across the moor and into the distance. I thought I'd be devastated to hear that news … that he'd found somebody else, but I'm not bothered in the slightest.

Miss Denby's sweet tinkling laughter was carried to Florence's ears as it caught on the wind and she couldn't help but wonder what Garrett might have said to cause it.

He never made me laugh, she thought – not once.

Chapter Fourteen

AMBROSE FLICKED THE reins and clicked his tongue and the horse pulled the bow-top wagon with ease out of the farm track and into the main road. The sound of clattering hoofs and jangling harness was music to his ears after two months of staying put in one place. Mind, Ambrose had no complaint, for the farmer had paid him well for the two months' work and he'd even considered staying on when he'd been asked. All that changed the moment Florence's letter arrived at the post office, though, and wild horses wouldn't hold him back.

It was late afternoon and growing dark when Ambrose drove his wagon through Thirsk and wound his way through the familiar market square to Long Street where he pulled his wagon to a halt outside Miss Wooten's house.

'It's a bit late in the day for visitors,' Eleanor Wooten said, with a startled expression on her face as she looked at the woman sitting opposite her on the other side of the fireplace.

Eleanor Wooten had been struck down with a severe attack of flu over the Christmas period. Her daily help did what she could, but she had family of her own to care for and was therefore unable to live in. It was only at her doctor's insistence she'd agreed, albeit reluctantly, to engage someone to live in; stubbornly refusing to go into hospital.

The attractive widow sitting opposite had fitted the post perfectly. Eleanor Wooten found her to be both courteous and kind, yet at the same time very hard-working. Her duties, besides living in, were to do the shopping and prepare supper occasionally. But the woman had proven she was no idler; taking it upon herself to assist her employer in every way she could, including assisting her in bathing and dressing. They'd laughed one day when Eleanor said in mock admonishment, 'I shan't ever wish to get well if you continue to spoil me like this.'

'Answer the door ... but don't invite them in before you come back and tell me who it is – unless it happens to be the doctor of course.'

'Ambrose!' Daphne cried in amazement. 'W-what on earth are you doing here?'

'Is it really you, Daphne...?' Ambrose's eyes widened with surprise. 'What on earth are you doing here?'

Realizing they'd both asked the same question – they laughed nervously.

'Daphne, who is it at the door?' Miss Wooten shouted from the sitting room.

'Just wait there – I'll let her know you're here.'

Eleanor Wooten was already on her feet and making her way across the room when Daphne returned.

'Who is it, then?' she said snappily. 'I thought I recognized that voice.'

'It's an Ambrose Wilson, Miss Wooten.'

'Good grief! Ambrose? Turning up here at this time of year? Well, I never did! Let the poor man in, then ... don't leave him freezing to death on the doorstep!'

Daphne showed Ambrose into the front room where Miss Wooten had returned and was sitting in her armchair. Her face broke into smiles and her eyes shone with delight when she looked at her dear friend Ambrose, and she clasped his hand warmly.

'Hello, Miss Wooten, forgive me for calling so late in the day, and ... so early in the year ...'

'Aw, sit yourself down, Ambrose,' she interjected. 'No need to apologize. You know you're always welcome whatever time of year it is. Although ... I must admit it's come as a bit of a surprise. Take your coat off, lad, and sit down and warm yourself through. Daphne, will you make a fresh pot of tea for our guest, please?'

'Yes, of course. Here, let me take your coat, Ambrose ...'

Ambrose divested himself of his damp coat and handed it to her.

'Thanks, Daphne.'

Eleanor Wooten sat back in her chair frowning. That sounds rather familiar ... *Daphne? Ambrose?*

'Excuse me, I know it's none of my business, but tell me, do you two know each other?'

'I'll leave the explaining up to Daphne,' Ambrose said, glancing at Daphne. Her eyes appealed to some part of him and her message was conveyed.

'Yes, we do know each another, Miss Wooten, but it's a long story,' Daphne said. 'I'll tell you all about it one day soon.'

'You don't have to explain anything to me – I was just curious, that's all. I'm nothing but a nosy old woman,' she chuckled. 'Now, Daphne, how about we have that fresh pot of tea?'

It wasn't long before Daphne returned. She placed the tray on the low table beside Miss Wooten's chair and started to leave.

'Please, don't go. Stay and have tea with us, Daphne,' Eleanor said.

Daphne placed a chair by the table and poured the tea; and when the three were settled Ambrose spoke.

'I'm back this way because I'm getting married.'

Now there's a bold statement if ever I heard one, Eleanor Wooten thought, and sat bolt upright. I always thought Ambrose to be the bachelor type. But there again, he's a handsome hardworking chap, and a good catch for any woman. I'd have set my cap at him myself sixty years ago, she thought, smiling.

'Congratulations, Ambrose! That's wonderful news,' Daphne said, getting up from her chair and dropping a kiss on his cheek.

Daphne's felicitations were a little too enthusiastic for Eleanor Wooten's sharp hearing; and the veil of uncertainty on Daphne's face didn't pass unnoticed.

'Congratulations indeed. Might I enquire as to who the fortunate young lady is who's managed to capture your heart, Ambrose?' Eleanor enquired.

His face beamed with pride. Ambrose liked the way Miss

Wooten spoke to him, it made him feel special, gentlemanly like.

'Daphne will have already guessed. She knows her well enough ... don't you, Daphne?'

Daphne nodded.

'It's Miss Florence Grainger,' Ambrose said.

'And does this Miss Grainger live in these parts?'

'Not so far away. She lives up on the moors, above Ryeburn. I'm on my way there now and I was hoping you'd permit me to pull my wagon into the orchard for the night, Miss Wooten. I'll be away at first light.'

'No, you cannot stay in the orchard, young man. Go and pull your wagon round the back and see to your horse then come back here. We've plenty of spare beds – you'll stay here where it's nice and warm.'

'Aw, I can't put on yer like that, Miss Wooten,' Ambrose protested.

'Oh, be quiet and do as you're told, lad,' admonished the old girl, 'and get a move on – it's almost dark! Then join us for dinner. If that's all right with you, Daphne?'

'Perfectly all right by me, Miss Wooten, I'll peel a few more potatoes before I see to Joseph ...'

A child's cry suddenly pierced the air.

'W-what ... who ... is...?' Ambrose looked from one to the other in confusion.

Daphne rose to her feet. '*That* is Joseph demanding his feed,' she replied, averting her eyes from his quizzical gaze.

'Here, let me take that,' Ambrose said, taking the tray from Daphne. 'Thank you for the tea, Miss Wooten. I'll see to the horses first, then take you up on your kind offer of a meal and a warm bed.'

Daphne went into the kitchen and Ambrose followed. He put the tray on the table, then turned to face Daphne.

'Why didn't you say something, Daphne ... to me ... or Florence? Yer know we'd have helped you.' He hesitated a moment before he spoke again. 'And what about the father, Daphne? Is it ...'

'Shhh ... don't say it, Ambrose. Don't say his name ... please

... Miss Wooten believes my husband died recently from injuries sustained during the war ... I–I don't want her to know anything different ... please, Ambrose. You won't say anything, will you? Promise me? I'm only here for another week or two then I have to look for another job and find somewhere else to live ... But meanwhile, my son and I have food and warmth ... a roof over our heads.'

Ambrose stared in disbelief at this distressed gentle lady. For that's what she was in his eyes, and always would be, a lady.

'And Florence ... I take it she doesn't know where you are ... that you've a child? She knows nothing?'

'She knew I was pregnant ... but that's all. I didn't tell her I was going away ... I knew she'd insist on helping me ... and I didn't want her to be saddled with the responsibility, a–and my disgrace ... or be a burden to her ... or to anyone else. So I left my job and moved to Thirsk where nobody knows me ... or anything about the humiliating circumstances I've found myself in.'

'Can I see him?' Ambrose asked. Then resting his hands on her shoulders he looked at her. 'And you're not alone anymore, Daphne ... You have me and Florence. You and your son are among friends.'

Daphne's eyes filled with tears as she looked into the kindest brown eyes she'd ever seen. 'Thank you, Ambrose. Florence is a very lucky girl ... as I'm sure she knows.'

Another scream from Joseph startled them and they both laughed.

'You can be Uncle Ambrose – that's if you don't mind being Joseph's uncle?'

'I'd like that very much, Daphne. I've no brothers left to grant me the title ... the war saw to that,' he added quietly.

Marjorie Denby went downstairs having changed out of her riding habit into suitable attire for lunch. As she crossed the hall she heard raised voices coming from the drawing room as she approached. The door was ajar; and curiosity getting the better of her she hovered on the other side and listened.

'For goodness' sake, man, you musn't betray your own class

mixing with the likes of her!'

'I'm fed up to the back teeth of being told by you how to live my life!'

'And … Marjorie?' Robin's voice was conciliatory when he mentioned her name. 'Doesn't Marjorie deserve some consideration and respect, hmm? God, Garrett, you can't go disappearing to Hamer Bridge whenever your cock fancies!'

Marjorie was rooted to the spot. *W … what a fool I've been … he doesn't love me … doesn't give a fig for me – never has! It would be a marriage of convenience. He's in love with that woman we met on the moor … I should have seen it … It was patently obvious….*

'Mind your own bloody business, Robin. I'm going to marry her, aren't I? What more can I do to bloody please you? Thought doing that would have got you off my back – for a while at least!'

Felicity walked onto the scene to find Marjorie standing outside the door eavesdropping. The two women stood speechless catching Garrett's final cruel barrage of words – it was too late – the damage was done.

'Marjorie … Marjorie, oh, how awful, I am so sorry … so very sorry …'

'Well, I'm not!' Marjorie announced. She thrust the door wide open causing it to slam hard and loud on the wall – both men turned suddenly. The shocked and grotesque expression on Marjorie's face communicated to Garrett she'd heard every cruel word of his damning conversation. He leaned towards his brother and fixed him with a baleful stare.

'Pleased with yourself now are you, Robin?'

'Ugh!' she laughed. 'Don't go blaming Robin for y–your callous nature! My parents were right about you, Garrett Ferrensby,' she admitted airily. 'You're a selfish brute.'

'I agree with them wholeheartedly,' Garrett said with a wry twist to his mouth.

Marjorie glowered at him, and removing the sapphire ring from her finger she flung it across the room. 'Can you order somebody to take me to the station, Robin?' she asked calmly, 'And straightaway if you will, please. I don't wish to spend a moment longer than is necessary in this house – I'll pack immediately.'

An unwitting Ivy Baxter entered the uneasy silence announcing lunch was now served.

'I hope you choke on it, you vile creature!' Marjorie snarled at Garrett and strode from the room.

'W–what?' stammered the bemused housekeeper.

'Miss Denby won't be joining us for lunch today, Ivy,' Garrett said.

Chapter Fifteen

'WELL, THAT WAS short and sweet, my dear. Good luck, Marjorie!' Garrett said, raising his glass to the horse and trap retreating down the drive with his ex-fiancée ensconced on board. He stood gazing out of the large drawing-room window through wine-sodden eyes and didn't hear the housekeeper enter the room.

Pondering the situation her employer had created for himself, Ivy Baxter stood watching Garrett for a moment. He's not been right ever since the traveller lass moved into Hamer Bridge.... As if owt could come o' that!

She coughed lightly. 'I've saved you a bit o' lunch. Are you going to have summat to eat? Mr Robin and wife have taken off and gone for a ride ... daft lot,' Ivy added, shaking her head. 'In this weather, I ask you! Sky's full o' snow ... I reckon Miss Denby's got away just in time before we're snowed up and blocked in again.'

'Hahaha ...' Garrett guffawed. And throwing his head back laughed till tears streamed down his face, then almost losing his balance, he staggered over to a table where a half-empty decanter of whisky stood and replenished his glass.

'Ivy, have you any idea how funny that is? *Her!* Marjorie snowed up here with this family for another week? Her papa would send in the cavalry to rescue her *from this wicked man!*' he said dramatically, stabbing his chest with his finger.

'You're drunk ...' Ivy remonstrated.

'Maybe ... but not drunk enough. If that stupid wench hadn't eavesdropped none of this would have happened ... the foolish woman. Ah, well, that's that, I guess ... it was bound to happen sooner or later. '

'At least have something to eat,' Ivy pleaded.

'Get out, Ivy, and stop fussing. Leave me alone. I'll be all right. I'll see you in the morning ... I promise you ... now go!'

Ivy left the room and closed the door behind her knowing she'd not be able to rest until he was safely in his room.

Robin and Felicity came back from their ride covered in a dusting of snow. The maid rushed to relieve them of their wet outer clothes. Ivy Baxter looked on and waited till the maid returned to her duties before approaching Robin and Felicity.

'Mister Robin, I know it's not my place ... but ...'

'But what?'

Ivy hesitated.

'Oh, for God's sake spit it out, Mrs Baxter!'

And that's why you'll never be a proper gentleman, thought Ivy, looking into his mean face. You're ignorant, unlike your brother. Mr Garrett might get drunk, but he'd never speak to a member of staff like that in a million years!

'I'm still waiting, Mrs Baxter.'

'Thought you should know Mister Garrett's still in the drawing room and he's in a bit of a state, like ... ahem,' she coughed nervously. 'I took the liberty of lighting a fire in the study for you and Mrs Ferrensby ...'

'Good. That will be all, Mrs Baxter,' he said, abruptly terminating the conversation.

'Why do you have to be so rude to Mrs Baxter, Robin?' Felicity asked when they'd withdrawn to the study. 'She does her best ... oh, I know she's not up to scratch, compared to our London housekeeper, darling, but considering ... there's no mistress of the house, so to speak. Oh, what a pity ...' Felicity sighed, 'Marjorie was the ideal woman for the position.... She'd have made the perfect sister-in-law too ...'

'You might as well forget all about Marjorie. When this gets out there won't be a woman standing who will touch my brother with a bargepole – believe me!'

'Oh, stop it and don't be so dramatic, Robin! There's always some impoverished well-to-do lady who'd consider taking him on. I can think of a few who'd be only too willing.'

Garrett woke up to pitch blackness. The striking of a clock notified him it was 2 a.m. The fire had died and the curtains weren't drawn, allowing the cold blast of winter to strike the glass and penetrate the room. He slumped forward in the chair and rested his throbbing head in his hands ... only the touch of his hands increased the pain. A wave of nausea swept over him and he waited ... unmoving and submissively until it passed. He cursed himself for getting into a drunken state again unable to recall events prior to his passing out.

Garrett pulled himself onto his feet, with the aid of his walking stick, and picked his way slowly across the furniture-cluttered drawing room and out into the darkened hallway.

The sound of groaning brought him to a sudden halt as he was passing by the study. He listened. There it was again ... He saw a dim light in the gap beneath the door and he took a step closer; the door was slightly ajar. Garrett peered through the small opening and saw that embers still glowed in the fire grate. He pressed the door open slightly wider so as to see into the room. The sound came louder now ... but it was soft ...

Then what he saw caused him to catch his breath.

Janet, the young housemaid, was lying naked on a rug in front of the hearth and by her side, leaning over her, was his brother. Robin was gazing down into the young girl's face while caressing her breasts. The girl had her eyes closed and her mouth was open as she released moans of pleasure.

Garrett forced himself to step away from the carnal scene and a self-assured smirk settled on his face as he considered the consequences of what he'd just witnessed.

You'll never talk down to me again, Robin. *Never!*

The next morning after snatching a couple of hours' sleep Garrett was up bright and early and the first down for breakfast. A maid was putting a match to the fire when he entered.

'Morning,' he said chirpily. 'It's Janet, isn't it?'

'Yes, sir,' she said, standing up.

145

'Well, carry on, Janet, don't let me interrupt your work. I know I'm up rather early, but when you've finished lighting the fire I'd like a full breakfast ... please.'

'Right, I won't be long, sir.'

Garrett picked up an old newspaper and pretended to read while eyeing the girl. God, she can't be more than seventeen years old, he thought, *if that!* Janet's stature was short and shapely with a tiny waist; and he'd already had the pleasure of sizing up her breasts which he recalled were ample and firm.

Garrett didn't hear Felicity enter the dining room and capture him leering at the housemaid from over the top of a newspaper.

'You're up early, Garrett. Good morning.'

'W-what ... Oh, good morning, Felicity, I didn't see you.'

'Just a boiled egg, please, Janet.'

Janet got to her feet and scurried from the room.

'Nice girl, that,' Garrett said.

'Yes, I couldn't help but notice your appreciation of her,' Felicity said, sneering.

Garrett smiled broadly at his sister-in-law. If only you knew how much your own husband appreciates her too, he thought. Yes, it shouldn't be too long, Felicity, before your visits to Agra will be either curbed or terminated ... and preferably the latter.

'Are you all right?' Felicity enquired, frowning. 'Or have you already started drinking this morning?'

'I'm feeling better than I have done in a long time.'

'Really! Now why does that surprise me, I wonder?' Robin said entering the room taking a seat opposite Garrett. He pulled the bell and when the maid came, ordered breakfast. 'Thank you,' he said curtly, not bothering to glance up at the girl.

You prat! And looking at him as if for the first time, Garrett perceived what a conceited prude and duplicitous degenerate his brother really was.

'Garrett ... are you listening to a word I'm saying?' Robin said.

'Listening? Of course I'm listening to you, old boy ... haven't I always? What's the matter with you this morning? Didn't you sleep well last night ... or did something keep you awake?'

'I slept very well, thank you! Now stop trying to evade my

questioning ...'

'Oh ... is that so?' Garrett interrupted. I thought you were *busy* in the study until the early hours. I happened to wake up, hung-over, *naturally*, and I popped my head through the study door and saw you ... Didn't want to disturb you, though ... thought it must be important business. You must be completely exhausted, Robin. Hmm, now, would you pass me the marmalade, please, Felicity ...'

Robin turned ashen and was suddenly lost for words.

'Looks like it's set fair today. Think I'll go for a ride ... you want to come along,' Garrett said to Robin.

Robin coughed and cleared his throat. 'Er, no,' he muttered, 'but, there is some business I do need to discuss with you today ... and if the weather holds we'll catch the train back to London, tomorrow.'

'Tomorrow? Why tomorrow? I thought we'd be here another week at least. My friends won't be expecting me ... and ...'

'Oh, do be quiet, Felicity ... I've business to attend to and constituents to see.'

'Well I never!' Felicity said huffily. And throwing her napkin down on the table she left the room.

The brothers sat in silence for what seemed a long time after Felicity left. Robin spoke first.

'Well ... you caught me out. What are you going to do? Tell Felicity?'

'No, not if you get off my back and mind your own bloody business in future,' Garrett replied.

'I see ... blackmail, eh?'

'Call it what you like, I don't give a damn.'

'Does this mean that gypsy girl will be brought into the picture?'

'Maybe. You'll have to wait and see.'

Garrett lit a cigarette and took a long pull as he looked at Robin – his face showing an expression of defeat ... and Garrett was suddenly overcome with guilt and pity when the door opened and the maid in question entered.

'Oh, I'm sorry, I–I thought you'd all finished and gone.'

'Well, as you can see we haven't so get out!' snarled Robin.

And Janet, whose body he'd enjoyed last night, hurried from the room.

The pity Garrett had experienced an instant ago was replaced with anger.

'I want you to leave here, Robin, and the sooner the better! Let's face it … there's no love lost between us. Also, when, or *if* you happen to visit, I would appreciate your behaving in a civil manner towards everybody under this roof – that includes the staff – and Janet in particular. God, Robin, how could you?' Garrett said, shaking his head. 'She's no more than a child, man!'

'She's no child … believe me!' Robin said.

'Well, she's not now you've corrupted the poor girl! You disgust me!'

Garrett got up from the table and left the room. He met the young maid in question loitering in the hallway with an empty tray waiting to clear the breakfast table and he opened the door to allow her in.

'We've finished here, haven't we, Robin?' Garrett said icily.

Robin rose from his chair and strode across the room where Garrett waited holding the door open for him. Janet gave Robin a sideways glance and smiled coyly at him as he walked past her.

'There, what did I tell you?' Robin said smugly. 'I rest my case. Did you see that look she gave me just then? A child indeed …'

Garrett took advantage of the clear weather and rode into Ryeburn to see his solicitor. If the weather turned nasty he'd stay at a hotel for the night which would excuse him from dining with Robin and Felicity.

The market square was virtually deserted apart from the occasional shopper. Garrett went to his solicitor's office and was able to see him right away.

Clive pulled a chair out for his client before taking his seat on the other side of the large leather-topped desk.

'Now what can I do for you, Garrett?'

'Bit of a sensitive matter … I want to know what has become of Daphne Bowman – and the child.…'

Clive Hatch's eyes almost popped out of their sockets. 'What?' he exclaimed.

'She didn't have an abortion. I saw her, Clive. And not so very long ago when I happened to be in Thirsk. She looked positively dreadful ...'

'B–but what about the money you gave her to get rid of it? It ... it's not your fault.' Clive rose to his feet struggling to find appropriate words. 'She had a choice!'

'Perhaps she did – and chose not to get rid of it – obviously ... Oh, for God's sake sit down and put your eyes back in their sockets Clive! This happens to be *my* child we're talking about!'

Clive sat back down and opening the bottom drawer of his desk withdrew a bottle of Scotch and two glasses.

'Believe me I don't normally drink at work, Garrett, but right now I need one.'

Clive drank deeply then looked at Garrett. 'What is it you want me to do?'

'I want you to make a few discreet enquiries about her; where she's staying, has the child survived ... and if so ... is it a boy or a girl?' He took a large swig and drained his glass. 'For all I know, I might have a son.'

'You mean you'd *actually* recognize the child as your own?' Clive said blankly.

'Just do as I ask, Clive,' Garrett said, rising to leave, 'after all, that's what I pay for.'

The weather held and the stable boy greeted Garrett as he rode into the courtyard.

'I 'ope you don't mind, sir, but I drove Master Robin 'nd his missus to t'station this mornin'.'

'Good thing I taught you to drive, then, Bart, eh?'

'Aye, 'tis that. Ah said to yer brother, t'snow's comin' again – ah can smell it. So 'e said 'e wanted to be off afore it came an' didn't want to be stuck up 'ere in t'moors.'

'Well done, Bart,' Garrett said, and walking back to the house, reflected that none of his staff would be sorry to see the back of either of them.

Sleep came hard that night for Garrett even with the copious amounts of alcohol he'd consumed. His thoughts whirled round like leaves on a windy day. What if he were never to marry?

Robin assumed should he and Felicity have a son then he would be master of High Agra ... Whereas, there is a possibility that I have a son of my own now – somewhere.

Since seeing Daphne in Thirsk that day, the possibility that he was a father invaded his thoughts over and over again.

Moth lay at Florence's feet in front of the blazing fire. The weather had changed dramatically two days ago when a deep low pressure delivered vast quantities of snow on a strong north-easterly depositing it on the North York Moors.

Her fingers were sore from stitching the rabbit skins piled high at the side of her chair. She'd fashioned hats, scarves, and mittens. Moth whimpered for attention and she leaned down and stroked the top of his head. He'd proved a wonderful companion – and provider. Most of the skins she was working on were those of rabbits hunted down by Moth whilst out on his nightly prowls.

The recent weather would delay Ambrose which disappointed her at first until it dawned on her that after they married she would relinquish the warmth and protection of her cottage for a life on the road. This would certainly be the last winter she'd spend with a solid roof overhead. Florence closed her eyes and wallowed in its warmth and comfort.

Chapter Sixteen

AMBROSE COULDN'T SETTLE and vacated the room at Miss Wooten's house after three days and moved back into his bow-top wagon in the orchard. The weather was abysmal, but he'd managed to keep himself busy digging a path through the snow from the orchard to the back of the house and clearing away the deep snow blocking the pathway at the front of the house. He brought in logs and kept the coal buckets filled. The paths were too icy and treacherous for Daphne to venture out and Ambrose took it upon himself to walk into town and stock up with groceries with the aid of a shopping list from Daphne.

'Won't you come back into the house till this nasty weather passes, lad?'

'No, I'm fine in the wagon, thank you, Miss Wooten. I like to be close to me 'orses – especially when the weather's bad. They get upset when I'm not about and seem to know I'm not in the wagon – it's as if they can smell me. I'm sorry to have put on yer all this time with the weather so bad ... the 'orses wouldn't make it to Ryeburn – never mind to Hamer Bridge.' Ambrose put his hand up. 'I know ... I know ... you don't mind, Miss Wooten. You're a generous woman and I'll be forever grateful to you; one day I hope I can repay you for your kindness.'

'Well ... there is something you can do for me ... That is if it's not asking too much, or putting you out of your way?'

Ambrose's eyes lit up. 'Anything, please, ask away.'

'The thing is ... last night Daphne and I got talking. She's not going to stay on here. Did you know that?'

'Aye, I'd an idea,' Ambrose said.

'Well, she's a mind to leave here soon. She was telling me how very fond she is of the lass you're marrying and she'd like to see her again. So, when the weather clears and you leave for Ryeburn, I was wondering if maybe you'd take Daphne along with you … and give the girl a bit of a break. The roads will soon be open and she could come back here after seeing her friend. There's a charabanc runs regularly from Ryeburn to Thirsk in fine weather. I'll not see Daphne short of money.'

'That's all very well, but are you well enough to be left on your own for a few days?'

'Oh, I'm well enough now, Ambrose,' she chuckled. And when she laughed he noticed a sparkle had returned, lighting up her eyes. 'I'm not short of help here. My housekeeper will come in every day. But I have to say this, I'll miss Daphne … She and the bairn would be welcome to stay here for good if they wanted to.'

'Have you told her that, Miss Wooten?'

'Oh, yes. But she said she doesn't want to stay around these parts … it's a shame,' Miss Wooten added sadly, then nodding her head gently she closed her eyes.

Ambrose sat quietly until she was soundly asleep and snoring softly before leaving the room. He sought out Daphne, who was busy in the scullery preparing vegetables for the evening meal while Joseph lay sleeping in his bassinet on the table.

'Hello, Ambrose.'

'Hello, Daphne. How's the little fella getting on?' Ambrose asked, smiling down at the sleeping child.

'He's well. Can't you tell? Just look at the size of him!' she said proudly. 'He'll soon be too big for the bassinet.'

'Daphne, the old girl's been telling me she's offered you a permanent position here … Tell me, why aren't you taking it? I thought you said that's what you wanted: security for you and Joseph? I know it's none of my business …' he said, putting his arm about her shoulder, 'but you're mine and Florence's friend … and right or wrong I feel it is *my* business, Daphne … and there's the little fella to think of….'

'All right … I'll tell you,' Daphne interrupted.

She turned to look at him and a twinge of jealousy suddenly hit her. She wondered if Florence appreciated what a fine catch she'd netted herself? Ambrose would never let her down or be unfaithful to her; he'd be her protector for as long as he had breath in his body. He was worth a hundred of the likes of Garrett Ferrensby who were two-a-penny.

'The brother and sister I was staying with … who rescued me and actually saved my life … and Joseph's, well, they wanted to keep him, adopt him and bring him up as their own nephew. Don't get me wrong, Ambrose, I was very grateful to them, but I didn't ask them to help me.' Her eyes suddenly welled with tears. 'They … they said I'd likely end up in the workhouse if I didn't do as they suggested … and I'd drag my child down with me. And what sort of life could I offer him? They tried to wear me down … Ambrose, convince me I wasn't a fit mother.'

'Oh, Daphne….' Ambrose's heart filled.

'Thirsk is a small town, Ambrose, where everyone knows everyone else's business. It's for the best to move away and make a fresh start … somewhere new for me and my son. And I can do that. I believe … it … it's achievable.'

'It is, lass, it's achievable … and me an' Florence will help you. That's a promise. Now, when I leave here, you come with me, all right? Then the three of us will put our 'eads together and work something out.' Ambrose then added jokingly, 'And three 'eads are better than two – even if they're only sheep 'eads!'

Daphne threw her head back and laughed. She hadn't laughed in a long time and, although the feeling felt alien, it felt good too.

'Oh, it's so good to have you here, Ambrose. You're just the tonic I needed. And I will come with you to see Florence, if that's all right. You know … Florence was the one true friend I had … and I would very much like her to meet Joseph.'

Although only five weeks old, Joseph woke up and opened his eyes when his mother spoke his name.

'Your aunt Florence will be that pleased to meet you,' Ambrose said to Joseph, whose eyes were locked on his mother.

'I'll let Miss Wooten know this evening that I'm going with you, then … Do you think this cold weather will last long?'

'No, now we're into February the sun's got some heat in it. We'll be away next week, you mark my words. There's a mild spell coming from the west. It'll take us a full day at least an' we'll have to be away at sunrise or mebbe a bit sooner. I've a couple of lanterns for the wagon.'

'We'll be ready whenever you say,' she said, lifting Joseph from where he lay. His nappy was damp and he needed changing and walking from the scullery she stopped and turned to her friend. 'Thank you, from the bottom of my heart, Ambrose,' she said. 'Thank you for everything.'

Chapter Seventeen

CLIVE HATCH BECKONED Miss Brown into his office.
'I'm expecting Mr Ferrensby this morning, Miss Brown. Show him straight into the office the moment he arrives, please. Thank you ... that will be all.'

Garrett was Clive's first appointment that day and he was not looking forward to seeing him. And besides which, he thought the man a bloody fool! Who the hell in his right mind would chase up a by-blow? Don't know what he's thinking of ... Could he be thinking of leaving the Agra estate to his bastard son? I'll have to do my damnedest to talk him out of it if that's the case ... God, his poor father would turn in his grave if he knew!

Garrett was shown into Clive's office and he sat down.

'Well, Clive, what have you got for me? Good news, I hope.'

'Err ... *you* might call it that,' he said quietly. 'I've made contact with a colleague of mine in Thirsk. I can't tell you his name for obvious reasons ... or the nature of our discussion.' The solicitor coughed. 'That would be highly unethical, but, what I can tell you is that Mrs Bowman gave birth to a son on the tenth January this year. It has been brought to my notice that she convalesced for a short period at the home of Agnes and Edgar Jones, residents of Thirsk – a local butcher and his sister – quite a comfortable family, monetarily speaking. After leaving there, she found temporary work with a Miss Wooten, also a Thirsk resident – a fellmonger by trade,' he said. Then with a look of distaste Clive handed Garrett an envelope containing both addresses.

'Be circumspect, Garrett, that is all I'd suggest ... And if I may be so bold as to add – it is what your father would also have advised.'

'I'll try and do just that, Clive. And thank you for your diligence in the matter.' And you may be as bold as you wish, Garrett thought, seeing as it's not your son. Garrett slipped the envelope into his jacket pocket and, saying goodbye, left.

The warm February sunshine made short work of melting January's snow and Thirsk market square thronged with a bustle of shoppers, horse-drawn traps, and automobiles.

Garrett located the butcher's shop. He stood gazing through the window waiting for the long line of customers to dwindle before entering.

'I'd like to speak to Mr Edgar Jones, please.'

'Aye, is that so? Well, that'll be me you want, then,' Edgar said, eyeing up the well-spoken toff on the other side of the counter. The likes of him didn't come in to buy, they sent their housekeepers instead.

'Arthur!' The butcher's yell procured another equally burly bloodstained man from a back room. 'See to t'shop a minute,' he told the man.

Garrett followed Edgar outside and up a narrow passage to the rear of the shop. The stench of dead animal flesh made Garrett's stomach turn and he wanted to retch, but he checked himself and lit a cigarette to mask the smell.

'Well, what yer after? We don't get the likes of you queuing up in our shop – not for meat anyway.'

'I want some information,' Garrett said.

'And what sort of information might that be, then?'

'I'm trying to locate a Mrs Daphne Bowman … and I understand you gave her refuge for a while.'

'You a relative of hers or summat?'

'Erm … no, not a relative, but I need to see her. I'm given to understand she had a child … a baby boy whilst living with you … and your sister,' Garrett added quickly. Edgar leaned back against the sun-soaked wall, enjoying the warmth of the bricks. He was trying to make out the man before him when Agnes appeared.

'Edgar! What's happening?' she snapped. 'Why aren't you in the shop?'

Edgar reluctantly eased his aching back from the wall.

'Agnes, this is Mr Ferrensby ...'

'Ferrensby, Garrett Ferrensby,' Garrett said, smiling at the stern-looking sister. 'How do you do, Miss Jones. I'm here looking into the whereabouts of Mrs Bowman and her child.'

'Well, she's not here. You go back to the shop, Edgar – I'll deal with this.'

Poor bloody Edgar, Garrett thought ... and poor Daphne, had shw been on the receiving end of this shrew's venomous tongue?

Agnes studied Garrett, and it wasn't long before she thought she saw the resemblance between father and son. It was the shape of his eyebrows that gave the game away.

'You're the father of the child, aren't you? I can see the resemblance as clear as day. You have the very same eyes ... and eyebrows ... arched like the bairn's are ... Well I never!'

Garrett was speechless at the woman's directness and at the same time he was experiencing a new sensation ... a wonderful sensation ... it was akin to pride.

'She said her husband died quite recently; said he was injured in the war. That was a load of baloney, wasn't it? It's you, you're the father. You married to someone else, then?'

'No,' Garrett replied, wondering what the hell he was doing standing here being interrogated by some bitter, dried up-old spinster?

'Thank your brother for me, please, Miss Jones, and good day to you,' he said.

It was the middle of the afternoon when Garrett pulled his car up in the front of a large double-bay-windowed house and turned off the engine.

He climbed out of the car and straightened his coat and, as he made his way slowly to the front door, he grew uneasy. What on earth will I say if she answers the door? Demand to see my son? I've no proof he's mine ... the birth certificate will state *father unknown*. He reached the front door and raised the heavy knocker ... something stopped him and lowering it back down gently, he turned away. He was startled when the door suddenly opened wide and a woman spoke.

'I've been watching you, and you've been standing there long enough to know you've got the right address.'

Garrett turned round to face an elderly woman standing in the doorway, whom he assumed was Miss Wooten.

'Well? What is it you're after? I haven't got all day and the heat's escaping through this door!'

'My name's Ferrensby, Garrett Ferrensby. I'm looking for a Mrs Bowman who I've been given to understand works here. I-I need to speak with her … it's important. You must be Miss Wooten?'

Eleanor Wooten was taken by surprise at the well-spoken gentleman driving an automobile and looking for Daphne. Not that she cared for the new-fangled machines; to her mind they were nothing more than noisy contraptions that leaked oil instead of good manure. She regarded Garrett with a curious interest. Her housekeeper was in the house upstairs turning over the bedrooms so it'd do no harm inviting him in, she thought … and I might well be doing Daphne a favour finding out what he's after.

'So you not only know Mrs Bowman … but you know my name too? I can tell you that Mrs Bowman does work for me, but she's not here right now.' Eleanor Wooten couldn't quite make out whether it was relief or disappointment she noticed flit across his face. 'Maybe you'd care to come inside for a minute … keep the cold out?' She'd sighted from the window that he walked with a limp and carried a walking stick.

'Yes, I would, if it's not an inconvenience. That's very kind of you, thank you, Miss Wooten.'

She led Garrett into the front sitting room where a fire blazed in the hearth.

'Would you care to join me in a sherry, Mr Ferrensby? I usually have one at this time of day … not the *done thing* at two in the afternoon, I know, but it helps relax me for the afternoon.'

'I'd like that very much, thank you. Do you mind if I smoke?' Garrett said.

'Not at all … I like the smell of tobacco – reminds me of when my brothers were alive.'

They sat quietly for a few moments sipping their sherry.

'You are naturally wondering why I've come here asking about Daphne, Miss Wooten. You're a prudent woman, I can see, that and there will be no pulling the wool over your eyes. I feel I can trust you.'

'Thank you, young man. I'll take that as a compliment,' She said, and they both smiled.

'So, I'm going to be honest with you,' he said, shifting in the chair. 'I'm the father of Daphne Bowman's child. He is my son.'

Eleanor's eyebrows shot up in disbelief.

'What has she called him ... please, I need to know?' he said.

'Joseph ...' she said. And quietly staring at him, the similarities between father and son slowly manifested before her eyes. 'Joseph Garrett Bowman ... that ... that's what you said your surname was, didn't you? When you introduced yourself ... Garrett? She almost died ... but you didn't know that, did you?' Eleanor said. 'Are you already married?'

'No ...' Garrett said, averting his eyes from her reproachful gaze. 'When will she back?'

Eleanor determined she'd divulged far too much information already regarding Daphne's situation. And if this man before her was the father of her child, and hadn't done the decent thing by marrying her, then Eleanor Wooten concluded he couldn't be that much of a gentleman – despite his grand attire and fancy car.

'I'm not sure when she'll be back. But if you'd care to leave your address, I'll tell her you called and Miss Bowman can decide for herself whether she chooses to write to you or not.'

Her tone had switched from one of friendliness to frostiness on learning of his bachelor status – conveying her desire that he leave and that the old lady was not about to disclose any further information.

Garrett rose and held his hand out to assist his hostess. She declined, and placing her hands on each side of the chair eased herself to her feet and led the way to the front door.

'Good day, Miss Wooten, and ... thank you.' Garrett held out his hand.

'Good day,' she said coolly, and, not taking his hand, closed the door.

Eleanor went back to the sitting room and stood in the window watching until Garrett's car disappeared from view. Then putting on her spectacles she looked at the calling card he'd handed her before leaving. Eleanor's heart sank when she read it. *Mr Garrett Ferrensby, High Agra, Ryeburn.*

'Ah, well,' she said, placing the card behind the clock on the mantelpiece, 'with Ambrose alongside you, lass … you'll not take any harm.' And because of her belief in Ambrose, Eleanor Wooten elected to relinquish any concerns for Daphne.

Chapter Eighteen

THE WEATHER WAS sympathetic, but the mileage demanding. With only a single horse to pull the wagon the journey was taking longer than expected, necessitating a second overnight stop. Dusk was fast approaching when Ambrose rolled the wagon and pitched camp on the wide open green of the picturesque village at Hutton-le-Hole.

'Stay put for a minute,' Ambrose said, clambering down. It wasn't long before he'd unharnessed the horse and set the chocks to stop the wagon from rolling back or forth on the undulating mounds that formed the village green.

Mother and baby were quickly transferred to the inside of the wagon where Daphne watched, spellbound, as Ambrose performed the customary ritual of lighting a fire in the tiny cast-iron stove before placing the kettle on the top to boil. He then produced two delicate china cups and saucers from a tiny cupboard and set them out neatly on a tray; by the time the kettle was boiling the small wagon was warm and snug.

'There you go, little fella,' Ambrose said, handing Daphne a bottle of warm milk.

'You don't need a wife, Ambrose,' Daphne joked. 'You can take excellent care of yourself.'

'Aye, you're right there, you know,' he said, grinning. 'I *can* take good care of myself. I can cook, clean up after myself … even wash my own clothes, but … you know what? I don't much care for only horses to talk to as company. A man needs a mate, Daphne, and mebbe that need's greater in a man than in a woman.

You women can bare yer souls; share yer fears and thoughts more easily than a man can … D'you know what I mean?'

'I do, Ambrose, and I also know you'll not find a better, kinder, nor more understanding woman to bare your soul to than Florence.'

'Aye, I knows that …'

Joseph cut their tête-à-tête short by letting out a piercing scream. They looked at him in alarm, then laughed. Daphne had been so engrossed listening to Ambrose she hadn't noticed the bottle teat slip from the baby's mouth and him writhing frantically to reclaim it.

'You sort the bairn out for bed and you can both sleep in mine … it's clean,' Ambrose said, pointing towards the back of the wagon. 'I've a stew ready to warm up for us that the housekeeper made on Miss Wooten's orders and insisted I fetched along. Think she thought you were gonna starve to death,' he said, and smiled with genuine amusement.

'I can't take your bed again!' Daphne protested. 'I'll be fine resting here …'

'Aw, for God's sake, lass, will yer do as you're told for once? I've slept under this wagon and on the floor of this wagon more often than I've slept in that bed. Now say when you want to go to bed an' I'll disappear for a few minutes and check all's well outside.'

'You're too kind, Ambrose, too kind … thank you …'

'It's what friends are for. Come on, let's eat, before we fulfil dear Miss Wooten's prophecy and starve to death!' he quipped, giving a hearty chuckle.

Ambrose banked the fire up for the night to keep the wagon warm for Daphne and the baby; both were sound asleep when he climbed back inside the wagon after seeing to the horse.

Daphne woke the next morning to the sun pouring through the tiny windows of the wagon. She'd slept well again and was feeling happy and refreshed. The cosiness, and the security of the wagon had taken her by surprise; she'd prepared herself for a period of considerable discomfort, whereas Joseph had woken only once through the night and she had been able to feed him, without disturbing Ambrose, with milk she'd prepared and tucked inside a sheepskin mitt to keep warm under the eiderdown.

Daphne heard Ambrose whistling outside and after dressing quickly, she fed Joseph and settled him back down again to sleep before she went outside.

Ambrose had lit a campfire and already made a pan of porridge.

'Good morning, Ambrose,' she said.

'Mornin', lass. Is it warm enough for you to eat out 'ere or do you want to be inside?'

'Oh, I'd love to eat outside.' Daphne sat on one of the two stools beside the fire. 'Hmm ... delicious, thank you, Ambrose,' she said, tasting the thick bowl of porridge laced with honey. He'd given her a large enough helping to sustain her for the day. She rested the bowl on her lap and looked at him. 'You know, when I woke this morning I could understand why you choose this way of life, Ambrose.' She took another mouthful of porridge and waited for him to say something, which he didn't. He sat silently and pensive and Daphne continued. 'I've loved these last two days ... being on the road with you ... It's been a privilege to be invited into your way of life. I've never slept so well or awakened as refreshed ... then to top all that – I've a different view each morning. It has been truly wonderful ... so peaceful, and to think, before we set out,' she said, laughing, 'I was actually dreading it.'

Ambrose put his empty bowl down and lit a cigarette. 'Ah, it's grand you've enjoyed it cos I was fretting a bit about takin' a gorgio alongside me. It pleases me to know you're not against the traveller way of life.' Then, taking a long pull on his cigarette, he said, 'And as for choosing it as a way of life, Daphne, I didn't choose it – it chose me. It's in my blood ... just as the settled way of life is in yours.'

Daphne insisted on clearing and washing their breakfast things while Ambrose damped out the fire before replacing the sod of earth back on top of the charred earth. When they climbed aboard the wagon and drove into the road Daphne glanced back over her shoulder. She wanted the memory of these last few days to be impressed on her mind for all time.

They passed through the village of Rosedale Abbey. Despite its name, Daphne informed Ambrose, there'd never been an abbey here – just a small Cistercian nunnery about eight hundred years ago – of which only a single stone pillar still remained. Then when he asked Daphne how come she knew about these things she was mindful of yet another aspect of their cultural divide. The gypsy children weren't educated as such; they attended the school of survival. In a primitive sense they learned how to endure the harshest of winters – honing the innate skill to poach fish, hunt down, snare; skin and gut their capture.

'Have you thought about where you'll move to?' Ambrose said

'W-what? Sorry, I was daydreaming … Not sure, to be honest.'

'Well, you and the bairn are welcome to stay with us until you get on your feet.'

'I know that, Ambrose … and I'll keep it in mind,' she said, and then changed the subject. 'Oh, I am looking forward to seeing Florence again … it's been such a long time.'

'Aye, me too, me too …' Ambrose replied; the ache to hold her in his arms and to tell her how much he loved her was almost too much to bear. 'Won't be long now, my love …' he murmured softly, 'another hour and I'll be there …'

Daphne turned and looked at Ambrose in astonishment – it wasn't her he was speaking to … he was talking to Florence … telling her he was on his way … and he'd be there at her side soon.

A surge of envy swept over her and she tried to imagine what it would feel like to be loved like that … My own husband never even told me he loved me – but there again … I didn't tell him I loved him either – because I didn't.

Daylight was fading fast and the wagon lurched as Ambrose guided it skilfully along the track through deep ruts. The day had been an arduous one for them and for the horse pulling the wagon up the narrow road from Rosedale Abbey that wound its way up onto the moor. It was steep and prompted them to disembark and walk beside the wagon for the duration of the climb.

'Please … do you think we can stop for a few minutes?' Daphne pleaded.

'No. Better not, lass,' Ambrose said, shaking his head. 'It's only a couple of miles now an' the going's easier. C'mon, get up there, lad!' he shouted, ignoring her plea. He cracked the whip noisily above the horse's head and the wagon lurched forward as the horse gathered speed.

The sun had gone down and the light was fast fading by the time Florence had finished bedding down the horses. She threw another lump of peat on the fire and put the kettle on to boil. The hare stew she made earlier was simmering gently and she peeled a few potatoes and dropped them into the same pot. Then she crossed the room and lit the lamp on the dresser on the far wall. The dimly lit room was now bathed with light and her attention moved to her reflection in the mirror-backed dresser. Florence barely recognized the stranger looking back at her. The pale face appeared more ashen framed by her jet-black hair. She moved closer to the reflection and looked into her own eyes; frantically seeking identification ... but saw only emptiness. Suddenly the pot on the range boiled over and hissed loudly, interrupting her preoccupation with herself.

'Blast!'

Moth began to bark. 'Stop it, I'm not shouting at you, Moth ... come here, boy.' She reached out to stroke him, but Moth paid no attention and darted to the door and barked even louder. Florence couldn't hear herself think with the deafening noise. Sooner than unlock the door she walked to the window. She saw two lanterns swaying in the dark, but it was only at the sound of cartwheels that she made out the shadowy outline of the horse-drawn wagon.

'Ambrose, Ambrose ... you're here!'

Chapter Nineteen

'ENID, WHEN YOU'VE done scouring those pans you can start on the potatoes. D'you think you can manage that without 'aving me standing over yer?'

'I'll manage,' Enid replied quietly while longing to yell, *I've been peeling spuds since I was four years old, I don't need anybody to stand over me now I'm fifteen!* But instead, she bit her tongue and raised her eyebrows concealed under her white frilly cap.

'Mr Ferrensby wants to see me in his study and I don't know how long I'll be,' Ivy Baxter said, untying her stained pinafore. 'And if I'm not back in twenty minutes get started on them carrots.'

Ivy knocked on the study door and waited.

'Come in, Ivy.' Garrett rose to his feet as Ivy entered the room. 'Close the door properly ... that's it. Now, come and sit by the fire next to me. There's something I want to discuss with you ... it ... it's of a rather personal nature, Ivy ... and, to be honest I don't know who else to ask. You've been with this family forever it seems, and I can trust you.'

Ivy shifted warily in the unfamiliar chair. She'd known it was only a matter of time before Janet's sexual favours concerning his brother would be brought to his attention. Flighty little madam! God only knows what her mam and dad will make of it if they find out what she's been up to ... Such decent people too, respectable church-going folk ...

'Are you sure you're all right, Ivy ... you look extremely worried? Are you?' asked Garrett.

'Yes. Shouldn't I be? It's Janet you're wanting to discuss, isn't it?'

'Err … Janet? No, not Janet, why? Do you want to discuss her? Is she not up to scratch…?'

'She … no, sh–she's fine …' Ivy stammered, 'I–I thought it must be something to do with …'

'No, you can rest easy there, Ivy,' he said, smiling, 'it's nothing to do with the staff. High Agra runs like clockwork, all thanks to you,' he assured her. Then rising from his chair he walked over to the dresser and returned with two glasses of sherry and handed her one.

'Here, drink this … you might need it.'

'Bit early in the day for me … but you're the boss. Thank you,' Ivy said, taking a large sip of the delicious golden liquid. She admired the crystal glass she held in her hand and the fine crystal decanters that she'd filled many times over the years – yet this was the first time she'd sampled it. She bought a bottle of the cheap stuff once a year for herself at Christmas which she imbibed on special occasions.

'What I'm about to tell you is highly confidential. But of course you know that … and as I said before, I trust you, Ivy.'

'Aye, well if you don't know where my loyalty lies by now … you never will.'

'Never doubted your loyalty, not once,' Garrett said, refilling his glass with the whisky on a small side table next to his chair.

'I've a son, Ivy.'

Ivy's glass remained suspended on her lips; she had been about to take another sip, but she drained the glass instead.

'You were right, I needed that.' Ivy looked at him and he was staring into the fire. He felt her gaze upon him and slowly turned to face her and his eyes were filled with tears.

'I want my son more than anything I've ever wanted in my life. I want him here … with me at High Agra where he belongs!' he said vehemently.

'And where's this son of yours now?' Ivy asked calmly, disregarding his displeasure at the situation.

'I don't know … not for sure. I know he's still in the area, though, and with ... with the mother.'

'And would the mother be Daphne Bowman?'

'Yes, it would.'

'Right then, now how do you think I can help you, lad?'

Garrett suddenly relaxed and sinking back in his chair looked at her. This was the Ivy whose advice he sought; the Ivy who called him lad; the Ivy who would steer him through this storm to calmer waters ... he needed her on his side.

'You could start by telling me what *you* believe is the right thing to do ...'

'The *right* thing to do?' Ivy said in astonishment. 'Marry the woman, of course! That's the right thing to do!'

'That day she came here ... she was upset, and very distressed, Ivy. Do you remember?'

'Yes, I do.'

'She came to see me that day to tell me she was carrying my child – and I told her I didn't believe it was mine ... so I sent her away. B–but the truth is, I knew all along it was mine. Daphne wasn't ... isn't the type to lie ... she's a good person.' He laughed softly, then continued. 'The trouble was – and probably still is, I don't love Daphne ... I ... like her ...'

'Do you like her enough to marry to lay claim to your son?'

'If she won't hand him over to me without – then ... yes, I'm prepared to marry her.'

'Aye, well ... that's if she'll 'ave you, mind.'

'That's why I need your opinion, Ivy,' Garrett said, smiling at her, 'because you don't mince your words.'

'And what about the lass at Hamer Bridge?' Ivy asked. He might think it impertinent of her to ask, but Ivy didn't care – this was a time for straight talking

'What about her?' Garrett lowered his gaze. He wasn't willing to discuss Florence with Ivy or anybody else.

'Do you love Florence?'

Ivy's candidness had completely taken him aback; he hadn't expected his feelings for Florence to form part of the discussion.

'This has nothing to do with Florence! This is about my son and ... and how to acquire custody!'

'Daphne and Florence are friends. Don't you think they both deserve to know where they stand?'

'Haven't seen Florence for weeks now and I'm not about to. There's nothing between us any more. W-what I felt for Florence is … is gone.'

It was a curious thing. Ivy would have sworn he was still besotted with the gypsy lass, but the hostility she saw in his eyes at the mention of her name told her otherwise.

'Ivy, I would like you to walk over to Hamer sometime soon and try to find out whether Miss Grainger has any knowledge of Daphne's whereabouts. Would you do that for me, please? She's more likely to tell you than me.'

'Yes, I'll do that. But give me a few days to mull it over. Now, I'd better get back and make sure Enid hasn't ruined them vegetables!'

Garrett rose and escorted his housekeeper to the door. He rested his hand gently on her shoulder. 'Thank you, Ivy, thank you.'

He closed the door behind her and replenished his glass. Tears stung the back of his eyes … and his heart ached.

'*Florence, oh, Florence …*' he said, whispering her name softly. If I could turn back time … and retract the cruel things I said to you … but it's too late … what's done is done.

The large cob was sweating after his long haul and steam was rising from the chestnut coat. Ambrose pulled on the broad leather reins and brought the wagon to a halt before leaping down. He ran towards the cottage where the door was suddenly flung open and Florence rushed out to greet him, running into his open arms. He lifted her off the ground and did two full turns before lowering her back down. Smiling, she lifted her face to him and his lips met hers. It was their very first kiss … and it was long and deep and a long time before Ambrose could ease his lips from hers. He gazed at her in wonder, and Florence's heart almost burst with joy; for when she looked into his eyes she realized she'd loved Ambrose from the start and wanted nothing more than to spend the rest of her life with him. …

'Florence ... my darling Florence ...' Ambrose whispered, threading his fingers through her black glossy hair.

'Shh,' she murmured, brushing her lips against his. 'Hmm ... you smell wonderful ... of horses and ... saddle soap ...'

Ambrose's kiss stretched into a smile on her lips. 'Is that so? Well, you smell wonderful too ... of rabbit stew.'

They drew apart, clasping hands and laughing. She was suddenly conscious of his leather-gloved hand and brought it to her lips and kissed it. The waiting horse shifted, causing the harness to rattle, before whinnying loudly. Ambrose let go of Florence's hands and rested his on her shoulders. He stopped smiling and his face became serious.

'Florence, I've brought somebody along with me ... a friend who wants to see you. I hope you'll not be disappointed ...'

Ambrose didn't finish the sentence: Florence wasn't listening. She was walking towards the woman standing at the side of the wagon. The two women reached out and fell into each other's arms weeping and sobbing.

'Am I dreaming? Is it really you, Daphne?' Florence said.

'It's me, Florence, it's me,' Daphne sobbed. 'And I'm not alone ...'

'Not alone?' Florence said, furrowing her brow.

'No. Come with me.'

Daphne took Florence by the hand and guided her inside the wagon where Joseph lay sleeping oblivious to the world outside.

Florence leaned over and gently pushed his shawl aside, and as she did so, she was in no doubt as to who his father was.

'This is Joseph.' Daphne said.

'He ... he's beautiful ... beautiful ... and Joseph's a fine name you've chosen for him.' Florence then turned to Daphne. 'And you, Daphne, tell me, how have you been? And where did you go? And why didn't you come and see me ... tell me, let me know you were leaving? I've been so worried about you all this time.'

'Later, later,' Daphne interrupted, 'let's talk later. But right now I'm tired. It's been a long journey and Joseph needs feeding. Are you sure you don't mind our staying a while ... putting on you like this?' Daphne asked, and her eyes brimmed with tears when she said, 'It's just that I had to see you before I leave … I wanted *you* to meet my son.'

In the semi-darkness and with only a feeble glow from the lamplight, Florence could see that her friend was not in the best of health. She thought her far too pale and much too thin; the dark circles around her eyes lent her a sickly, ghostlike appearance. 'C'mon on, let's get you inside and warmed up in front of that fire,' she said taking Daphne's arm. 'I've a stew cooking on the range.'

After unloading Daphne's belongings into the cottage, Ambrose led his horse and wagon into the barn. The horses stirred in their stall at his approach and Ambrose walked over and patted their necks.

'Hello, Ginger, remember me, do yer, lad? And my … you've grown into a fine animal, young fella … Now what was that fancy name she gave yer, eh? Dancer, yes, that's what she called yer … Not thrown her off your back then yet – have yer?'

'No, he hasn't!'

Ambrose spun round to see Florence had entered the barn and was standing close behind him with Moth at her heels.

'Aww … come here, will yer, woman … God, you don't know how much I've missed you.'

Moth growled deeply as Ambrose pulled her towards him making them chuckle.

'Yer can stop that bloody game for a start!' Ambrose said, feigning annoyance at the dog. 'Better get used to me cos I ain't going anywhere … and there's gonna be a fair amount o' kissing goin' on!'

Moth obediently dropped to the floor and lying down placed his head between his front paws.

'That's more like it. Good boy.' Ambrose reached down and rubbed the dog's head. 'Now you can watch.'

'Moth will grow to love you … almost as much as I do …' Florence said. Her face was close to his … and they breathed each other's breath.

'And I love you more than life itself …' He lowered his head and his mouth covered hers. Her lips were warm and soft and, when she placed her arms around his neck, he pulled her closer against his body.

One of the horses snorted loudly and Ambrose reluctantly released his hold on Florence. 'We'd better go back,' he said, 'Daphne will wonder what's keeping us.' His need for her in his loins was painful.

God only knows how I'm going to keep my hands off her, seeing her every day!

'Daphne's feeding and bathing the bairn ...' she said.

Ambrose looked into her eyes and saw a hunger for bodily satisfaction that equalled his own; the pupils in her eyes were so dilated with desire they practically eclipsed the blue iris.

'Let's get married as soon as we can ... I can't wait, Florence ... I can't ...' Ambrose's hand cupped her breast and she caught her breath. 'To be with you every day and not able to make love to you is too much to ask of any man ...'

He reached inside his jacket pocket and produced a small leather box.

'I've brought you something ... I hope it fits.' Ambrose grasped the box in his gloved hand and opened it. He removed the ring and slipped it onto Florence's third finger.

'Oh ... Ambrose, Ambrose it's ... it's beautiful!' She gasped, raising her hand to examine the exquisite brilliant cut sapphire.

'Couldn't be anything but a sapphire to match your eyes ... An' if it doesn't fit, we can call at Manfield's jewellers in Thirsk and get it altered.'

'It fits perfectly ... it's the most beautiful ring I've ever seen in my entire life ... Thank you ... thank you ...'

'Nah, thanks for saying you'll marry me. I'm the happiest man walking right now. So what d'you say we get married as soon as we can?'

Florence flung her arms round Ambrose's neck – almost unbalancing him with excitement. 'I say yes ... yes, yes ... and the sooner the better!'

Chapter Twenty

THE MONTH OF March arrived caressing the moors with unusual springlike warmth. Daphne wiped her hands on her rough apron. There were only the outside windows and paintwork to clean and the cottage would be spick and span for Florence and Ambrose returning from their honeymoon in Scarborough.

After considerable pleading Florence managed to persuade her to stay on in the cottage at least until they returned. Daphne agreed when learning a young lad called Rob from Rosedale Abbey would be staying – and sleeping in the barn. He was a brawny, broad-shouldered lad. He would see to the horses, milk the goat, and help Daphne. Daphne invited Rob to share his meals in the cottage with her but he declined, saying he was used to taking his meals alone. Nevertheless, Daphne found it a comfort knowing Rob was within calling distance should she happen to need him.

She had just put Joseph down to sleep at mid-morning when there was a knock at the door. Moth barked and Daphne's hand shot up to her throat. Where was Rob? Ambrose had given him strict instructions not to allow any visitor to the cottage without Daphne's permission. The door opened slightly and Moth let out a low growl.

'Anybody home?' a woman's voice called.

Daphne took a deep sigh of relief.

'Quiet, Moth! Stop it!'

Daphne opened the door. The woman standing before her

looked familiar, but she couldn't quite place her.

'Yes?' Daphne asked politely.

Ivy Baxter's eyes flew open in disbelief when Daphne Bowman opened the door. She was the last person she expected to see. 'Err … is … is … Florence at home?' she stammered.

'No, she's away for a few days. She's on her honeymoon, as a matter of fact. Is it important, or anything I can help you with? Wait a moment …' Daphne said, cocking her head to one side. 'Don't I know you from somewhere? Your face … you look awfully familiar.'

My God! Florence married! Garrett can't know nowt about it … He'd have said summat … Well, I never, the gypsy lass … gone and got hersel' wed. He'll be past himself when he finds out!

Ivy quickly gathered her wits and brought her attention back to the present.

'Aye, you mebbe do remember me. We've only met once before … and very briefly. I'm Ivy Baxter, the housekeeper … up at … at … High Agra,' she said hesitantly, holding out her hand.

'How do you do,' Daphne said, shaking her proffered hand. 'I'm Daphne Bowman, a friend of Florence's'

'Sometimes I drop in on Florence,' Ivy explained. 'Only now and again like … for a chat an' a cup o' tea.'

The painful memory of that day she went to High Agra and told Garrett she was pregnant came flooding back. Daphne recalled seeing the old lady quite clearly now. It was she who'd given her a pitying look as she tore from the house sobbing.

Taking into consideration the housekeeper had made the effort to pay a visit, Daphne concluded it would only be polite to invite her in for tea. Florence would wish her to be civil to her friend.

'Please, do come inside and I'll put the kettle on. Any friend of Florence is a friend of mine … I hope.'

Once inside and sitting comfortably by the warm, freshly blackened range, Ivy couldn't help but admire the charming interior living room. It was immaculate, from the shiny copper pans dangling from big brass hooks above the range to the highly polished furniture and the pretty flowered curtains adorning the two small windows.

174

When Daphne went into the scullery, Ivy's eyes scoured the room in search of evidence of an infant, but there was nothing to suggest a baby lived there. Daphne returned shortly with a tea tray and placed it on the small table between them; it was as Daphne readjusted the cushion behind her that Ivy noticed a baby's matching hat and mitts tucked behind it.

'Oh, you've a child, then?' Ivy said.

'Yes ... I have a son.'

'Is ... is he here with you?'

'Yes. He's asleep in the bedroom. Well, he was,' Daphne said, rising from her chair when a cry from the child confirmed his presence. 'Moth's barking must have woken him. I'll go and fetch him.'

'There, there ...' Daphne's soothing voice calmed the baby she cradled in her arms. She crooked her little finger and placed it to his mouth and Joseph started to suck in earnest.

'He's hungry again ... would you mind holding him while I heat him some milk?'

'No, no, not at all ... I'd love to. Oh ...' Ivy gasped, and her heart caught when she looked at the child. There could be no doubt this was Garrett's son; they were Garrett's distinctive grey eyes that beheld hers beneath those characteristic, well-defined eyebrows.

'He's beautiful. What's his name?'

'Joseph,' Daphne said proudly as she decanted the fresh goat's milk from a jug into the saucepan before placing it on the range.

'Joseph ... now that's a fine name your mother's chosen for you ...' Ivy's tender words and rocking was rewarded with coos and gurgles of pleasure from Joseph – instantly bewitching her before she grudgingly handed him back to his mother.

Daphne settled back into her chair and Joseph sucked heartily and noisily at his bottle while both women looked on and smiled. The bottle was soon emptied and Joseph asleep on his mother's lap.

'I'd better be off,' Ivy said. She'd become stiff with sitting and pulled herself to her feet slowly. 'It's been grand seeing you again ... and thank you for your hospitality and the tea.'

Daphne rose from her chair and walked to the door with the

baby resting against her shoulder.

'I'll tell Florence you called when she gets home.'

'Aye, do that. Goodbye, young Joseph,' Ivy said placing her hand on the baby's back. 'And I pray God keeps you both safe from harm ... always.'

'W-what beautiful words of comfort, Mrs Baxter ... feels like you're blessing my child,' Daphne said, her eyes welling. 'Thank you.'

'I am. And it's Ivy. You can call me Ivy.'

The sound of the front door slamming signalled Garrett's return to Edith, the maid; she arrived just in time to relieve Garrett of the riding coat he'd divested.

'Tell Mrs Baxter I wish to see her in my study – straight away, Edith!'

'Yes, sir,' Edith said, scurrying off to find the housekeeper. The metal tip of Garrett's stick sounded on the tiled floor as he limped down the hall to the study, and the maid wondered what could have happened to put him in such a foul mood?

Garrett looked at his pocket watch and replenished his glass. He'd been waiting half an hour already and there was still no sign of the housekeeper – God damn it! Where in the blazes has that bloody woman got to – it's almost midday!

Ivy Baxter knocked on the study door and waited.

'Come!' Garrett said sharply.

Ah, so Edith was right in saying he's annoyed ...

'Sit down, Ivy.' It was an order.

'Yer wondering why I aven't reported to you soon as I got back from yonder cottage?' Ivy said, nodding in the direction of Hamer Bridge. 'Well, I needed to chew it over a bit, quiet, like, in my own mind.'

'Oh, don't be so damned exasperating, Ivy!' Garrett stood up and filling a glass with sherry handed it to her. 'Here, drink this. I want to know everything that was said.'

Ivy glanced at the clock on the mantel, wishing she were in the kitchen preparing lunch rather than having to tell him Florence Grainger was wed.

'Oh, forget the time, we can eat later!' Garrett snapped impatiently. 'Well ... c'mon, what did you find out?'

'Miss Grainger wasn't there ... b-but Daphne Bowman was. She's staying a few days while Florence is away ... on her honeymoon ... sh–she's gotten herself married ...' A wave of pity flooded Ivy as she watched Garrett slump back in his chair. And when he spoke his voice was a mere whisper.

'Florence ... married, you say...? Are you absolutely certain? W-whom has she married? Do you know, Ivy?'

'No, an' I didn't think it was my place to ask. Daphne didn't say. It's more than likely to be that gypsy fella who comes visiting her sometimes ... Ambrose summat or other, I think his name is. They're better stickin' to their own kind if yer want my opinion ...'

Ambrose Wilson's face swam before his eyes as he recalled the handsome-looking gypsy. The man had been pleasantly polite whereas he recalled he had been downright rude.

'You're probably right ... Ivy,' Garrett said, his senses already somewhat anaesthetized by alcohol, bestowing his voice with a gentle, philosophical quality. 'She's better off with her own kind ...'

Daphne's situation had been forgotten for the moment with the news of Florence marrying; and Ivy decided now was the time to deliver the news.

'Daphne is at Hamer Bridge *with* the baby. He's called Joseph,' Ivy said.

'*Joseph ... Joseph*,' Garrett repeated ... inscribing it in his heart and mind. 'Did you see him?' he asked excitedly, leaning forward in his chair and grasping Ivy's hands in his own.

Ivy nodded.

'And...?' he said.

'A-and ... he's the mirror image of yourself ...'

'Honestly?' Garrett's face shone with pure happiness on hearing this and his mouth stretched into a wide smile across his face, and his eyes glistened with tears of sheer joy.

'Yes, honestly,' Ivy said. Then grinning madly, she boasted, 'And I held him while she prepared his bottle ... he is so beautiful

... perfect.' Ivy's eyes misted over recalling his scent, the softness of his skin, and the feel of his downy hair when her lips kissed the top of his head.

'And she's a good mother ... Daphne?'

'Yes, she's a fine mother,' Ivy assured him. 'Make no mistake, your son's in good hands,' she said.

And returning to her duties, Ivy vacated the study, leaving Garrett to ponder his next move.

Garrett replaced the almost empty whisky decanter back on the side table. It was important he remain sober and keep a clear head – there was much to consider and his first port of call would be his solicitor. His son's existence changed everything.

The heir to High Agra must come home and take his rightful place.

Chapter Twenty-One

GARRETT WAS UP early poring over documents at his desk in the study when Janet walked in without knocking. She still hadn't seen him sitting there when she knelt at the hearth and started scraping out the ashes. Garrett sat silently – watching her. The girl stopped her raking and lay the brush and pan down on the hearth. She yawned widely and stretched her arms high above her before resting her chin on her chest and slowly circling her head … After completing her ritual, and while still in a kneeling position, she removed an envelope from her apron pocket and opened it. From where Garrett was sitting it appeared to be a two-page letter. He was about to reveal his presence, when Janet suddenly giggled.

'Aww … Robin …' she sighed.

'Robin!' Garrett yelled, causing Janet, who was still on her knees, to spin round and topple over in the process.

She leapt to her feet. 'Sorry, sir … I'm so sorry … I didn't know you were in here, sir.'

Garrett had stepped round to the front of his desk and crooked his finger beckoning her forward. The maid's face was flushed deep red with embarrassment with eyes ready to pop from their sockets. She was breathing hard and fast and her bosom rose and fell … Garrett couldn't drag his eyes away. She was ripe … and it had been so long … weeks … he needed a woman.

'Don't be afraid of me … I didn't mean to scare you, Janet.'

Garrett moved closer, and reaching out to her, he gently stroked her lower arm. 'Do you miss Robin … hmm?'

The maid nodded.

'Well, Janet, Robin won't be coming back to Agra for a long while. And we all get lonely sometimes ... but I think maybe you and I know how we can remedy that ... don't we? For a start we can lock the door ... it's still early ... and nobody will ever know.' Garrett walked to the door and turned the key; and when he turned around, Janet had removed her apron and unbuttoned the front of her dress. She then sprawled out on the rug, waiting; an inviting smile playing on her mouth.

'Tut-tut ... you are a naughty girl ...'

Janet laughed and pulled Garrett down on top of her ... and whispering into his ear, said, 'I've been pining for you to want me ... like your brother does...'

'God, you're a wanton woman ...' Garrett said, moving inside her, his need heightened by what she'd just said. And as the sensation swelled it was impossible for her to think or speak any longer ... she moaned with pleasure as they climaxed together and Garrett's spill of completion ran hot and sticky against her thighs.

After changing into riding attire and eating a hearty breakfast, Garrett sent orders for his horse to be saddled. Yesterday all Garrett could see ahead of him was an open space of loneliness; now twenty-four hours later, his sexual exploits not only relieved him of physical tensions, but the news that his son was at Hamer Bridge galvanized his objective.

Daphne hummed as she cradled Joseph in her arms. And after only a few minutes she gazed down at him and saw he'd fallen asleep. She carried him to the crib in the bedroom, murmuring softly, 'Your Aunt Florence and Uncle Ambrose will be home tomorrow, sweetheart ... and then we must think about the future.'

The tea was still hot and she poured herself another cup. Daphne had given a great deal of thought to what she might or might not do over the last three days. She had a little money put by, but that would only pay for her and Joseph's board and lodge for a month at the most. She had also written to Miss Wooten saying she would call to see her sometime during the next fort-night – for it appeared winter had at long last released its hold on the moors.

Daphne looked about her, thinking how much she'd miss the dear little cottage. Florence had created a lovely home here for herself which she was now going to share with Ambrose. And deep down she wished she and Joseph could stay for the coming summer ... Hamer Bridge would be the ideal place to raise a child, Daphne thought, and would have been tempted to stay had Florence not married and been living on her own still. But that wasn't to be – marriage changed everything, and it was only right the newly-weds have their home to themselves.

Daphne rose from her chair and went outside. She leaned her back against the wall and closing her eyes basked in the late February sunshine. The sound of a lark singing resonated in the air and a smile spread across her face. She breathed deeply; the smell of earth ... and a sense of new beginnings pervaded her.

The distant whinny of a horse disrupted Daphne's pleasant interlude from reality. She shielded her eyes from the sun and looked to where someone on horseback was riding along the lane that led to High Agra.

Daphne hastily disappeared indoors. She'd not given Garrett Ferrensby a thought since arriving at Hamer. Why on earth would she? *She* had been both father and mother to Joseph from the moment Garrett chose to disown him. A lump caught in her throat, and quite unexpectedly, out of nowhere, fierce emotions threatened to overwhelm her before tears gushed from her eyes relieving the pressure within.

And when the sound of wailing reached her ears she realized it was her own.

Daphne didn't know how long she'd been sitting there gazing into space, but the fire was low and Joseph had wakened, he was cooing in his crib. And, although she was spent and exhausted from crying, Daphne perceived a deep inner calm had replaced the turbulence within her.

The peat bucket was empty and Daphne collected Joseph from his crib and went into the barn to find Rob to ask him to fill it.

181

She'd had no reason to go into the barn since Rob was doing all the fetching, carrying, milking the goat and bringing the milk into the house for her. She glanced around delighted to see he'd tidied up. Not that it was a mess before – for Florence worked hard. Not only at keeping the cottage scrupulously clean, but also the outbuildings. There were some heavy jobs, though, that Florence couldn't manage to do, like shifting the heavy metal implements that lay rusting in a corner. And as she looked to where the rusting heap lay, Rob was working and leaning over some contraption with a hammer in his hand.

'Hello, Rob!' Daphne hollered over the din as he started hammering the metal.

Rob stopped what he was doing when he heard her call and stood up. He was covered in dust and grime and grinned widely when he saw Daphne had Joseph in her arms.

'Hello, little man.' Rob's dirty finger stroked the baby's cheek. Daphne was about to protest when Joseph smiled up at him.

'Aw ... d'you think the little fella knows me?'

'I'm sure he does, Rob,' Daphne said, smiling back at Rob. The simple lad had a kind heart and she was grateful to have him around.

'Will you bring me some peat in when you've finished whatever it is you're doing, please, Rob?'

'Aye, I'll come now. I can finish this later ... it's for you and the bairn,' he said shyly. 'I thought you'd enjoy a walk out wi' t'bairn if yer had summat to push 'im in now t' weather's faired up like. Yer can't carry 'im o'er far. But with this, yer can push 'im o'er t' rough bits o' moor.'

Daphne turned her attention to where Rob had been hammering and saw it was a perambulator. The body looked clean enough, and there were only a few tears on the leather inside. With a good wipe down and a blanket it would do well. It's not as though I'm going to be venturing into Ryeburn or Kirkbymoorside pushing it.

'Thank you, Rob. That was very thoughtful of you to think of me ... and Joseph.' She ran her fingers along the side where an exquisite engraving was partially visible, but had worn away.

Daphne imagined it to have cost a lot of money when new. 'I'll take him out as soon as it's ready. It's not too cold and the fresh moorland air will be good for him.'

'I'll bring it over as soon as I've 'ad me dinner.'

Daphne closed the fire down on the range. It was still only two o'clock and Rob had delivered the perambulator as promised. On a second viewing of the contraption parked in the middle of the floor of the tidy living room it looked ready for the scrapheap. Beggars can't be choosers, Daphne reminded herself. And besides she didn't want to disappoint Rob after his efforts. She lined it with a brightly coloured crocheted blanket which was long enough to hang over the sides and hide most of the wear and tear. Then she took a pillow from her bed which she laid Joseph on before covering him with a warm white shawl.

Daphne set out in high spirits, but pushing Joseph along the moorland track was proving not to be quite as straightforward as she had hoped. Whenever she inadvertently steered one of the wheels into a rut it had to be freed by hand. After half an hour her hands were covered in dirt and Daphne thanked God there was nobody about to see her in such a state besides Moth.

Rob insisted Moth accompany them and warned Daphne not to venture from the track as the wheels might become stuck. Daphne, although having lived close to the moors for many years, had never ventured onto them and as she inadvertently climbed higher she carelessly strayed from the beaten track.

Rob was growing more worried and upset by each passing minute. Daphne hadn't returned home from her walk and his stomach ached, notifying him it must be teatime. He went into the cottage and built up the fire for her return and when he went back outside a man was standing at the door with a large dog. The man looked at him in surprise.

'Who the devil are you? And what are you doing here?' he demanded.

'Ah works 'ere. What d'you want? She's not come back wi' bairn.'

'W-who has not come w-with the bairn?' Garrett asked,

speaking slowly, but also extremely irritated at having to converse with an imbecile. Bloody typical of Florence he thought, employing a village idiot!

'Mrs Bowman. I made 'er a prambu... thing for 'er to push t'bairn on t'moor an' she's been gone a long time ...' Then, shaking his head fretfully, he said, 'an' ah 'aven't 'ad me tea yet.'

'Saddle one of the horses for me. Now, lad! And be quick about it! I'll go find her ... and the boy.'

Rob started to run to do the man's bidding but then stopped dead in his track. He turned, and looking at Garrett, asked him. "Ow d'you know it's a boy? Ah didn't tell yer.'

'Oh, for God's sake does it matter?' Garrett snapped back impatiently. 'Just get a bloody move on, lad, if you don't want Mrs Bowman and ... and the *bairn* spending a night on the moors!'

And with that terrible thought in mind Rob hurried off and returned a few minutes later with Dancer saddled up.

'Which way did they go, do you know?' Garrett said.

'I told 'er to stick to t'road. She's taken t'dog wi' her. E'll know 'is way 'ome.'

'Right ... Come on, then, Dancer, let's see what you're made of and how well she's trained you. 'You, too, Bruno!' Garrett shouted kicking his heels into the horse's side – and the lively gelding took off at a fast canter with the Great Dane lolloping behind.

Garrett took out his pocket watch. He'd been searching for half an hour now without luck. A cold, damp mist had drifted in from the sea and descended on the moor. Dancer pawed the ground. The spirited horse had been deprived of exercise much of the winter and was enjoying himself.

Infernal woman! I'll give it another half-hour then I'll go back and get up a search party. Garrett had walked and ridden the moors all his life and knew them better than anybody. He recalled Daphne once telling him she hadn't walked on the moors before and that it was her wish to do so. Well, you've got your bloody wish, Daphne ... but it's a damn pity you took my son along with you.

The mist thickened as the darkness fell, and with a heavy

heart, Garrett turned his horse for home. When he reached the familiar rocky outcrop he reined Dancer to a halt. Bruno was having a job to keep up with the sprightly horse and in need of a short rest to catch his breath.

He didn't hear anything at first – it was only when Bruno started whining that Garrett knew he'd heard something. He strained to listen, but there was nothing.

'You heard something, Bruno, didn't you?' he said. 'Hush … quiet, boy … listen.' Garrett's voice was gentle but firm and the dog obeyed. Bruno stood stock-still, listening intently along with his master.

Within a few seconds the sound of a muffled bark penetrated the mist.

'Is it Moth, Bruno?' Garrett said. Bruno was unable to contain his excitement a moment longer and burst into incessant barking, drowning out that of the other dog …

'Go see … go see … slowly … slowly … now …' Garrett instructed the dog. Bruno set out with his nose to the ground and his ears pricked while Garrett followed close behind on Dancer. The horse picked his way sure-footedly over the precarious terrain. Garrett was beginning to think his dog had him on a wild goose chase when he suddenly raised his head high and frantically sniffed the air before barking wildly.

'Daphne! Daphne Bowman! Can you hear me?' Garrett yelled loudly.

For a few seconds there was complete silence but then a female voice called out feebly. 'Help! Help! W-we're here … please hurry …'

Garrett urged Dancer towards the sound, which came from somewhere not far away.

'Daphne! Keep talking so we can find you! Moth! Moth!' Garrett shouted the dog's name which triggered a response. It wasn't long before Bruno discovered the forlorn band huddled together in the damp heather exposed to the elements.

'Daphne, oh my dear God … you poor soul,' Garrett said, climbing down from his horse. He ignored the excruciating pain shooting through his leg and leaned down to where Daphne lay with Joseph asleep in her arms. 'Come, we must get you and the baby back home ...' He helped her to her feet. 'Here, put this on,' he said removing his coat. 'You're wet and cold.' Garrett then quickly made a sling with the crocheted blanket and tied it round himself before placing the child inside it next to his own warm body. 'I'm going to climb onto the horse, Daphne, and then I want you to use whatever strength you have to hoist yourself up behind me. Do you understand?'

Daphne nodded, too cold and exhausted to speak, and did as Garrett requested. Only a few moments ago, she'd been convinced nobody would ever find them on the moor, or come looking for them in the dark – and calmly accepted that death would be their fate. What was happening right now in her confused mind appeared as nothing more than a dream.

'Take us home, Bruno, good boy,' Garrett said, and the cold and bedraggled group made their way over the moor.

Garrett could feel the strong beat of his own heart against his son's body. He held the reins in one hand allowing the other to stroke Joseph's back; gently pressing him closer to his own chest. He glanced down at the hidden bundle and smiled to himself.

You are my son, Joseph ... my son and heir.

Chapter Twenty-Two

IT WAS DARK and late by the time Garrett reached the cottage. 'Boy! Boy! Where are you?'

Rob came running from the barn.

'Is she all right?' he said, taking the horse's reins.

'Yes. Now look sharp, lad, and follow me up the road to High Agra. Miss Bowman and the child will be cared for there until F ... Miss Grainger returns. You can bring the horse back.'

'A've not eaten owt yet.'

'My housekeeper will give you something to eat. Now look sharp and don't stretch my patience!'

Daphne wasn't aware of anything other than the rhythmic motion of her body welded to Garrett's back and her arms wrapped around him holding fast. She was afraid to open her eyes when the horse came to a halt and the motion ceased; lest the dream would end ... and the nightmare begin again.

Mrs Baxter came out onto the terrace to see what all the commotion was. A look of horror came to her face when she saw the gardener and stable boy carrying a body between them.

'W-what on earth's happening? And why in God's name aren't you wearing a coat? You'll catch your death!' Ivy rebuked. Then she saw Garrett was carrying a small bundle in his arms ... and the bundle moved. Her hand shot to her mouth and she gasped out loud. 'What are yer doing w-with that bairn? Lord bless us and save us! Pass him to me, now, c'mon, I'll see to 'im.'

Garrett handed the baby over to Ivy. 'Have a fire lit in the guest room next to mine immediately, Mrs Baxter. Oh, and bring milk for the child … Now, where did I put that damn bottle…?' Garrett ran to where his men were holding Daphne and he rummaged in the coat pocket she was wearing where the bottle was still half full.

Daphne suddenly opened her eyes and grasped hold of Garrett's arm as he was about to leave her side. He looked at her and she was trying to say something but her voice was weak. He leaned close, placing his ear next to her mouth. 'What is it, Daphne? Tell me … please,' he said softly.

'The milk … goat's milk … for the baby …' she said throatily before closing her eyes.

Garrett gave the bottle to Ivy, then looked about him. He yelled. 'Boy!'

'Aye, I'm still 'ere!' Rob replied. 'An' mi name's Rob, not *boy*,' he added indignantly. 'Mrs Bowman treats me proper … she does. She's wot yer'd call a good-natured woman. An' ah thowt yer should know that.' Then turning his back on Garrett, he walked away, saying, '*Now* I'll go fetch t'goat's milk for t'bairn.'

Garrett stared after the youth open-mouthed. He hadn't the time right now, but if he had, he'd have reprimanded the lad for speaking to his betters in such a manner. But right now he was in dire need of a large whisky.

Ivy Baxter ordered fires to be lit in the study, the guest bedroom, and the master's bedroom. Mrs Bowman was too tired and weak to tend to the needs of her baby so Ivy had the maid fetch an old crib from the attic and put it in her own bedroom. She heated the milk which the hungry infant guzzled down and then tore up a cotton sheet and changed the baby's soiled nappy before laying him down to sleep on her bed while a blanket aired for his crib. When she went downstairs to the kitchen she was pleased to see Rob had returned with a churn of milk. Edith had sat him down at one end of the kitchen table with an enormous plateful of ham, cheese, pickles and bread.

'Thank you,' Rob said politely, smiling at Ivy when she entered the kitchen.

'You're welcome, Rob. An' there's apple pie in the pantry. Edith, I'm sure Rob can make use of that. Come back in the morning for breakfast after you've milked the goat, Rob. All your meals will be prepared for you here until Miss Bowman is fit to go home ... or at least till Miss Grainger returns home from her honeymoon.'

'Ta very much,' Rob said through a mouthful of food, dropping crumbs across the table as he spoke.

When Daphne woke the next morning in the strange room she didn't know where she was at first. Her first thought being she was in Thirsk at the home of Agnes and Edgar Jones. But this bedroom was far bigger and grander than the one there. A fire blazed in the grate and the curtains had been drawn back. She rose from her bed. Her legs felt wobbly and she walked gingerly to the window and when she looked out recognized at once that she was at Garrett's home, High Agra. Snippets of the previous day slowly crept back. Garrett had rescued her and Joseph. They'd got lost on the moor ... he'd saved their lives. But where was he? Joseph! Where's my baby? Who's looking after him? And for some reason, Daphne didn't feel fearful for his safety ... she just desperately wanted to see him. There was a robe hanging behind the door and Daphne quickly slipped it on and went downstairs. She shivered as she tiptoed across the tiled hall floor which was icy cold beneath her bare feet. There were voices coming from the far end of the hall and Daphne walked towards them. Rob was the first to see her.

"Ello, Mrs Bowman ... is you all right?'

Edith and Janet turned to where an ashen-faced woman stood in the doorway. Her robe had fallen open revealing a thin see-through nightdress which had Rob's complete attention.

'I'll go get Mrs Baxter for yer,' Edith said, leaping from her chair. She hurried to the housekeeper's office off the kitchen and returned in seconds with Ivy.

'Come with me, Mrs Bowman,' Ivy said calmly, leading her gently away from the others. 'You'll be wanting to see your son, are you? He's upstairs asleep.'

'Yes, please ... I do.'

Daphne allowed Ivy to guide her back up the stairs and into her room where Joseph was sleeping peacefully. Her eyes filled with tears at the sight of him and she gently stroked his cheek.

'Come on, let's have you back in bed and resting. The bairn's thriving. Rob's fetching goat's milk over twice a day – and I'll see to him so's you can get plenty of rest. You need building up.'

'W-where is Mr Ferrensby? He saved our lives ... but you know that, don't you? When you see him will you ask him to come and see me, please? I-I'd like to thank him personally.'

'Aye, I'll do that as long as you promise me you'll get back into bed and rest. I'll fetch the young 'un along for you later.'

'Thank you. Thank you very much ... I'll never be able to repay you for your kindness.' Then, taking Ivy by surprise, Daphne leaned forward and kissed the woman on her cheek.

Clive Hatch shuffled the papers in front of him and replaced them on his desk. The client sitting opposite had been standing waiting outside when he arrived at work an hour ago. The fire wasn't lit yet and the office was still cold and his secretary wasn't due to start work till 8.30.

'Sorry to have barged in on you so unexpectedly, Clive, but as you can see, it's of utmost importance. If you can just sign and witness that for me, please,' Garrett said, gesturing to the hand-written draft laid on his desk. 'It will suffice until you've drawn up a professional document detailing my wishes.'

'Is this a wise move, Garrett? Ought you not to wait a few weeks ... I know it's none of my business, but—'

'That is correct, Clive. It is none of your business. Now, will you sign that?' Garrett asked, stabbing the papers on the solicitor's desk, 'Draw up a document as requested, or, do I take my business elsewhere and find another solicitor who *will* do my bidding?'

Clive picked up the pen on his desk and signed the papers.

'Now, if you will sign this, please ... then I'll be on my way,' Garrett said, shoving another piece of paper under the solicitor's nose.

'I-I will have to read it first!' Clive said.

'If you must. I have already signed it ... and it requires your signature to witness it ... and Daphne Bowman's, of course. I'll get her to sign it today.' *Blast!* Garrett thought. *He'll not sign it once he's read it!*

'B–but she hasn't signed it yet, Garrett ...' His eyes widened in horror as he scoured the wording. 'I'd be struck off for signing this ... its perjury!'

'I'll take my business elsewhere, then.' Garrett swooped up the papers from the desk. As he reached the door and opened it to leave Clive stopped him.

'All right, I'll do it, on one condition, though, Garrett. You return to this office in two days with that piece of paper – with or without her signature on it.'

'I'll see you in two days, Clive.'

Although Garrett had rescued his son and held him close he hadn't actually looked at his son's face ... nor touched his flesh. And when he walked into the housekeeper's room and saw him a surge of excitement rushed through his body and filled him with the most wondrous feeling he could ever have imagined. Garrett trembled as he reached down and gently stroked his son's hand. Joseph instinctively reached out and grasped his father's finger – and Garrett gasped with delight.

'Yes, I am your father, Joseph,' he said. His son's eyes met his and they held one another for a long while. And then Joseph frowned and knotted his brow ... causing those Ferrensby eyebrows to meet in the middle – in that moment Garrett saw his own reflection in his son and smiled.

As much as Garrett wanted to, he couldn't delay paying Daphne a visit any longer. He'd put it off for as long as was politely possible. Ivy said Daphne had asked to see him. She'd also informed him Florence had returned home with *that* husband and Florence had sent word for Daphne to return to Hamer Bridge where her *friends* would care for her.

Garrett heard the clock in Daphne's room strike five when he tapped softly on the bedroom door.

'Come in.'

Garrett stepped into the room. Daphne was sitting on the side of her bed with the crib positioned next to it and Joseph fast asleep.

'Ah, good, I see you're in better health since I last saw you, Daphne,' Garrett said. His mouth twitched, forcing a smile. He was surprised by how nervous he suddenly felt in her presence. Daphne had recovered better than he'd first thought. The vulnerable woman he'd wooed and made love to all that time ago no longer existed; it appeared motherhood and hardship hadn't diminished her as he imagined. When he'd glimpsed her, heavily pregnant, that day in Thirsk – she'd looked ready for the scrap-heap.

He would have to tread warily to realize his goal.

'Yes, I'm as good as new. Thanks to you and your housekeeper … and your dog,' she said with nervous laughter. 'I–I know that neither of us would be alive had you not come looking for us. I'll be forever in your debt … thank you for saving our lives, Garrett.'

'Oh, no, no …' Garrett said, shrugging his shoulders. 'Believe me I only did what anybody else would have done.' As he spoke he wandered across the room and stood at the side of the crib. He glanced down at his son. A light puffing sound emanated from cupid-shaped, pouted lips with every breath.

To stop herself from trembling as she observed Garrett, Daphne fisted her hands and pressed her fingertips into the palms until it hurt.

He knows … he knows. He knows Joseph is his son!

'Would you like to hold him?' Daphne said softly. Her voice was tender as when speaking to her child.

'Very much … yes, I would …'

Daphne carefully lifted Joseph from his crib and placed him in his father's open arms. They exchanged anxious glances when their hands fleetingly touched. Garrett sat down on the side of the bed while Daphne stood by the crib. A flush came to her cheeks when he looked up and caught her watching him.

'He's a fine boy. And you're an excellent mother by all accounts, I hear … so my housekeeper tells me. Not that I'd expect anything less from you …'

So that's why Mrs Baxter called to see Florence, Daphne thought. He was making enquiries …

'Daphne … I think we need to talk and discuss the future,' he said uneasily.

Daphne felt the blood drain from her face and her senses started to slip away; her legs turned to jelly. Fortunately there was a chair beside the crib and gripping the sides she sat down and tried to appear calm. Then she took a few deep breaths before looking him directly in the eye.

'So you accept Joseph is your son?' It was more a statement than a question and there was nothing soft or forgiving in her manner.

'Yes.'

Daphne lowered her gaze to where her hands rested on her lap. In the next few seconds she recalled the pain and suffering she'd endured the last year; and especially the rejection of herself when carrying his child. She'd vowed not to allow the past to taint hers, or her son's future ... But was that at all possible? she asked herself.

'Why?' Daphne asked, her voice rising. 'Why now ... after all this time? You knew I was carrying your child that day I came here. But you didn't want to know then, did you ... Oh, no. Let's get rid of her – and her bastard brat! Buy her off with money! Money you sent *via* that horrible solicitor of yours. Well, let me tell you now, I've not touched a penny of it ...'

Spent and exhausted, rivers of tears from stored, pent-up anger streamed down Daphne's face.

Garrett laid Joseph down in his crib. He knelt down in front of Daphne and took her clenched fists in his hands and held them until her sobbing subsided.

'I'm sorry. And I know sorry doesn't change the fact that I-I abandoned you ... and my child. But ... let's not allow *my* mistake to dictate our son's future. He deserves that at the very least, don't you think? Ouch!' Garrett cried out in pain, but then managed to smile when Daphne looked at him with genuine concern on her tear-stained face. 'My bloody leg's killing me kneeling down here!' he said, and clambered to his feet.

'I'm sorry too,' Daphne said, feeling rather ashamed of her outburst. 'And you're right of course. Our son does deserve both our consideration ...'

'Rest now, Daphne ... we'll talk tomorrow, or when you're feeling up to it, eh?'

'I'm thinking of returning to the cottage tomorrow, now that Florence is home.' Daphne watched Garrett closely, waiting for his reaction. He averted his eyes from hers but not before she saw a light flicker in his eyes at the mention of her name.

Chapter Twenty-Three

'AND WHERE'S MY *Romani chi* (gypsy lass) riding off to this morning?' Ambrose called to Florence, who emerged from the barn with Dancer.

'We're off for a gallop *Romani chal* (gypsy lad),' Florence replied. And sidling up behind him where he stood touching up the paintwork on some cart-shafts, she kissed the back of his neck. 'I'd invite you to come with me ... but we wouldn't get much riding done, well ... not on the horses!'

'You're a wicked wanton woman, Florence Wilson!' Ambrose said, turning round kissing her full on the mouth. The desire he felt for his wife frightened him at times. On their honeymoon they'd made love every day. Ambrose had been pleasantly surprised at his wife's enthusiasm and prayed every day it would never ebb. His hands now slowly slid round to the front of her and he started unbuttoning her jacket and she pushed him away, laughing. 'Promise me you won't be long, eh?' he said, caressing her breasts through the tweed jacket. 'Lord knows how I'm gonna keep my hands off yer when Daphne and the bairn's back.'

'I won't be long, *Perino* (sweetheart),' Florence said. And hoisting herself up onto Dancer's back she tightened his girth whilst he was walking off. 'See how keen he is?' she called back to Ambrose, and blew him a kiss.

Had someone told Florence that one day she would be as happy as she was now she'd have laughed at them. But it was true. Ambrose was a kind and considerate husband ... both in and out of the bedroom. Florence smiled, recalling how he'd made gentle love to her that first night; assuming that it was her first time. He hadn't asked her so she didn't tell him she was no longer a virgin. But when he made love to her she found herself comparing him with Garrett: Ambrose's lovemaking made her feel safe, loved and cherished, whereas Garrett's lovemaking was fuelled by hot passion and lust.

She reached a rise in the moor and pulled Dancer to a halt. The wind had lost its bitter edge and an early spring had brought a welcome change in the temperature. Her eyes scanned the deserted moorland and a barn owl ghosted past on silent wings. *I've grown to love these moors …* Florence thought wistfully, *and I don't ever want to leave … Oh, please fall in love with them too, Ambrose.*

Lost in thought she hadn't heard the horse's approach. It was only when she heard his voice she spun round in her saddle.

'These are our moors at their most seductive, don't you think?'

'What are you doing here?' Florence retorted, while wondering what he meant by *our moors*. She'd never forgive him for the insults hurled at her the last time they were together. He'd made his position quite clear where he stood regarding her people.

'I might ask you the same thing, Mrs … erm …'

'Wilson. Mrs Ambrose Wilson!' she said. And yanking Dancer's reins Florence wheeled him round. But Garrett was too quick for her. He reached out and grabbed the horse's bridle.

'Now, now, don't be childish, Florence,' he said, his tone condescending. 'It's not very becoming, especially in a married woman.'

'Please, let go. My husband's waiting for me and expecting me home very soon.'

'Well, he can damn well wait five minutes!'

'No, he can't!'

'He loves you *that* much … does he? My … my, well, I must say, Florence, I can hardly blame him …' Then as he let go of the bridle, she spun Dancer round and Garrett slapped him sharply on his rump making him shoot off at high speed.

'Go on, boy … take her home!' Garrett bellowed after them.

Florence galloped along the moor until reaching a safe distance. White sweat coated Dancer's neck. Florence dismounted and led the horse to a nearby water trough used by the sheep that grazed the moor all year round.

As Dancer quenched his thirst Florence cupped her hands and rinsed her face. She hadn't been prepared for seeing him again and it had come as an enormous shock to her. And when she leaned down and rinsed her face again she realized she was sobbing loudly.

Oh, why, why do I feel like this when all he's ever brought me is misery – and poor Daphne, staying with him... let's hope she'll be back soon.

Florence tied Dancer to a fence post. She felt emotionally drained from crying and upset by seeing Garrett. It was important Ambrose didn't know she'd been crying; and she lay down in the springy heather and closed her eyes to rest awhile. And it was in the still silence of the moors where nothing intruded into one's thoughts save the familiar song of a skylark, that Florence admitted to herself she still had feelings for Garrett.

Garrett was in the drawing room and rang the bell. He was sorely disappointed when he saw it was Janet and not Ivy.

'Yes, sir?' Janet asked coyly.

'Oh, Janet, it was Mrs Baxter I wanted to see, not you. Go and ask her to come now, please. Thank you.'

Janet left the room miffed at Garrett's dismissal. Huh ... thought he'd be pleased to see me. Put me in me place good and proper, he did! Well, he can go find his pleasure elsewhere, he can!

''E wants to see you, not me,' Janet informed Ivy.

'As if I've not enough to do in this place ... Doesn't he know that's the reason you and Edith were taken on ... to ease *my* workload!' Ivy stopped what she was doing and looked across at Janet. 'An' why have you got a face on you like a slapped backside, eh?'

'It's nowt. Nowt you'd want to know about, any road!'

'I'm only askin' what's upset yer, lass, so I'll have less of your lip!'

'Sorry, Mrs Baxter, it's, err ... that time o' the month ... that's all.'

'Aye … well, let's hope they keep turning up every month!' Ivy said, leaving the kitchen.

'Bloody old dragon,' Janet hissed quietly, pulling a face.

Janet was finding her time at High Agra insufferable. The nights were long and boring until Robin had waylaid her one evening and shown her that boredom could be pleasurably alleviated. Now he'd gone back to London and it was looking like it might have been a one-off with Garrett … Hmm, mebbe he'll take more interest when that Daphne woman and 'er bairn buggers off back to t'cottage.

Ivy knocked on the drawing-room door and walked in.

'Oh, Ivy, come in. I wanted to speak with you … not the maid.'

'What's so important you couldn't send a message with Janet?'

Garrett sighed inwardly. Why must bloody Ivy take me to the brink of my patience?

'I'm inviting Miss Bowman to join me for dinner tonight and thought you should know … all right?'

'H-has anything been sorted yet … regards the bairn?'

'No, not yet, Ivy. That's why she's having dinner down here with me. Needless to say it's a very delicate matter … and there's much to discuss. We'll dine at seven, Ivy. Thank you.'

Daphne was inspecting her drab and shabby clothes when there was a light tap on the door.

'Come in.'

The housekeeper stood in the doorway. 'I've a message from Mr Ferrensby,' she said, looking past Daphne and craning her neck at the crib.

'Joseph's awake, Mrs Baxter. Come and see him,' Daphne said. And taking her by the arm drew her into the room.

'Dinner's being served in the dining room at seven o'clock and Mr Ferrensby would like you to join him in the drawing room at six-thirty for drinks beforehand.'

'Thank you, I'd love to, but I'm afraid I've nothing to wear, only the old clothes I came in which you kindly laundered for me. Will they do?'

Ivy looked her up and down. 'That's no problem, you come with me.' She led Daphne a short distance along the landing into another bedroom. Ivy opened the door of a large mahogany wardrobe packed with ladies-wear for every occasion.

'I can't wear these ... surely, they must belong to somebody,' Daphne exclaimed.

'They do, they belong to the other Mr Ferrensby's wife. And they won't be coming back for months ... if at all. Ah, now here's something simple if it bothers you that much,' Ivy said, slipping a cream silk blouse and a plain black velvet skirt off a coat hanger and tossing them onto the nearby bed. 'Or this,' she said, holding up an expensive green evening dress.

'I think this will do nicely ... if it fits me,' Daphne said, holding the blouse and skirt next to her and ignoring the evening dress.

'Yes. And if it doesn't fit come back and wear whatever you want.'

'Thank you again for your kindness ...' Daphne said.

'Aw, think nothing of it. Now look sharp. I'll keep an eye on Joseph for you tonight – I've bits of sewing I can get on with.'

Garrett was waiting in the drawing room for Daphne. When she walked through the door he was taken aback at the transformation and thought she looked positively elegant; he could hardly take his eyes off her.

'Good evening, Daphne.'

'G-good evening ... Garrett,' Daphne said nervously, calling to mind how unwelcome she'd been in this drawing room less than a year ago.

'What will you have to drink?' he asked, walking to a side table.

'A dry sherry would be very nice, please.'

Garrett handed her a glass; and touching her elbow directed her to an armchair by the fire before sitting down opposite. Daphne's heart skipped a beat at the touch of his hand and his proximity. She inhaled the familiar scent of his cologne and was transported back to a time – a feeling – she believed she'd obliterated from her memory a long time ago.

'You look lovely this evening,' Garrett said. Then cocking his head to one side added, 'Motherhood ... becomes you, Daphne.'

'Thank you,' Daphne replied shyly, and blushed as Garrett's eyes appraised her from head to toe.

She'll never hand the child over, he thought, looking across at her. Garrett touched the pocket on his jacket where it bulged slightly containing the document he intended asking her to sign tonight and realized the chances were it wouldn't see the light of day.

Garrett rose from his chair and refilled both their glasses.

'I may as well come straight out with it, Daphne. The thing is ... I don't want you and ... and our son to return to the cottage. I–I'd like you both to stay here. I'm asking you to marry me. Will you marry me, Daphne?'

Daphne was speechless and wondered had she heard him right. She saw the Adam's apple bobbing in his throat as he waited anxiously for her reply and knew then she'd heard correctly.

'I–I don't understand.'

'What is it you don't understand, Daphne?'

'What I don't understand is ... you made it perfectly clear in this very room only months ago,' Daphne reminded him, having found her voice, 'that you wanted nothing more to do with me, or ... or your child.'

'Well ... I've changed and now I want to make amends,' he said.

'Oh, I see ... and why now?' Daphne enquired, suspiciously.

Garrett gave a self-deprecatory laugh and shook his head from side to side slowly. 'I'll admit to you, Daphne, because I know there's no pulling the wool over your eyes. High Agra needs an heir. And that heir is here ... right now ... asleep upstairs,' he said, pointing to the ceiling.

Daphne polished off her sherry and handed the empty glass to Garrett. 'May I have another one, please?'

A knock on the door silenced them and a maid entered.

'Dinner's served, *sir*,' Janet said, glaring at Garrett.

'Thank you, err ... Janet,' Garrett said, striving to say her name, yet relieved Daphne had her back to the door and was therefore spared the piqued look on the maid's face. 'We'll be there in a few minutes.'

'You're serious, aren't you?' Daphne said, picking up where they'd left off after the door closed behind the maid.

'Of course I'm serious!' Garrett said. 'I've never been more serious about anything in my entire life.'

'I need to give it some thought ...' Daphne said calmly.

'What is there to think about?' Garrett asked with equal calm. 'You wouldn't cut your nose off to spite your face ... and deprive Joseph of his rightful place, would you?'

'I didn't say no, all I said is that I need to think about it. Is that a problem?'

'No, not a problem at all ... take whatever time you need.'

'I'm going back to the cottage while I consider what you've said.'

'No! Don't do that ... c-can't you do your thinking here?'

'You mean carry out some sort of charade ... parade around this house pretending to be the lady of the manor? No, I'm sorry, Garrett, but I couldn't. And besides, Florence is expecting us to return and I can't let her down ... she's a good friend.'

'All right,' Garrett conceded, 'but promise me, please, you won't take too long. Our son's future awaits him – and so does ours.'

After dining together that evening and when Daphne had retired to her bedroom, Garrett withdrew to his study. He congratulated himself. And cradling a large glass of whisky in both hands he pondered the possible consequences of the evening. Although displeased about her returning to Hamer Bridge tomorrow, along with his son, he felt certain that his proposal of marriage would be accepted. And as the whisky worked its magic, transporting Garrett into a dreamlike state ... he recalled the perfect nights of lust they'd shared together at the hotel ... in Daphne's bedroom. Garrett chuckled to himself. No, Daphne, no indeed, he thought, a lascivious expression written on his face, I certainly wouldn't be averse to resurrecting that part of our relationship.

A gentle tap on the door caused Garrett to jolt. A maid entered the room and walked across the room and stood in front of him. He glanced at the clock on the mantel which said it was almost midnight.

'Can I get you anything ... or do anything for you, sir ... before

I go to bed?'

When you're forty you'll be a fat, grotesque little woman, but right now you epitomize the fullness of youth ... firm round breasts and round buttocks.... He was about to refuse, then Janet opened the buttons of her dress, revealing her nakedness beneath, and reaching out he drew her to him – burying his face in her large white bosom.

'Oh, Janet, Janet ... this has to stop,' he murmured into her flesh, 'you do realize that, don't you?'

'Yes, I know ... so let's enjoy one another while we can, eh?'

'Yes ... now go and lock the door, my dear girl ... my dear, dear girl ...'

Chapter Twenty-Four

A MBROSE ROSE EARLY and went into the barn. He walked over to the stack of rabbit skins and carefully examined each one before separating them into two piles for market the next day. One pile was perfect and the other flawed. The perfect skins would fetch good money while the remainder were to be picked over and sold for pennies.

Ambrose tied the skins into their respective bundles and tossed them onto the cart. Florence would be expecting him back for breakfast and if he wasn't in soon she or Daphne would come and call him.

Something had changed in Florence. And he could only think that she no longer wanted to take to the open road as they'd planned – having acquired a taste for the settled way of life. There had been little privacy since Daphne and the baby moved back into the cottage. And while he and Florence slept on a mattress on the living-room floor, Daphne and Joseph occupied the bedroom.

Another month and then we have to leave because that's my way of life ... and always has been. It was Florence's too before she'd money to buy this place. She's my wife for God's sake! Surely to God Daphne and the bairn can stay here if Florence wants to keep this place on ... An' who knows what Daphne will do? She might even decide to wed that posh mush (man) from the big 'ouse. Aye ... and God help her if she does. I can't stand the bloody mush myself.

But there's one thing for sure ... my wife's gonna be travellin' the road alongside o' me. An' any chavvies (children) we 'ave won't be brought up among gorgios.

Florence walked into the barn and was about to call Ambrose,then stopped. She saw him leaning over the back of the cart with his arms folded with a worried expression on his face. She walked right up to him before he noticed she was there.

'Ah, my *Romani chi*, I'm coming in now. I didn't hear you ...'

'That's because I didn't say anything. Are you all right, Ambrose? Y-you looked worried ... *it traishes mande* (it frightens me) to see you like this ... Ambrose?'

'Aw, don't. There's nothing for you to be *traishe* of, c'mon, let's go and eat.'

They left the barn together laughing when Ambrose joked, 'I could eat a horse and then look round for you!'

After breakfast Ambrose went back into the barn to finish loading the cart.

As Florence cleared the table Daphne folded away the bedding from the night before. The two women worked well together in the limited space they shared. With Daphne's hotel experience and Florence's practical skills, it seemed there was nothing they couldn't tackle together.

Daphne finished clearing away the breakfast things and set about preparing a rabbit Moth had brought home last night. Florence placed a bucket in front of Daphne to drop the giblets in. And when the smell reached her nostrils Florence retched and heaved into the bucket.

'Oh, my goodness, let me help you, sit down, Florence!' Daphne said, guiding Florence a nearby chair.

'Water, please ... a drink of water and I'll be fine,' Florence said. Her face was ashen and she had bags under her eyes. Daphne passed her a mug of water which she sipped slowly. 'I'm all right now ... honestly, don't look so worried.'

'Maybe you should see a doctor ... I'll go with you today if you like?' offered Daphne.

'No. I'm fine now ... it's passed, look,' Florence quipped, smiling at her friend, whose face was full of concern. 'Must have picked up a bug in that hotel we stopped at on our honeymoon cos that's when it started. But I'm absolutely fine now,' Florence assured her and resumed her chores.

Daphne studied Florence closely where she was cleaning brasses at the far end of the table. The colour had returned to her face ... yet on closer scrutiny, Daphne noticed her waistline had thickened and her breasts were plumper. In fact Florence was altogether ... larger ... rounder ...

I don't believe it! She's pregnant!

After gutting and skinning the rabbit Daphne put it on the stove to simmer with a few vegetables. Then she slipped quietly into the bedroom where Joseph lay sleeping and sat on the side of the bed. She had a strange feeling something was not quite right and needed to think. Does Ambrose know his wife's pregnant? she wondered.

Joseph let out a squeal. Daphne lifted him from his cot and laid him on top of the bed and changed his soiled nappy. Looking down at her son, she smiled, thinking how nice it would be for her son to have a friend living close by with whom he could play should she decide to accept Garrett's proposal of marriage – when realization dawned.

It isn't Ambrose's child! It can't be ... Florence hasn't seen him for months ... B-but who, then? Whose child is it...?

Florence hung the shining brasses back and stepped back to admire her handiwork. She took great pride in keeping the cottage clean and tidy. But since Daphne had moved in with them the place didn't stay tidy for long. There were always piles of washing and buckets of nappies soaking about the place.

'I'm finished here for now, Daphne,' Florence said, putting her head through the bedroom door. 'It's a grand day, I'm going up the moor for some fresh air. You put your feet up for a bit and rest, I won't be long ...'

'All right ... see you later, Florence.'

'You look a bit peaky ... are you all right?' Florence asked.

'I'm fine. Now off you go while the weather's nice and I'll put my feet up and feed Joseph.'

Florence called to see Ambrose in the barn on her way.

'Take Moth with you,' Ambrose said. After what had happened to Daphne he found himself worrying whenever Florence took off onto the moors alone. He'd never voiced his fears out loud to his wife, knowing she'd instantly slap him down. 'You know how he loves to run on the moors,' he continued.

'All right, c'mon, Moth.'

'Aren't you forgettin' somethin'?' Ambrose said, grinning.

'An' what might that be?' Florence turned back and walked into Ambrose's open arms which enfolded her and he kissed her on the mouth. 'Be careful ... I know you don't like me saying that but I couldn't live without you, me darlin' – not now ... not ever.' He cupped her breast. 'Hey, what's this?' He took a step back and assessed her. 'Are you putting weight on?'

She ignored his question and smiled through trembling lips.

'Not that I mind ... cos there's more of you to hold.' Ambrose's eyes crinkled with laughter and he pulled her near again.

'I'll not be long,' she said, freeing herself from his embrace. 'I'll give you a hand when I get back.'

Any doubts Florence had harboured for the past three weeks faded fast. She was pregnant with Garrett Ferrensby's child. Tears trickled down her face as she strode aimlessly across the moor with Moth at her heels. How on earth was she ever going to explain it to Ambrose when there was nothing to explain? She couldn't justify what happened. Would he still want her? Could he bear to rear another man's child? Looking at it day in day out for the rest of his life?

I'd never have married you, Ambrose, if I'd known I was pregnant ... Oh why, why, did I allow a man I hardly knew to touch me?

The answer to her question was immediate – requiring no forethought.

'Because I loved him ...' she cried aloud, 'I loved him – that's why ...'

After some time Florence dried her tear-stained face with her handkerchief and headed for home. The warm sunshine breathed its springtime magic over the moorland where evidence of new life abounded. Florence concluded that should never leaving these moors be the price she paid for her sins – then so be it.

She suddenly stopped dead in her tracks. There was an

inconspicuous adder lying coiled on a small boulder, and the warm spring sunshine had succeeded in enticing the snake from its six-month hibernation. Florence had been told by a number of local people about the snakes inhabiting these moors. They said a bite from one could kill you if not treated straight away. She stepped back a few paces and admired the handsome creature with its greyish brown body and distinctive black zigzag pattern on its back. Florence caught sight of Moth suddenly; he was bounding towards her and she quickly ran off in the opposite direction to where the adder lay sunning himself.

'Moth, come on, boy!' Florence yelled, and Moth raced after her delighting in her playfulness.

Coming down from the moor she saw they had a visitor at Hamer Bridge. Florence's heart pounded in her chest. It was someone from the travelling fraternity. The bow-top wagon pulled up in front of the cottage. It was painted in brilliant colours forming a strong contrast with the muted landscape.

Oh, my God, please … not Ambrose's family …

'Visitors?' Florence said to Ambrose, who walked up the lane to meet her. 'Who is it?'

'Ah, now wait and see,' he said, teasing her.

Florence groaned inwardly. There were times, like right now, when Ambrose could be extremely annoying. What was she supposed to do? Jump for joy? His parents didn't approve of her before, and would approve even less when they discovered she was pregnant.

'Eeh, you'll be cock-a-hoop!' Ambrose wore a ridiculous grin on his face. For a minute she thought he might even blindfold her to heighten the surprise.

He opened the front door and Florence stepped inside.

'Mena? Mena Hall!' Florence raced across the room to where the old lady was sitting by the range with a cup of tea in her hands. The fortune-teller put her cup down and embraced Florence.

'Oh, Mena, it's so good to see you … What are you doing this way travelling on your own…?'

'I'm not on me own, lass, oh no, I've got young Harry wi' me.'

Mena pointed to the far end of the room where a boy of about fourteen was sitting at the table stuffing his mouth with bread and cheese. Florence hadn't noticed him with all the excitement.

'Hello, Harry. You lookin' after my friend all right, eh?' she said.

'Aye, old Mena's on her way to Scarborough where she 'as cousins livin'. Not settled in a 'ouse, like you,' the young lad added sarcastically. 'They don't move round any more cos they're too old to.' He spoke truthfully and therefore nobody was offended; and least of all, Mena. But Daphne, a silent witness of Romany culture taking place, was shocked at his outspokenness and gasped aloud. 'Mena's cousins spend their days' *dukkering* (fortune-telling),' Harry continued, ignoring Daphne's displeasure. 'An' the old woman's goin' to spend what time she has left in this world working wi' them.'

'Ah can speak for meself, 'Arry, thank yer very much. Now, Florence, is it all right if me an 'Arry stays 'ere for a day or two to rest up the *grai* (horse)?'

'You can stay as long as you want ... can't she, Ambrose? And you can sleep in the cottage if you like ...'

'Nay, lass, I couldn't sleep in a 'ouse if yer paid me in gold ... We'll be fine in the wagon, thank you.'

'There's the barn, which is nice and dry,' Florence said, turning to Harry.

'That'll be grand. Ta very much.'

As Ambrose pulled the cart to a halt in Ryeburn, he said to Florence, 'Here we are then, love, I'm at your service, just tell me what to do and I'll do it.' He felt slightly concerned for his wife. She'd hardly spoken a word since leaving Hamer Bridge, and when she did speak he sensed tenseness in her voice.

Florence hadn't stood the market since last autumn and had visited the town on only very few occasions for supplies when the weather permitted. And Ambrose, having never stood a market before, looked to Florence for direction. He jumped down, and guiding the horse, he backed the cart into a designated area before taking the horse across the market square to a livery stable. When he returned it was to find Florence surrounded by customers. He stood at a distance and watched his wife as she interacted with the townsfolk. And he was suddenly subjected to a twinge of envy when realizing she had somehow succeeded in embracing both worlds – both the Romany and the gorgio way of life. Ambrose noticed her smiling and animated when the customers engaged her in deep conversation. The people of Ryeburn were obviously delighted to see her back at the market again after the long winter break.

The roar of a car engine distracted his attention from his wife. A man climbed out from behind the wheel and strode confidently to where Florence stood – Ambrose recognized him immediately.

It's her neighbour … the bloody toff!

He was about to rush over and tell him to push off … but something held him back. Ambrose waited and carried on watching. Florence was agitated when the man approached her and the customers she'd been speaking with stepped aside, displaying deference to him. Ambrose was livid when Florence's fists clenched at her side and her face contorted with anguish. The man had reached out and taken her hands in his, but she snatched them away quickly. Then, when Garrett Ferrensby threw his head back and laughed at this gesture, Ambrose sprinted across the square and was at her side in seconds.

'Florence … is everything all right?' Ambrose asked, barging his way in front of Garrett. Florence's eyes swam with unshed tears and she groped blindly for a handkerchief to catch them before they fell.

'I'm all right … honestly. And Mr Ferrensby's just leaving.'

'Am I?' Garrett said, with a mischievous smirk on his face.

Ambrose spun round to face him. The anger he felt inside was ready to explode. 'Yes, you're going right now, mister … that's if you don't want your face rearranging. Now piss off!'

Garrett ignored Ambrose's bullying tactics, and looking directly at Florence, he said. 'Do you want me to leave, Florence?'

'Yes …' she whispered. 'Please go.'

The small crowd that had congregated parted, allowing

Garrett to pass; then turning, they stood gaping after the man from High Agra, wondering what the hell was going on.

Florence couldn't look Ambrose in the eye when she spoke. 'If you see to the ones wanting to buy skins ... an' I'll see to the others.'

Ambrose nodded and walked away; grateful for the distraction of two women drawing him into a long discussion about the skins they were inspecting.

Mena's young companion Harry declined Daphne's invitation to eat indoors, saying he preferred not to. And it was with relief she carried a plate of food out to the barn for him.

It was like living with a house full of foreigners, Daphne thought, listening to them converse in their Romany tongue with a smattering of English thrown in – she'd be pleased to see the back of them when they left tomorrow.

Mena coughed loudly and Daphne turned just in time to see her spit a gob of phlegm into the fire and it made her retch.

The old woman picked up the poker and stirred the fire.

'You don't much care fer the likes of us d'you, missus?' she said, folding her bony hands on her lap. 'Even though yer friend's one of us ... Mebbe yer've closed your mind to that side o' Florence ... eh?'

Daphne stood up straight from where she was setting the table for their lunch. 'No, you're quite wrong. I've never given Florence's background any thought. Now would you like to sit up at the table and join me for lunch ... or prefer to stay where you are?' Daphne asked curtly, changing the subject.

Mena hauled her arthritic body from the chair to the table. Daphne pulled out the chair for her; and as she did so, a strong odour of unwashed flesh floated up to greet her. And Daphne vowed, should she get through the next half-hour without vomiting – it would be nothing short of a miracle.

Mena ate a hearty repast as Daphne picked at the food on her own plate, while surreptitiously dropping bits onto the floor for Moth, who lay at her feet waiting for crumbs to fall his way.

As soon as Mena finished eating Daphne suggested she relax

by the fire and she would bring her a cup of tea.

'Mek it a strong one, lass – I don't drink dishwater,' Mena demanded without a please or thank you.

Had this *ignorant woman* not been a friend of Florence, Daphne would have told her to leave immediately. Instead, she put the kettle on and cleared away the table while waiting for it to boil and prayed for strength to keep a still tongue.

The gypsy lad brought his empty plate back and sauntered into the cottage uninvited wearing dirty boots. He sat down in the armchair opposite Mena by the fire. Then speaking to Daphne as though she were the hired help, said, 'Where's me cuppa tea to wash me dinner down, missus? An' don't be all day!' he added jokingly.

Daphne bit her tongue and stepped between the pair of them and lifted the heavy kettle from the range and was in two minds to pour the boiling water over them both! She mashed the tea and poured Harry's into a metal mug.

'There you are ... I'm sure you'll prefer to drink yours outside,' Daphne said, and with a sardonic grin on her face she opened the front door for him to leave.

Daphne handed Mena a cup of tea and sat down at the table. She surveyed the gypsy woman, who carefully decanted the tea from her cup into the saucer before allowing it to cool and slurping it noisily. Daphne tried to imagine Florence conducting herself in a similar vein, and couldn't. She concluded it must be a case of vast cultural differences within these ethnic groups.

Joseph cried out, jolting Daphne from her musings. She left the table and went into the bedroom to see to him.

'I'll wash up while you see to t'bairn,' Mena said.

Daphne heated some milk and settled into an armchair to feed her baby. And it wasn't long before Mena returned from washing up and settled down beside her and an agreeable silence filled the room; interspersed with the pleasurable sound of Joseph sucking greedily on his teat.

'He's a handsome babby,' Mena said, grinning toothlessly. She reached out a dirty gnarled finger and stroked the child's cheek. Daphne didn't recoil as she thought she might, and she smiled at the old lady, thinking, maybe she wasn't so bad after all.

'T'bairn's father's not far away ... an 'e loves the little *chavi* (child).'

'M-my husband died!' Daphne said defensively. 'F-from injuries ... sustained in the war.'

Mena didn't respond straightaway. For a long while with a vague wistfulness in her eye she stared at the woman sitting opposite her.

'Mind your step ... lass. That's my advice to yer ... mind your step ...' Mena said. And her voice was gentle. Then she rose from her chair and wrapped a shawl about her shoulders to leave.

'W-would you read my palm, please...?' Daphne asked nervously.

Mena turned. Her own heart ached for the gorgio woman she looked at. A shadow of hope in the guise of a smile flitted across Daphne's face escorted by a faint mist of tears in her eyes.

Mena shook her head. 'No, lass, no ... I won't. But take heed o' what I say an' mind yer step.'

Daphne gazed after her – her heart heavy – as she walked out of the door.

Mena took refuge in her wagon. She'd spent an entire day and night trapped in those four walls which was more than enough. She drew on her clay pipe deciding tonight she'd sleep in her own bed and set out early in the morning.

The woman was filled with pity for Daphne. It seemed no matter how hard she tried it was impossible to rid herself of a chill that had fastened about her heart when she'd looked into the gorgio woman's face.

Chapter Twenty-Five

THE DAY WAS coming alive with birdsong as larks and curlews greeted the morning sun. Florence and Ambrose stood waving their farewell to Mena and her young companion waiting until the bow-top wagon disappeared over the horizon and into the distance.

Nothing had been mentioned so far of yesterday's events and Ambrose couldn't delay it any longer. He decided he'd wait until their friends had left before asking Florence if something had gone on between *him* and her.

I've every right to know!

'We need to talk, Florence,' he said, not looking at her as he spoke. This wasn't a request. It was something Ambrose had to have sorted – and quickly.

'Yes … I know … but I–I don't know what Daphne's doing today … if she'll be around or …'

'Or what?' he snapped. 'I'll be working in the barn. I'll see you in there when yer brings me my dinner.'

Ambrose didn't wait for an answer and strode off into the barn where he could lose himself in work for a few hours.

Florence went back inside the house and began cleaning out the scullery. She emptied all the shelves and scrubbed them down and was putting things back in place when she saw Daphne leaning against the door watching her.

'Why didn't you say you were pregnant? I thought we were friends.'

Florence's face looked deathly white against the blackness of her hair. 'I-I didn't know … not for ages,' she confessed, her voice faltering. 'Ambrose doesn't know yet …'

'Oh, God … I am so sorry, Florence …'

'I'd never have married him had I known … never. He deserves better than that.' Florence wrung her hands together and burst into tears.

'Come on … there now … it'll be all right,' Daphne said, putting her arms about her. 'I'm sure he'll love you just the same …'

'No. That's where you're wrong,' Florence said, pulling away, looking directly at Daphne. 'He'll never forgive me. He might say he does … and we might even stay together … but he'll never forgive me. Gypsies can be the most unforgiving people on God's earth if their woman is unfaithful … or breaks a moral law according to their culture … We're different, Daphne! Surely you've noticed … you've seen what Mena was like. They're all set in their ways. I've kicked over the traces and broken free from a lot of their rigid thinking and narrow ways since my mother died and I had to fend for myself. And Ambrose, maybe he is a gentleman … but he's a gypsy first and foremost and he carries their ways through to the marrow in his bones.'

This was the first time Florence had spoken to Daphne about her people and their culture before and Daphne was shocked by her friend's despair of being forgiven.

'I'll stay here with you … that's if Ambrose's foolish pride won't allow him to forgive … We'll be fine – we'll stick together, Florence. I won't ever abandon you. I promise … And our children, they'll grow up together and be friends – just as we are. We can make it work, Florence!'

'If only … if only …' Florence said, wiping her tears. 'My first loyalty is to my husband. I have to be honest with him … and hold nothing back.'

She didn't enquire as to who the father of her child was, although Florence would have told her had she asked. Daphne could only surmise it must be one of the market traders she'd become friendly with at Ryeburn.

And my God, can I empathize with her. It gets lonely on your own … very lonely.

Florence filled her morning doing the jobs she disliked the most; considering them partial atonement for her sins. It was whilst doing this that it dawned on her Ambrose had displayed nothing less than deep compassion for Daphne and her situation. Maybe *he* will forgive me. But how forgiving would Daphne be when she learned Garrett was the father of her child? Oh, what a mess it all is … just look at the havoc Garrett Ferrensby's wrought!

By the time it was noon, Florence was bursting to get the meeting with Ambrose over with. She could manage without him financially – and he likewise. They'd go their separate ways and Florence would pretend the last few weeks had never happened and their marriage would be over. There was no way she would ever be accepted back into the travelling community, but she didn't mind that. She loved the moors and Hamer Bridge. That would suffice.

'I'll take that, thank you,' Florence said, taking a plate of food from Daphne. 'Wish me luck.'

'Good luck, my friend,' Daphne said, kissing her on the cheek. 'And remember whatever happens … all will be well. We have each other, right?'

Florence entered the barn. Ambrose had groomed Dancer till his coat shone like polished jet and was finishing off pulling his mane.

'Oh, he looks magnificent!' Florence said. She handed Ambrose the plate of food and stood back to admire Dancer. Smiling she turned to Ambrose. 'Thank you …' she said. Then her face grew serious, remembering why they were in the barn and not in the cottage dining together.

'Have you eaten?' Ambrose asked.

'No, I–I'm not hungry … I'll eat later. After … after we've talked.'

Ambrose sat on a three-legged stool and ate his meal in silence. Florence perched on the side of the cart. She felt the sweat trickle down between her shoulder blades as she waited for him to finish eating. When he'd finished he put the plate down on the floor and took a large swig of tea, then wiped his mouth with the back of his hand.

He looked at her.

'Were you and 'im lovers?' he asked. His tone was harsh and disparaging.

'I wouldn't say lovers ... I ...'

'How long was it going on for, then?'

'Nothing was *going on*. It was only the once ... that I'd lain with him.' Florence's face burned with shame and she turned away. She knew it didn't matter what she said because in his mind – his traditional gypsy mind – she was heaping insult after insult upon him.

'Oh, I see ... only once, eh?' Ambrose threw his head back and laughed loudly – but there was no mirth in his laughter. 'A mistake, was it?' he said bitterly. Then grabbing Florence by her arm he forced her to look at him. 'Look at me! It wasn't a mistake marrying me, was it? Bloody muggins 'ere!' Ambrose snarled. 'And what if you'd got yersel' pregnant, eh? What then?'

Daphne bowed her head, and whispered, 'I am pregnant ... I've just found out.'

She didn't feel the pain when he slapped her hard across the face – only relief. And she wanted him to slap her again and again to ease the pain of her guilt.

'I promise you ... I'd no idea. I know it won't make any difference ... but please, you must believe me when I say that I love you, Ambrose ... I love you with all my heart.'

He stared at her for a long time; then dropping his face into his hands, he was powerless to still the rising tide of tears that gathered in his eyes.

'Leave me be ...' he said, his voice rasping. 'Please ... just leave me be.'

Ambrose slept in the barn the following nights. And to avoid Florence he would slip into the cottage when he saw her crossing the yard going to milk the goat.

'Are you all right, Ambrose?' Daphne was standing by the range.

'Aye ... I'll live,' he said.

'I've a stew on the go. You'll have some, won't you?'

'No, I couldn't eat a thing, lass, but ta very much. I've come for this,' he said, opening the corner cupboard and taking out a full bottle of whisky. 'Me head's needing some peace and quiet.'

'Florence loves you, Ambrose ... I know she does. She's broken ... and so are you. I can tell. Are you prepared to stand by and allow one mistake to get in the way of happiness?'

Ambrose swung round and glared at Daphne. 'Loves me, you say? Loves me? Hah! Well it wasn't me she was thinkin' of when she opened her legs for that stuck-up bastard who lives up there, was it? I've a good mind to go up there and give 'im a bloody good hiding! That man's poison to everyone he touches!'

Daphne swayed and grabbed the fireside chair to steady herself.

'What? Y-you mean to tell me that Garrett Ferrensby is the father of Florence's child...?'

Surely I must be dreaming; Florence wouldn't ... she couldn't.

'Awww ... Daphne ... Daphne ... lass, I'm sorry, I'm sorry ... yer didn't know, did yer? She never said? Oh ... no, come away 'ere.' Ambrose stepped forward to comfort her, but she blocked him with both her hands and he stepped back.

'No,' she said, 'Please ... don't say you're sorry ... it's not your fault. I'm all right ... honestly.' Then taking a deep breath, and swallowing the lump in her throat, Daphne stood erect.

Ambrose was silent and didn't know what to say.

'I was making plans for Joseph and myself away from here anyway. That was before I got sidetracked, deceived, or whatever you choose to call it. So please don't feel sorry for me, Ambrose. I loathe pity. I simply loathe it!'

'There's nowt pitiful about you, Daphne. You're a lady. And owt I can do to help yer, let me know. I'm sorry to be the one to tell yer, sorry to me very heart.'

Ambrose gathered up the bottle of whisky from the table and went back to the barn to anaesthetize his pain.

It had been three whole weeks since Daphne and Joseph left Agra. Garrett had anticipated hearing from her within a few days and her leaping at his proposal – and not dragging it out like this. He then speculated that Florence and her thug of a husband might have discouraged her. A stab of pain shot through him as he recalled seeing Florence. He sensed a change in Daphne ... a subtle shift of power had taken place and it was she who held the reins that shaped his destiny.

He sealed the envelope containing the letter he'd written and rang the bell by his desk.

'Oh, good,' Garrett said when Ivy Baxter entered his study. Janet was the last person he wanted to see right now. 'I'm pleased it's you, Ivy. Tell the stable boy to take this letter to Hamer Bridge immediately, please. And emphasize it be handed directly to Mrs Bowman and no one else.'

Ivy glanced down at the envelope. 'This place hasn't been the same since she and t'bairn left,' she said.

'No, you're right, Ivy ... it hasn't.'

Daphne opened the front door.

'Yes?' she asked, recognizing the workhand from Agra.

'I've to wait an' tek a letter back,' the boy said, handing her an envelope.

'In that case wait here, please.' Daphne closed the door and went into the living room. She sat down at the table and tore open the envelope.

My dear Daphne, Garrett had written – and a faint smile played on Daphne's mouth.

I sincerely hope you will see fit to visit High Agra soon and let me know your answer regarding my proposal of marriage. I have missed you and our son more than you will ever know since you left here. If I beg on bended knee would you consider gracing me with your presence and dining with me this evening?

If that is the case – I am begging you. Please, do say yes.

Affectionately yours,

Garrett.

Daphne folded the letter and put it in her pocket and paused for thought. Florence would be back soon. She'd gone to market on her own today. Ambrose had loaded the cart up with goods and harnessed the horse for her that morning, but didn't accompany his wife. He'd slept and eaten in the barn of late; he called at the cottage only when Florence wasn't around. This was to make sure she and Joseph were all right, although they never discussed the current situation. It was evident to Daphne that Florence was ignorant of the fact she had learned who the father of her child was. And Daphne chose not to enlighten her.

Daphne wrote a short reply to Garrett saying she would call tonight at 6.30, but not to send someone to collect her as she preferred to walk.

Daphne walked to the window when she heard the clatter of cartwheels. Florence was back from market. She was about to go and see if she required any assistance when Ambrose strode from the barn and towards her. She saw them exchange glances, then Florence started to walk away, but Ambrose reached out and pulled her back. Florence turned to him with her head bowed. Ambrose was saying something to her and he reached out and placed a finger beneath her chin and raised her head to look at him. He'd stopped speaking and was smiling at Florence. Florence nodded to him, then stood watching as he led the horse and cart into the barn.

Oh, Ambrose, you are a good man ... too good for Florence ... She doesn't deserve you, thought Daphne. *You should have chosen me instead. No, no airs and graces necessary where you're concerned ... no, you're a gentleman through and through. If only Garrett Ferrensby had been blessed with a smidgen of your goodness....*

After witnessing the intimate scene of Ambrose and Florence from the window Daphne accepted her time at Hamer Bridge was limited and she needed to make a decision.

She hurried from the window pretending to look busy when Florence burst into the room, her face wreathed in smiles.

'Tea?' Daphne asked.

'Yes, please. Oh, Daphne, isn't it wonderful?' Florence had crossed the room and was hugging her. Daphne felt the protrusion of Florence's swollen abdomen pressing into her and wanted to recoil but didn't. 'Ambrose has made up with me!'

'That is wonderful news, Florence, I'm very happy for you.'

Daphne forced a smile and freed herself from her tight embrace. 'I was wondering,' she asked, turning away and putting the kettle on to boil. 'Would you mind looking after Joseph for a couple of hours this evening?'

'Of course not, I'd love to. Why, are you going out somewhere?' Florence frowned, eyeing Daphne, curious to know where she could possibly be going to on an evening here on the moors!

'I've been invited to have dinner with Garrett Ferrensby,' Daphne said. Florence stiffened and the smile she'd burst into the room with vanished.

'If you can't watch him I can take him with me … Rob's fixed the perambulator. I can wheel him up in that.'

'No. You go … me an' Ambrose will watch Joseph. I–I'll go to help Ambrose see to the horses … I'll have a cup of tea with him later.'

That surprised you, didn't it, you cow? Daphne's eyes were dark with rage. And were it not for hurting Ambrose she would have rushed from the house and told Florence what a whore she thought she was.

Chapter Twenty-Six

WHEN THE SUN dipped below the horizon a fluorescence of colours spilled over into the western sky, flooding it with reds and purples of every hue. And although there was a cool nip in the March air, there was not a breath of wind.

Daphne strolled up the track. She was carrying a lantern for the short walk back in the dark. But it was a clear night and when the moon came up it would be almost full and she mightn't need to light it. She passed through the tall wrought-iron gates and onto the gravel drive. She hadn't gone far when High Agra came into view. The dark weathered stone on the west side of the house glowed pink in the reflection of the sunset. Daphne glanced down at her attire; and for the first time since becoming acquainted with Garrrett, she no longer minded.

Ivy Baxter answered the door to her with a genuine smile and a warm welcome. She ushered Daphne through to the drawing room where Garrett was waiting. He walked across the room to her, but his smile dissolved when he saw she was alone.

'W-where's Joseph?' he asked.

'I didn't want to break his routine …' Daphne replied. 'Florence is taking care of him until I return. I–I'm sorry if you're disappointed.'

'No … not at all disappointed,' Garrett lied. 'Come, sit by the fire. It's chilly outside.'

Garrett helped Daphne out of her shabby coat, then handed it to Ivy.

'What will you have to drink?' he asked, rubbing his hands

together nervously. 'Ah, yes, I remember now – your tipple's sherry, isn't it?'

Garrett poured their drinks and sat down.

Daphne was no longer in awe of the man sitting beside her and viewed Garrett objectively. She was no longer impressed by his grand house or his fine clothes. Oh, yes, I'll marry you – that's for certain. And *my* son will have what is rightfully his ... and when he's old enough ... I will let him know what a cruel and selfish bastard his father is.

She took a large swallow of her sherry and smiled at him.

'Well ... have you reached a decision, Daphne?' Garrett put his drink down on a small side table and picked up her hand and stroked it gently.

Daphne mistrusted the mocking humour she felt rising and spoke quickly to stop from laughing. 'I have, Garrett ... and my answer is ... yes. I accept your offer of marriage.'

'Oh, Daphne, Daphne ... Thank you. You've made me the happiest man alive! And I can promise you, you won't ever regret it.' He leaned across and kissed her on the cheek.

'I know I won't, Garrett,' she replied. *But you may.*

Dinner was announced and they proceeded to the dining room.

'Ivy. I want you to be the first to hear the good news,' Garrett said. 'Daphne has agreed to marry me.'

'That *is* good news ... my warmest congratulation to you both.' Then turning to Daphne, Ivy said, 'It'll be grand to have a bairn running round the place and laughter filling the silence.'

'Thank you, Mrs Baxter.' And when she looked at the housekeeper she saw she was genuinely happy Daphne would soon be mistress of High Agra.

All was silent and there was no light at the window when Garrett walked Daphne back to the cottage. They stopped before reaching the front door.

'I'll see you in a few days, Daphne,' Garrett said. He drew her to him and kissed her on the mouth. 'We made a good couple together ... once, remember, Daphne? No reason we shouldn't again … is there?'

Daphne kissed him back, then pulled away. 'No reason at all, Garrett. I'd better go in now.'

Florence stood watching them from the window in the darkened living room and felt physically sick when she saw them kiss. When Garrett walked away Florence rushed into the bedroom where Joseph lay sleeping and waited until she heard the front door close softly. She pinched her cheeks and patted her hair down neatly then went into the living room.

'Has Joseph been all right?' Daphne asked her.

'He's been grand. I gave him a bottle of milk and changed him about half an hour ago,' Florence said, pointing at the clock on the mantel and avoiding making eye contact.

'I'm getting married soon,' Daphne said cheerlessly, looking directly at Florence. 'Are you happy for me?' she asked.

And in the pain-filled pause that followed a charged hush settled over the room.

The women stared at one another, neither noticing Ambrose had entered the house and stood in the doorway listening.

'Ah, that's grand news, Daphne!' he said chirpily. He stepped casually into the room. 'I'm very happy for yer … that's if you're happy.' Ambrose kissed Daphne on the cheek. 'Ain't that right, my love?' He put a protective arm round Florence's shoulders, and squeezing her, he said, 'We want our friend 'ere to be happy don't we?'

Florence made no comment.

'Thank you. I'll be leaving in a day or two …' Daphne was smiling and speaking to Ambrose. 'You'll be pleased to have the place back to yourselves. But I won't be far away.' Then looking at Florence, Daphne said, 'And … thank you for letting me stay here with you and for making me and my son feel welcome. It's rare to meet a person with generosity such as yours in this world today, Florence …'

Florence, pale and impassive, looked back at Daphne through lifeless blue eyes.

'C'mon, lass.' Ambrose steered his wife from the room. 'We'll see you in the morning, Daphne,' he called over his shoulder.

'We've a bed made up in the barn for tonight.'

Florence nestled into Ambrose and pulled his head down to her and kissed him on the mouth. He rolled onto his side and faced her. 'God, I've missed you,' he said. 'An' I never want to close my eyes at night ever again for as long as I live without you there at me side.'

'Me neither,' Florence murmured.

'We need to talk about the future ... do what's right.' Ambrose had raised himself onto his elbow and was looked down her. 'We can't stay 'ere ... you do realize that, don't yer, Florence?' He felt her body stiffen at his words, but continued. 'Be best for both of us ... and for the bairn,' Ambrose said. He rested a gentle reassuring hand on her swollen abdomen. 'And ... whether yer like it or not,' he added, 'it's best for Daphne. So, I'm asking yer, Florence. Will yer leave this house an' tek to the open road with me – an' 'ave no regrets? Cos there's no room for regrets in this life.'

Every part of her was screaming, *No, I don't ever want to leave this home I've created – I don't want to leave this wilderness I love ... that I've become part of ... I want to gallop across the moor ... feel the wind in my hair ... and the cold rain lashing my face ... No, no I don't want to leave here!* But Florence heard her voice say, 'Yes, I'll take to the road with you.'

'And the bairn?' she asked, searching his face for any sign of resentment, but instead she saw only kindness and concern.

He was caressing her stomach and smiling down at her. 'Oh, you don't have to fret about the bairn. I'll be a good father to it ... an' I'll love it, cos it's thine, an' it'll be mine ... that's a promise.'

Although she was uncertain of much in life, Florence would stake her child's life on Ambrose being a man of his word.

The next morning Florence felt a marked change in her mood. During the night she had awakened quite suddenly with a fluttering sensation in her abdomen. She gasped with elation at the new awareness of the child within communicating with her and she roused Ambrose from a deep sleep to share in the unique and beautiful experience. *Life is pleasant,* Florence thought. *Life is good.*

By midday Daphne was packed and ready to leave.

'Will you have something to eat before you go?' Florence

asked. She was preparing sandwiches for Ambrose.

'No, thank you – I'm expected for lunch at the house.'

'We're not staying,' Florence said in an attempt to dismantle the barrier between them.

'Really? Well, please don't leave on my account,' Daphne said scornfully. 'And as you're obviously unaware ... I should inform you that I *do* know who the father of your child is. Ambrose told me. Oh, don't look at me like that! He thought I already knew; yes, he's a good man, Ambrose ... and you were right that day when you said he deserved better than you.'

Florence carefully laid the breadknife on the board. She turned to look at Daphne, who was glowering at her, her face twisted with contempt and hatred.

'Garrett doesn't know you're pregnant and I want it to stay that way,' Daphne hissed vehemently. 'Do you understand?'

'Leave.' Florence spoke calmly – too calmly. She felt afraid of her own rising anger now. 'And don't you ever darken my doorway again ... you vicious, vicious cow. Do you understand *me*? Now get out of my house before I put a gypsy curse on you and yours!' Her glistening blue eyes smouldered black with a rage she'd never been subjected to before.

The contempt on Daphne's face switched to fear at the mention of a gypsy curse and she ran out of the cottage. Florence turned to the window in time to watch Daphne and Joseph leave Hamer Bridge on a pony and trap.

God, please ... don't let me ever lay eyes on that woman again.

Florence placed her hands on her breast to still her thumping heart.

''Ave you got me a sandwich ready? An' why's Daphne and 't'bairn gone without sayin' ta-ra?'

'Oh, she said to say ta-ra,' lied Florence. 'You might see her again before we leave ... but maybe not. She won't want anything to do with the likes of us ... not now. Are you bothered?' she asked, looking at him.

'Nah, I've got you,' he said, swinging her round full circle before pulling her into his arms. 'And we'll soon have our own *chavo* (child) to cherish.'

'I love you, Ambrose ...' Florence whispered.

'Aye ... you know what, I believe you do.' Then scooping her into his arms they both laughed as Ambrose carried her through to the bedroom. 'But you'll 'ave to prove it ...' he said, laughing.

'Willingly ...' Florence purred.

Chapter Twenty-Seven

JANET TOOK A long draw on her cigarette. 'It 'asn't tekken *her* very long to put on a few airs and graces, 'as it?' she said to Edith as they prepared for bed in their shared attic room.

'Aw, stop moaning and give over, Janet. At least she's not as bad as that bitch 't'other poor bugger's married to,' Edith responded.

'Oh, you give 'er enough time an' you'll see ... Aye, she'll be worse than any of 'em, mark my words – her type usually are. Them that comes from nowt and never 'ad a penny to scratch their arses wi' – they're the ones to watch.'

'What are you complaining about anyway? You're not badly done by 'ere.'

'Mebbe not,' Janet said. 'But I ain't 'anging around to look after her bastard brat!'

'Put that cigarette out. Mrs Baxter will go barmy if she finds out you've been smokin' up 'ere and you'll be given the boot for nicking 'em.'

''Aven't nicked 'em. 'E gives me 'em ... Garrett.'

'Aye ... an' I can well imagine what you give 'im in return,' Edith muttered under her breath before snuggling down and burying her head beneath the blanket. 'Now let me get some sleep, Janet, for God's sake!'

Adapting to her new status as the mistress of High Agra proved to be an effortless transition for Daphne. There was just the staff situation to remedy and then she would be able to relax and fully enjoy her position. Maybe Garrett and she could take a trip abroad? Paris would be nice ... we could employ a nanny to look after Joseph. But the first thing she must do is get rid of that awful girl Janet. She was trouble, that one. Daphne suspected Garrett had been dallying with the girl before she'd taken up residence. Although quite commonplace among the gentry, Daphne concluded, she wouldn't stand for it. So, young lady, I'm very sorry to disappoint you, but it is no longer *the* done thing – not whilst I'm in charge!

The clock struck 11 a.m. Daphne changed into her new riding habit and went along to the stables. Garrett had insisted she learn to ride straightaway, stating, 'What on earth is the point of living out on the moors if one is unable to ride out and enjoy their beauty?' Daphne unfortunately was not as taken with learning to ride as her husband imagined her to be, but she didn't want to disappoint him.

And when she had the desire to see the moors, she preferred to walk.

Garrett was walking back to the house from the stables when they met.

'Ah, I see you're heading off for a riding lesson, Daphne. That's good. Hopefully shouldn't be too long and we can ride out together. Oh, and who's looking after my son?'

'Janet is taking care of him for an hour.' Daphne took enormous pleasure in watching Garrett flinch. Yes, Janet is good enough to bed when the fancy takes you ... not good enough to look after your son though, eh?

And that was another thing about him that was starting to irritate her. Joseph had suddenly become *his* son – not *theirs*.

'I've been thinking, Daphne, isn't it about time we employed a nanny to take care of Joseph?'

The opportunity she'd been waiting for now presented itself. 'Yes, I quite agree. And I also think we should let Janet go. It's come to my notice she doesn't appear to be happy here ... not since *my* arrival.'

'Really? I can't say I've noticed, to be honest. Maybe you're right. But please, do discuss it with Ivy first. Nobody goes over Ivy Baxter's head – not even you, my darling!'

That was the first time he'd referred to her as 'my darling'. Oh, I like that very much … *my darling.* Daphne smiled at him and proffered him her cheek. She looked at him in genuine surprise when he turned her face to him and kissed her on the mouth instead, causing her heart to race.

Garrett saw the question written on her face, and said mildly, 'I'm very fond of you, Daphne … and happy we're married, and not only because of Joseph. I thought it important to let you know that.' Then taking her hand he gently squeezed it. 'Enjoy your ride.'

Daphne stood gazing after her husband as he walked back to the house with his unfamiliar gait. And as she stood watching him, she wondered, had she misunderstood him all this time?

Daphne re-enacted the scene of his kissing her and what he said, many times that day, searching for the sincerity behind his words.

If you do come to love me, Garrett – then it must be more than you ever loved Florence … I'll settle for nothing less.

Garrett didn't remove his dirty riding boots, leaving a trail of muddy footprints on the freshly polished tiled floor, but went directly to the nursery where Janet was tending Joseph.

She looked at him in surprise when he walked in. His face was flushed from riding and his shirt was half in half out of his mud-splattered riding breeches.

'What yer doing up 'ere? Yer don't normally come to 't'nursery,' Janet said.

Hearing the broad-Yorkshire accent and seeing her in the raw light of day Garrett questioned his sanity for taking her to his bed. Daphne was right, she had to go. But it was vital he ensure she left quietly.

He gathered Joseph up in his arms. 'Look, Janet, it appears my w–wife has an inkling something's been going on between us,' he said. 'It would be better for you if you left and hand in your notice to Mrs Baxter … today.'

She was about to protest and he stopped her.

'Say you've been offered a position closer to home. And I will see to it *personally* that you are extremely well recompensed for agreeing to do this – along with an excellent reference. I'm sorry if you're not happy about it, Janet, but I have no choice. There, you have it.'

Janet wasn't stupid enough not to realize she wouldn't find another job should she be dismissed without a reference. It would be nigh impossible to find work anywhere – especially if 'is cow of a wife put it about I was a trollop.

'I'll miss yer, sir … and our little get-togethers,' Janet said, and lowering her eyes managed to blush. 'An' I'll do it for you cos I don't want you to get into any bother … and besides I was ready for off, any roads; can't say that I like your missus very much.'

'That's a good girl, Janet. I knew you'd see sense.'

Garrett made his way to the study rubbing his hands gleefully. He couldn't help but congratulate himself on the progress he'd made today. Daphne was *almost* won over … and as soon as he convinced her of his worthiness he'd have her sign the document naming him as Joseph's father. But … until that was done, he must ensure his wife's happiness – at any cost.

Florence gave the last of the brasses a final polish before wrapping each one carefully and packing them into a wooden box. Her next task was to wax every stick of furniture which would then be covered in dust sheets. Ambrose had wanted her to sell the cottage, but she stuck to her guns, refusing, and saying, no, we might be glad of it before we leave this earth.

The plan was to leave the moors sometime in the next fortnight. Their first stop would be Thirsk where Ambrose would pay a call to Miss Wooten. And Florence would call and see her solicitor in the town regarding instructions for Hamer Bridge. Then they would head northwards to Appleby, stopping off at Stoneygill on the way to visit Florence's mother's grave.

Moth sat looking at his mistress with doleful eyes. She stroked his ears and he placed his head on her lap. The dog seemed to sense a sudden change in his surroundings; like the rug that was always in front of the range which he sprawled out on every day had been rolled up and stored away. Everywhere was too clean and sterile.

'I know, lad, you're missing the old place already, aren't you, boy? Me too, Moth ... me too ...'

'Dog'll be fine as soon as we're back ont' road,' Ambrose said.'An' the sooner the better, I says, looking at the pair of you! Now give over with yer maudlin, Florence. You'll mek that poor bairn you're carryin' miserable afore it arrives.'

Florence turned and smiled at him. He was good at doing that, making her smile.

'I know ... I know, you're right.' She sighed.

'Let's get away while t'weather's good. What d'yer say, eh?' Ambrose crouched down in front of his wife taking both her hands in his own and waited patiently for her reply.

Where did he get this from? This inexhaustible supply of love that he has for me? Florence wondered. And suddenly Daphne's words broke through, echoing in her thoughts. *Ambrose is too good for you ... you don't deserve him.*

'Florence ... sweetheart, what do you say?' Ambrose spoke softly.

'Do you really love me, Ambrose?' Florence asked, over-whelmed with a powerful sense of insecurity, and her lip trembled as she spoke the words.

'Aw ... come on, lass, you know I do.' He pulled her into his arms and held her fast a few moments before pressing her from him. 'Look at me now!' he said, the tone of his voice serious. He raised her head so their eyes met. 'An' I want you to get this into yer 'ead. I love you more than life itself ... an' never ever doubt my love for you – cos it's a gypsy's love, d'yer hear that – a gypsy's love? Not some gorgio's love that'll be there one day and gone the next. D'you understand what I'm sayin', Florence?'

Florence nodded. 'Yes ... I understand,' she said, beholding his dark eyes that blazed with passion ... for her. He was like no one else on earth.

'We'll leave whenever you want ... I'm ready to go from this place now.'

The rain had eased. Ambrose slipped a bridle over Dancer's head and led him from the barn. Ambrose wouldn't permit Florence to ride again until after the baby was born. She stood watching him from the open doorway.

'You go steady now, exercising that horse o' mine,' she called, 'cos I was robbed blind by some gypsy horse dealer at Topcliffe Fair last year and paid him a fortune!'

'Aye, the other way round, yer mean. You got 'im for next to nowt cos you flashed those bonny blue eyes at me,' Ambrose quipped.

'Wish you'd put a saddle on him, he's used to it.'

'Mebbe he is, but I'm not,' Ambrose said, grabbing hold of Dancer's mane and leaping onto his back. 'So stop your complaining, woman,' he joked, 'and be grateful I'm not chargin' yer for exercising this *fine* expensive animal of yours.'

Florence feigned offence and laughed. Ambrose blew her a kiss before trotting Dancer out of the yard and towards the open moor.

On reaching the summit he reined the horse to a halt and climbed down. Ambrose looked around him and saw nothing; nothing ... only emptiness. He thought it the bleakest, most depressing place he'd ever seen.... Then as he stood gazing, the sun suddenly broke through, and the barren moorland came alive and was instantly transformed into a landscape of spectacular beauty. Cloud shadows danced over the moors transported by a gentle breeze and skylarks flew high above, their song competing with the call of the curlews.

Now I see what you see ... I understand why you love the moors ... Florence, I understand you not wanting to sell Hamer Bridge....

That day for the first time in his life, Ambrose Wilson was ambivalent about taking to the road. He wrestled with the uncertainty of leaving the cottage, even though in his heart, he knew they needed to make a fresh start away from Garrett Ferrensby.

His mind was still in turmoil as he rode into the yard and he dragged his scattered thoughts to the present as Florence walked up to meet him.

'Not a bead of sweat on you,' Florence said, running her hand over Dancer's coat, then whispering into the animal's ear, said laughingly, 'Too afraid to gallop without a saddle, was he?'

'Never been *traishe* (afraid) of owt in me life,' Ambrose said, climbing off the horse. 'Not until now, anyroads.'

Florence, surprised by his words spun round to face him. She'd never known him look as serious or solemn as he did at that moment and wondered had he changed his mind about her ... and the child. But then he gathered her into his arms and she breathed a deep sigh of relief.

Holding her close, Ambrose said, 'Out there alone on the moor in that wilderness ... I can understand why you love this God-forsaken bloody place, Florence. An' what I want to say is this. If you want us to stay put ... and live 'ere, we will.'

'Oh, my darling, darling Ambrose ...' she cried. Tears streamed down her face, wetting Ambrose's cheek pressed to hers. 'I can't ever thank you enough for saying that ...' She turned her face and drew his lips to hers and kissed him long and deep. 'I don't have to give it a second thought ... but thank you; thank you for loving me enough to give up a ... a way of life. But I've given you my answer – we leave here as soon as you're ready.'

It was then Ambrose's turn to be stunned into silence.

Chapter Twenty-Eight

DAPHNE WAS AT the bottom of the stairs when she heard laughter coming from the study. She was about to go and see who it was when Janet emerged carrying a small suitcase in one hand and a small package in the other.

'Bye … sir,' Janet called to Garrett in a too-familiar tone for Daphne's benefit before closing the study door.

'You are leaving, I see. Good luck,' Daphne said. She didn't move towards the girl, but remained standing where she was at the bottom of the stairs.

'An' good luck to you, missus,' Janet sniggered. 'I was ready for off anyway; I'm no nursemaid.'

'No. You most certainly are not!' Daphne said sharply.

Daphne's indignation rose when the girl turned her back on her. Then instead of leaving by the servant's entrance she strode straight out through the main door.

Daphne crossed the hall and walked into the study. Garrett was sitting at his desk leafing through papers. He hadn't heard her enter and looked up in surprise when she spoke.

'The girl's gone, then?' Daphne said, staring into the fire. 'Marched straight out through the front door and not a thank-you in sight!'

She's not a great deal to thank you for besides losing her bloody job! Garrett thought. 'I'll put an advert in the Ryeburn Press to replace Janet … and also a nanny for Joseph.' Daphne's face remained expressionless until he spoke again. 'I was wondering if maybe you wouldn't mind interviewing the applicants, Daphne. After all you are in charge of the household.' He turned away and walked over to a side table and poured a sherry for himself.

Daphne spun round, smiling brightly. 'Oh, yes, I'd be more than happy to do that. Do you really mean it, Garrett?'

'Of course I mean it, darling.'

He's doing it again ... calling me darling. 'I'll join you in a sherry if I may.'

'That's settled, then,' he said, handing her one. 'I'll drive into Ryeburn first thing tomorrow morning and place an advert. You know, Daphne, I didn't realize it until now, but this is what's been missing in my life – someone like you. And, although initially ... it was a ... a marriage of convenience, I genuinely feel that we are quite well matched. Don't you?'

The thrill of his words made her heart skip a beat and Daphne gripped her hands tightly on her lap when they shook with excitement. Eventually she said. 'Y-you've taken me by surprise, Garrett ... I never thought I'd hear you say anything like this ... but now you have – I must agree with you ... I believe we're quite well matched too.'

'I'm pleased you're of the same mind as me, Daphne.' Garrett leaned forward and gathering her clenched hands held them in his own. 'We can be a real family now ... you and me, and our son.' He gently pulled her towards him and kissed her tenderly on the mouth. 'And there's something else,' he said, reaching into his pocket and producing a slim leather case, which he handed to her. 'I want you to have this ... I hope you like it ... it was my grandmother's.'

Daphne opened the case. She was startled and her breath caught in her throat. Inside it was the most exquisite diamond necklace.

Garrett regarded her keenly. *Hmm ... so that's what it takes? A diamond necklace to secure a son and heir ...*

Daphne looked at him through eyes glistening with unshed tears. 'I d-don't know what to say ... I – I'm utterly speechless ...' she said, stumbling over her words. 'You won't regret marrying me ... Garrett ... I promise you.'

'I know that, Daphne. Here, let me replenish your glass.'

With his back to his wife she failed to notice a glint of triumph in Garrett's eyes.

And that night for the first time since they married they shared the marital bed.

'Would you look after Joseph for a couple of hours, please?' Daphne asked Ivy the next morning, who was clearing away the breakfast things. 'I know your hands are full while we're two staff down but I have a riding lesson I don't wish to miss.'

Ivy Baxter's face lit up at the prospect of spending a few hours with Joseph, who had become a favourite with her. 'I never mind looking after the little fella,' she replied, smiling from ear to ear. 'He's as good as gold for me and no bother at all.'

'Shouldn't be long before both positions are filled,' Garrett said to Daphne from behind a newspaper. 'I'll drive into Ryeburn this morning while you have your riding lesson. Oh, by the way, darling,' he said, lowering the newspaper and smiling across at his wife. 'If you'll not mind popping into the study with me for a few minutes … it almost slipped my mind,' he added, casually. 'There's something I need you to sign for me before I drive into Ryeburn.'

Daphne stood in the cool April sunshine waving farewell to Garrett. She watched the car disappear down the gravel drive and then made her way to the stable block. Her body was still tingling with delight from Garrett's gentle lovemaking. And she felt giddy with a happiness that penetrated all her senses. She'd also signed the document this very morning, decreeing Garrett the father of her son and, therefore the legal guardian of *Joseph Garrett Ferrensby*.

Her happiness was complete.

'I'm sorry, but I've changed my mind… I shan't be having a riding lesson today. I'm going for a walk instead,' Daphne informed the stable hand.

'Let me saddle up another horse and tek you out on a lead rein, then – cos Master Garrett won't like me not following out 'is orders,' he said nervously.

'No, I said I *do not* choose to ride today,' she rebuked. 'You have my permission to tell Mr Ferrensby that I insisted.'

Standing by the horse which was saddled and waiting, the lad touched his forelock. 'As you say, ma'am,' he conceded, yet somewhat confused. Then turning the horse around walked it back to the stable.

Daphne's body was demanding physical exercise. She wasn't used to a life of ease – and a long walk would release her of the excess energy rushing through her; and trotting steadily round a courtyard and being led like a child was not the answer.

She strode off purposefully. And once out of sight of the stables away from prying eyes, Daphne slowed her step and started to enjoy her walk. After an uphill ascent and reaching a plateau of exposed moorland she halted occasionally to appreciate the sweeping landscape. When I've learned to ride properly, she mused, Garrett and I will ride out over these moors together ... and when Joseph is a little older he'll join us.

Florence cast her eyes around the starkly furnished room. The range she'd blackened that morning was covered in rough hessian sacking to protect it from any damp and rust. And the thick heavy curtains she'd made for the windows were drawn to block out the sunshine and to prevent anybody from looking in through the windows after they had left.

Especially him who wanted to buy the place, she thought bitterly.

'You about ready, Florence?' Ambrose asked, entering the room and standing beside her. Once upon a time he'd not have believed those beautiful blue eyes could ever look as solemn as they did now. He rested a comforting arm round her shoulders. 'Hey, nobody's died, lass, 'ave they?'

'No, Ambrose, nobody's died ... mebbe just a little part of me. It no longer feels like home any more, not now with everything packed away ... does it?'

'It doesn't, no, yer right there,' Ambrose said, and then turned to face her. 'Come on, let's lock up and get away ... an' give over maudlin', we're in for a right grand summer.'

Florence locked the cottage door and dropped the key into her skirt pocket which she would leave with her solicitor in Thirsk.

Dancer whinnied and shifted restlessly in the new unfamiliar harness Florence had invested in the previous week. She climbed up and sat on the side of the cart with her legs dangling over the edge.

'You lead and I'll follow,' she called to Ambrose, who guided the bow-top wagon to the front.

'You'd better mean that?' Ambrose shouted, and laughed cheerfully.

Florence smiled back, but was choked and couldn't reply.

Ambrose clicked his tongue. 'Giddy up, boy!' he said. Ginger Dick lurched forward, pulling the heavy wagon – and Dancer followed.

The sound of jangling harnesses carried on the wind reached Daphne's ears.

She looked about her, but couldn't see anything. Then shielding her eyes from the glaring sun she scoured the moorland, curious to know where the sound was coming from. In the far distance she noticed a narrow moorland track snaking over the moors. Then she spotted it. There was no mistaking the alien colours of the bow-top wagon – swaying and rattling as it lumbered along. Behind the wagon she saw there was a cart that was being pulled by a black horse. Daphne recognized the animal immediately. It was Dancer. The animal was as dark and as beautiful as his owner. Watching them leave Daphne felt both glee and sadness. With Florence gone any competition for Garrett's affections would also be gone. The threat was removed.... Yet, at the same time, Daphne couldn't help but feel a deep sense of loss.

Although it was impossible to make out the figures of the two people she had come to love – and to lose, Daphne raised her hand, bidding them happiness and a fond farewell. And when she turned and walked away ... an unchecked tear slid down her cheek.

As Daphne started for home she was more subdued than when she set out.

She crouched down in the heather and kept very still. The

young roe deer hadn't seen her and emerged from behind a clump of gorse. Daphne had often eaten venison at the hotel where she'd worked, but had never seen a deer before. And as she gazed at the elegant deer, she decided she could never eat venison again.

She moved slightly and the doe spotted her and bounded off with graceful agility.

Daphne stood up to leave but her foot caught fast in a tangled mass of heather roots and she pitched forward. And as she fell she felt a sharp stinging bite on her ankle.

'Argh!' she cried. Then as she hit the ground her hand on a fell on sharp rock and she was bitten once again – this time on her hand. Daphne screamed out aloud when she saw two adders slither off through the undergrowth. She attempted to stand but her ankle was too badly sprained, or possibly broken, and wouldn't allow her. She rolled onto her back. It wasn't long before she lost all track of time... and taking a final glance at the blue sky Daphne's thoughts were of her son. 'Joseph ...' She whispered his name softly ... and as the venom spread rapidly through her body ... Daphne closed her eyes ...

Ambrose brought the wagon to a halt and pulled the brake on. They'd reached a rise in the moor and Ginger Dick was sweating and Florence drew the cart to a stop behind the wagon.

'Ginger's thirsty,' Ambrose said. He jumped down from the waggon and filled a pail from a water-jack fastened to the back of the cart.

Florence sauntered a short distance onto the moor with Moth at her heels while Ambrose tended the horses. From where she was standing if she screwed her eyes up she could make out the faint outline of High Agra.

Having captured it in her sight, Florence continued to stare for a long time; and she placed a hand on her protruding abdomen when she felt her child suddenly leap.

'You listening ter me, Florence? I've asked yer twice already if you want anything to drink!'

'I'm sorry, Ambrose ... er, no, thanks. You ready to be off again now?'

Florence climbed back onto the cart and glanced back over her shoulder to where she'd spent the last year of her life.

Would she miss it? Yes. Would she ever return? Maybe ... one day.

But you will return ... my child. For you are part of this place ... you belong to High Agra.